THE CRAZINESS HAD STARTED THEN. The lessons from the Book, the services in a religion that had never been part of a church, the daily trips to the Churn.

Addy had hated it all.

A branch brushed against Addy's robe, pricking her thigh. She pushed the branch away, the needles sharp against her palm, and was about to go back inside when something caught her gaze.

A man walked around the cliff. From this height he was tiny, more a bird's-eye view of a man than a man himself. Still she could make out a few details.

His black hair was plastered against his skull, his clothing wet and pasted against his body as if he had been in a downpour and failed to dry off. He walked with his head down, hands shoved in the pockets of his pants, his shoulders huddled forward as if to protect himself against an unseen threat. His walk had no real purpose, yet he wasn't ambling as some did on the beach. He almost appeared to be pacing, or walking as she had once seen Spence do, walking and staring at the beach instead of crying.

Spence. The man on the beach reminded her of Spence.

Spence who died fifty years ago.

Because of her.

Also by
Kristine Kathryn Rusch

Sins of the Blood

Façade

Snipers

Spree

Alien Influences

The
DEVIL'S CHURN

KRISTINE KATHRYN RUSCH

*wmg*PUBLISHING

The Devil's Churn

Published 2013 by WMG Publishing
www.wmgpublishing.com
First published in 1996 by Dell Publishing,
a division of Bantam Doubleday Dell Publishing Group, Inc.
Cover and Layout copyright © 2013 by WMG Publishing
Cover design by Allyson Longueira/WMG Publishing
Cover art copyright © Andreykuzmin/Dreamstime,
William Langeveld/Dreamstime
ISBN-13: 978-0-615-92519-6
ISBN-10: 0-615-92519-7

This one, too, is for Mom.

Acknowledgments

Thanks on this one go to Kristin Kiser for her insights and patience; Nina Kiriki Hoffman for the constant inspiration; Marian M. Rusch for the information and the stories; Julius Schwartz for introducing me to all the VIPs and, more important for taking me under his wing; Jenny Goodnough for seeing the heart of the novel; and Dean Wesley Smith for accompanying me on each and every trip to the Oregon Coast.

Author's Note

On the Oregon Coast, between Yachats and Florence, is a formation called the Devil's Churn. It is a wild, dangerous, beautiful place, a crevice in the rocks where the ocean swirls and churns and sometimes snatches the unwary into its grasp.

The town of Dory Cove does not exist. Lovers of the Oregon Coast must add an extra ten miles of coastline between the Devil's Churn and Yachats. For those who have read my novel *Façade,* the town of Dory Cove is about fifty miles south of another fictional coastal town, Seavy Village. The highway that travels between them is named 101 just like the real coast highway, but unlike the coast highway, this 101 lies on the dark side of the imagination.

The
DEVIL'S CHURN

1

ADELAIDE HAWTHORNE TAYLOR RUSTIN leaned against the cold iron railing that surrounded the stoop at Dunstaff's Funeral Home and longed for a cigarette. She hadn't smoked in thirty years, not since her second husband, Donald Rustin, plunged to his death from the eighth floor of Memphis's Peabody Hotel on Thanksgiving Day 1959, leaving behind a bottle of sixteen-year-old scotch, his naked and sleeping mistress, and $35,000 of real and unpayable debt. Addy had smoked for two weeks straight, a cigarette for each unpaid bill. Then, sick and shaky from the nicotine, numbed by the betrayal, she had stacked the bills in a corner, placed a newspaper open to the want ads on top of them, and flushed her last pack down the toilet.

She hadn't had a cigarette since, hadn't even wanted one. Until now.

The sun was setting over the town of Dory Cove, its golden rays illuminating Highway 101, but leaving the front door of Dunstaff's in shadow. Cars with out-of-state plates sped down the highway, ignoring the thirty-five-mile-an-hour signs posted on the north and south sides of the town. Vacationers, traveling through, seeing the Oregon Coast as a series of roadside motels and seashell shops, never stopped long enough to look for the real towns behind the touristy chintz.

Dory Cove was almost unrecognizable from the place Addy had left in 1939.

Only the ocean remained constant, its roar a demon that had haunted her dreams ever since. She had spent most of her adult life in prairie land, thinking at first it would take the memories of the ocean from her. But the ripple of wind across the tall grass had made her think of a quiet sea, and the howl of summertime tornadoes had brought back the fear of angry water. She couldn't escape the memories.

Her mother hadn't made things easy, dying fifty years after the Storm, forcing Addy to return when the next Storm was due.

The brown-painted metal door opened beside her, and her daughter Lisa peeked her head out. She was Addy's youngest, born in the days when Donald and Addy still had dreams of a life together. The youngest, one year shy of forty, her hair cut in a modified Louise Brooks bob that curled beneath her eyes and hid the encroaching gray.

"Mom, they're asking for you inside."

"I know," Addy said, wishing everyone would leave her alone. She was doing her best—better than her best actually, since she had come to tonight's visitation when she had only planned on attending tomorrow's funeral—but the cloying scent of flowers, the sterile sympathetic music piped from overhead speakers into the funeral home's blond-wood chapel, the sight of her mother—her all-powerful mother—shrunken and lifeless in the best casket Dunstaff could supply, made Addy's skin crawl.

Lisa slipped all the way out and let the door close. She shivered in the shade's coolness. "You know," she said, "Grammy would have wanted to be buried on the ocean-side of the cemetery."

"She wanted to be tossed into the Churn," Addy said, allowing the sarcasm into her voice.

"Mr. Dunstaff said that's illegal." Lisa spoke with a seriousness Addy hadn't expected. She had thought her daughter would laugh at her grandmother's foolishness. That Lisa didn't made a small tendril of fear run up Addy's spine.

She crossed her arms and frowned, trying to be as serious as Lisa. This discussion obviously meant something to her. "It's not illegal if we cremate her."

Lisa shuddered visibly. Fire was the enemy of water; they both knew that. Addy's mother, Olivia, would never have allowed herself to become ashes. "Mom," Lisa said. "An ocean-side plot. That's not too much to ask."

"I can't afford it," Addy said.

"We could all chip in. It's not that much, and you know how much it would mean to her."

"She's dead, Lisa. It would mean nothing to her now." Addy could imagine the cigarette between her fingers, the bite as she drew nicotine into her lungs. Numbness, that was what she was longing for, a chemical numbness that gave her energy but didn't allow her to feel.

"I think you're being perverse about this, Mom," Lisa said.

Addy almost denied it, then she looked at her daughter. Lisa had her grandmother's eyes, wide and blue, set close to her small nose, with dark brows that accented her long, dark lashes. Lisa lived in Salem, and she had traveled to Dory Cove every week to spend an hour or two with her grandmother, something Addy had never been able to do.

"Maybe I am being unreasonable," Addy said.

"Good," Lisa said. "Then you'll reconsider?"

"No," Addy said in her firmest voice. "Not ever."

* * *

BILLY MALONE balanced his straight-backed chair on two legs, brushing his head against the faded cedar slats beside his office door, and tipped his fedora over his face. He lit his pipe with shaking, arthritis-crabbed fingers and stared down the highway at Dunstaff's. Addy Hawthorne had been standing in the twilight chill for nearly an hour, leaning against the cheap wrought-iron rail that Michael Dunstaff, Jr., had been unwilling to replace since Billy had warned him about it twenty years before. A lawsuit waiting to happen, Billy had called it then, and Michael had turned his slate-gray eyes, already lined with disillusion at being back on the coast pursuing his father's business, toward Billy and said, *Ready to show off that newly minted law degree, boy?*

3

And Billy, whose newly minted degree was already five years old, had stared at the man young enough to be his son, and said in his best Amos 'n' Andy drawl: *I was jes' tryin' to be neighborly, Mr. Dunstaff, suh.* Dunstaff had had the grace to flush, but never to apologize. And if Dunstaff's hadn't been the only mortuary in town, Billy would have refused then and there to enter it.

But to refuse meant never having the chance to say good-bye to old friends, and he couldn't stomach that. For each coastal family that had treated him as something less than human, another had treated him with decency and respect.

There were a number of blacks on the coast now, but when Billy Malone arrived in 1935, he had been the only one, a twenty-year-old without a friend, who had run as far as he could without jumping into the ocean. At first it was poverty that made him stay—he didn't have enough money to return to Texas—and then Dory Cove had gotten into his blood. Even when he'd made the news in 1965 as both the oldest graduate from the University of Oregon Law School and the oldest black man to ever attend, heady days when he was famous throughout the Northwest and had had job offers from Seattle to San Francisco, he returned to the Cove. He had learned, in his years in Eugene, that he couldn't bear to be away from the ocean.

Despite the pain it had caused.

He'd missed his chance at making any more headlines. Mostly he helped his neighbors with small problems—absentee landlords, out-of-state suits. He had never gotten rich, but rich hadn't mattered. The education had.

Still, sitting on the porch of his office, the sun setting over the Pacific, staring at Addy Hawthorne, he felt twenty-four years old and lost again, like he had been on the day he had helped her load her battered brown suitcase on the train to Portland.

She had left that day and hadn't returned for fifty years. Now she stood down the street from him, smaller than he remembered, but still agile, her long brown hair replaced by a silver cap of curls, her last name twice changed to something he couldn't recall, and he felt as if the moment he had been waiting for all of his life had finally arrived.

* * *

CHARLIE WINTER turned his 1978 Oldsmobile into the driveway behind Dunstaff's. The spring rains had left potholes in the gravel, and Charlie hit each one, cursing as the Olds' ancient shocks failed to absorb the impacts. He was already annoyed that he had to come to Dunstaff's—Michael's idea of handicapped access was a plywood board over the second set of stairs leading into the front door—but Charlie had known Olivia Hawthorne his entire life, and he couldn't stomach not paying his respects.

He could have gone to the funeral, set for tomorrow morning, but he felt he had to come to the visitation as well. Olivia had tried to help him with his flashbacks, and even though her potions hadn't worked, she was one of the few who had tried to help him.

One of the few who had even noticed him.

He owed her for that alone.

He parked as close to the narrow sidewalk as he dared, then opened the heavy door and swung his legs out. His right leg was artificial. His left was his own, but getting more and more useless. The shrapnel the doctors in Hawaii had decided to leave under his skin was sensitive to the damp, the cold, even to his moods.

Some days he could barely get out of bed for the pain.

He grabbed his cane—he'd be damned if Addy would see him with crutches—and used it as a lever to pull himself out of the car. He wore his second best suit—he was saving his best for the funeral tomorrow—and he had slicked back what remained of his hair with Vitalis.

The cane wobbled in the gravel, and he had to swing his right leg to keep his balance. Thank heavens it hadn't rained in the last week. Dunstaff's plywood board was dry, not nearly as slippery as it could have been. Still, even with the asbestos mat Michael had stuck to the board in the mid-eighties, the thing would be slick.

Addy stood on the porch. She wore a black skirt and a white blouse, schoolgirl clothes that made her seem young despite the silver curls on her head. Her daughter Lisa, the former hippie, Olivia's pride and joy, stood next to her. Addy took a step forward as if to help Charlie, but Lisa held her back.

He gritted his teeth and gripped the iron railing that was rusting away in the salt air. The railing shook as he leaned his weight on it, but he had no choice. When he got inside, he'd remind Michael that as the population of Dory Cove aged, the need for good handicapped access would grow greater.

He climbed the ramp like a man in his eighties instead of one in his sixties. The rubber tip on his cane gripped the mat, but his shiny dress shoes slid. Only the strength in his arms and shoulders kept him upright. He kept his gaze on the ramp, unable to face Addy.

The last time he had seen her, he had been drenched from the storm, exhausted and terrified, tears running down his face. Spence had drowned in the storm-tossed waters of the Churn, Addy screaming, Billy reaching for him, Evelyn standing back, her hands over her face. Charlie had done nothing. He had been too far away. Finally, too late, he had run up the path for help. The memory still lived in his legs, but it felt, upon reflection, like a memory that belonged to someone else. And perhaps it did. Young Charlie Winter, the one who could run and cry, had died five years later when he stepped on a Jap mine on Iwo Jima.

When he reached the top of the ramp, Addy was waiting for him, her slender hand outstretched. "Charlie?" she said, sounding surprised.

He looked up to see pity and sorrow mingling in her eyes. Her face had the delicate lines of a rich man's widow, of a woman who had never faced the salt of the sea. He ignored the hand she had extended to him, and as he gained his balance on the creaky porch, Lisa said, "I didn't know you two knew each other."

"We don't," Charlie said.

Addy let her hand fall to her side. "Charlie," she said, "we were friends once."

He shook his head. "I was never your friend, Adelaide."

As he pulled open the heavy metal door, he heard Addy's sharp intake of breath. Served her right for abandoning them all after the Storm, leaving Dory Cove and never coming back. Served her right. She hadn't even bothered to stay for Spence's funeral, and she had been his girl, his very best girl. He had died with her engagement ring, newly bought, in his pocket.

* * *

THE TIMER BUZZED, the sound covering the wrap-up of the day's news on *All Things Considered*. Evelyn Brand shut off the timer, tucked a strand of still-dark hair behind her ear, then pulled on her oven mitts. The kitchen smelled of chocolate cake. Olivia had loved Evelyn's chocolate cake with marshmallow frosting, and Evelyn thought it only fitting that there be some at the memorial service in the morning.

Addy had elected to hold the meal at the Senior Center, an oddity for the coast. Addy claimed that Olivia's house wasn't big enough to serve a meal, and she was probably right. But Evelyn couldn't help wondering if there was something else behind it. Addy had never liked that house, even though she had been born there.

She hadn't even returned when Evelyn wrote that Olivia was so sick. Addy had sent Lisa in her stead.

Evelyn had nursed her own parents through long bouts with cancer, had seen her husband through years of heart disease and high blood pressure, and watched her child die from a fall off the rocks outside the Cove. She couldn't imagine leaving a loved one in someone else's hands, not when death was always hovering near.

But that was Addy. She never stuck around for the bad times. She had been on the run since she was nineteen years old.

Evelyn pulled out the battered metal cake pan that she had had since her wedding in 1943, and set it on top of the stove. The cake looked done, its top brown and firm, receded from the pan's sides, but she took a toothpick and checked anyway. She plunged the pick into the middle of the cake, then pulled it out. The pick came out clean. She set the pan on top of the cooling rack and closed the oven door with her hip.

Her kitchen was large—it had once seated her family comfortably—and the big bay windows overlooked the ocean. She took off her apron and hung it on the peg near the door, then went to the window as she always did, to watch the sun disappear over the horizon.

Olivia had taught her that custom, taught both Evelyn and Addy when they'd been growing up together in the tiny town of Dory Cove. In those days Olivia used to take out the Book and read to them, teaching the girls both the magic and the religion that belonged to the Churn. Already Zeke Hawthorne, Addy's father, was missing, had been since the early thirties when he took his small fishing boat too far out to sea. Each night Olivia would stand at the windows of her kitchen and watch the sun go down.

Someday your father will come back, she'd say to Addy.

Addy never questioned it. Evelyn wasn't sure Addy believed it. But Evelyn did.

How'd you know? Evelyn had asked once, when she was seventeen and thought she understood everything.

Olivia's eyes had turned dreamy. *The sun will glow green and the sea will become hard as stone. And he'll walk up from the deep.*

Evelyn had never asked again, but she had never forgotten. A few times she had seen the green glow over the ocean: once in 1945, once more in 1960, and last in 1977, and she wondered what demons had emerged from the deep. Those years transients died near the Churn, and tourists reported seeing a beautiful man with a tail for legs searching for something on the Churn's rocky shore.

Olivia had never seen the glow. She didn't believe anyone had seen the beautiful man. When Evelyn asked in 1945, Olivia had accused her of making the story up. *I would know,* Olivia had said. *I watch, and I would know.*

Behind Evelyn the radio blared the news theme. She sighed and stepped closer, feeling the chill of the evening radiate off the window glass. The sun was setting, sinking quickly behind the horizon, as it always did here, as if someone had the sun on a string and was yanking it beneath the water.

At the last minute the light reflected green across the sea. Evelyn's breath caught. She half expected to see Olivia on the waves, walking to the deep, searching for the husband who had been missing for half a century. Instead where the light touched the ocean, the water was smooth as glass. She felt that if she could get closer, she could see below the surface to the fish, the wrecked ships, the sandy bottom. But she was on top of a hill, across 101, almost a mile away.

The green glow was a solid path, leading to the Churn. She picked up her binoculars and put them against her face, their cold metal a shock. She blinked and then her eyesight adjusted. As it did, a man lifted himself on the solidness of the green as a person would do to get out of a swimming pool. Her heart was pounding, and she quickly put the binoculars down.

It couldn't be Zeke. Not after all the decades Olivia had waited for him. It wouldn't be fair that Zeke would appear a few days after Olivia died.

She had to look. She owed it to Olivia to look. She brought the binoculars back to her face, scanned the glow, but could see no one.

The man had vanished.

Then the sun dipped behind the horizon, and the glow faded as if it had never been.

She scanned the water, searching for a tiny bobbing head. Nothing. The surface was covered with sea foam. Waves broke across the top, their pattern regular and comforting. The sea had never been flat. She had imagined it all.

Imagined it because she had been thinking of Olivia, whom she would miss.

A lump rose in her throat. She put the binoculars in her holder and leaned against the window. The ocean appeared dark and sinister now, not the friend she usually thought it to be.

"Olivia," Evelyn murmured, feeling the power of a dream unfulfilled. Then she sighed, turned her back on the darkening sky, and went to frost the cake.

2

THE HOME ADDY was born in had been built on a sand cliff overlooking the Pacific Ocean. The house had been big for its time—a kitchen, two parlors, and a bedroom on the first floor; three bedrooms on the second. The house had originally been made of Douglas fir. By the time Addy realized what a firetrap her mother was living in, she had no money to do anything about it. She had had to wait until the mid-sixties to send money for the remodeling, and then she had sent the cash to Evelyn Brand with strict instructions for its use. Evelyn had begged Addy to return and convince her mother to make the changes, but Addy had refused. A year later Evelyn had sent photographs of the house's new look. Her mother had stood in each, glowering angrily at the camera. Addy had thrown the pictures away.

She hadn't gotten to see the changes until this week, the week of her mother's death.

The house Addy remembered dated from the 1930s. The exterior was the same: the Victorian styling, the wide porch surrounding the front, the dormers on the second floor, and the long roof that extended down the front like a slope. The new siding looked like a new coat of paint, and the windows were different—double-paned and made of reinforced glass.

The interior, though, the interior almost belonged to someone else.

The living room still held the deep cranberry furniture her mother had received as a wedding present. The matching rug was thin with age and faded near the windows. The long, uncomfortable sofa was covered with doilies and handmade pillows. A television set stood where the radio used to be, and a digital clock spun the time on top of it. Photographs of every family member graced the walls where her mother's seascapes once hung.

The dining room furniture was the same, the thick oak table with its heavy, rounded legs and matching chairs, one of which still bore the scar from Addy's fall at the age of three. Her mother's bedroom smelled of mothballs, old woman, and illness. The double bed with its feather mattress was covered with handmade quilts, but the seascapes lined the walls in here. Someone had placed a cot at the foot of the bed and an extra dresser beside it.

Addy had chosen to sleep in her old room upstairs and had tried to avoid the kitchen as long as she could.

For the kitchen held the most memories for her: when she thought of the house, she thought of her mother, standing tall and proud at the kitchen windows overlooking the sea, watching the sun set and waiting for the green glow that would bring her husband back. The house was built on a cliff over the beach, with a large stone retaining wall built around it. Her mother's garden hid inside the wall, and often her mother would go outside at twilight to pick vegetables for dinner and to get a better view of the sea.

But not all the memories were of her mother. Some were of the stove, a mammoth room-dominating cast-iron creature, in which a fire burned constantly.

The kitchen smelled of baked bread and wood, smells Addy had always associated with home. Smells that were missing now.

For the kitchen had been completely redone. The windows overlooking the sea were floor-to-ceiling panes that brought in light. The cross-hatched panes were protected from shattering by subtle reinforcements.

The kitchen had been widened: the woodlift from the cellar was gone, no longer needed now that the stove was heated with electricity. The stove itself was a tiny modern thing one-eighth the size of the one Addy remembered, and a refrigerator stood beside it. The icebox room had been remade into a breakfast nook, with an even better view of the sea.

Addy didn't notice the greatest difference until the morning of her mother's funeral. She had stumbled into the kitchen, made a pot of French roast with her mother's Mr. Coffee, and had taken a donut from the box Lisa had bought at the bakery on 101. Addy had stood in the kitchen holding her steaming mug and staring at the changes, then she had gone into the breakfast nook.

Her breath caught in her throat. For a moment she thought she had misremembered her life, her past, her entire being. And then she realized what had happened.

The garden was gone, replaced by a row of shrubs bent easterly with the wind. The shrubs looked thin, and as she approached the window, her coffee mug clutched in her chilled hand, she realized that they were thin because nothing protected them from the wind.

She took a sip, more from nervous habit than out of desire, and found the coffee too hot to drink. She set the mug on the blond wood table next to her plate, rubbed her hands on her robe, and opened the kitchen door.

Immediately the sea sounded closer. What had been a gentle lulling a moment before had become a roar. The wind caught and teased her hair. Her mouth went dry. She hadn't looked at the sea, really looked, since Spence died.

Initially she had been afraid to, afraid that with one glance she would retrieve her mother's Book and look for spells. And then, after Addy had left Dory Cove, she thought she was safe.

She had seen the sea when she arrived, peeking through buildings and around trees like a misbehaving child, but she had chosen not to look at it, not to think about it. The sea was ever present in Dory Cove. In some ways the sea was Dory Cove. But she had thought she would make it through these next few weeks without really seeing it, without really letting it touch her consciousness.

She had been wrong.

The sunlight on the waves made the water look blue. The line between the sea and the sky had blurred; she couldn't find the horizon. The air smelled of salt and adventure, and for a moment, her heart leapt with that childish energy, the energy that had led her from the house every morning until she turned twelve, the energy that made her walk barefoot on the cold sand, and play in the dangerous waters, and laugh at the waves.

She remembered that feeling as if it had never left. In those days the sea had been part of her, and she part of it. Her mother used to sit on the beach and watch Addy frolic in the cold water, laughing as she called Addy part fish.

Then the sea had taken her father, and it seemed friendly no longer.

Spence had taught her to look at the sea like a wild creature, unpredictable, beautiful, dangerous, with a life of its own. She had started walking on the sand again when the Storm—

She shook the memory from her, envisioned it leaving her mind on the trail of wind. Above her a gull floated, its wings bent to catch the drafts. If she half closed her eyes, she could almost believe that someone had painted it there, a white brush stroke against a vivid blue canvas.

The door slipped from her hands and slammed against the side of the house, startling her. Someone had put the door on backward, so that it caught the wind instead of protecting from it. She stepped down the concrete stoop, took the door handle, and shoved the door closed, only to find herself standing in the remains of her mother's garden.

Two rhododendrons had been planted against the side of the house, their flowers almost past their bloom. The ground was sandy, the grass scraggly, as if it had never found purchase after the garden was removed. The shrubs barely came up to Addy's thighs. They were ugly green-gray things, twisted by the constant wind.

The retaining wall was long gone. What had once been a large cliff-top had become barely big enough for the family's house. Wind, erosion, and storms had nibbled away at the cliff face, making it part of the beach below. She wondered how long ago her mother had planted the shrubs, what sort of vain hope some "expert" had given her about stopping erosion, about preventing the sea from stealing her property inch by inch.

Addy followed the remains of the ancient garden path, rabbit thin now, the stones that her father had laid in the year of her birth windrounded and cracked.

She stopped at the edge of the shrubs and stared over them at the years of destruction beyond.

A dozen shrubs still littered the cliff face. They lay on their sides, roots exposed to the early-morning sunlight, sand covering the branches like the fingers of a possessive lover. Scattered beyond them were bits of the retaining wall, rough-edged stones and broken bits of mortar. An entire section of the wall rested near the base of the cliff.

The beach had expanded here, becoming almost as big as the public beach in the center of the town. The cliff had become sand, the sand flattened into beach, the beach merged with the sea.

She swallowed convulsively, two, three, four times, then gulped air. It caught in her diaphragm and worked its way back up—a hiccup, then another, a nervous habit she thought had disappeared with childhood. She held her breath, her heart pounding against her chest, and stared at the curving lines the water had left in the sand.

Someday the sea would take the entire cliff, the house, the furniture, and all the memories. Someday soon.

The wind toyed with the curls on her forehead, gently playing with them, feeling her the way a blind woman would touch a long-lost friend. Time passed so quickly now. It seemed like only yesterday she had been an impatient teenager, unable to understand her mother's obsession with the sea. She could touch that emotion, feel it as immediately as the wind against her face. If she closed her eyes, she could see her mother, sensible skirt blowing against her high-button boots, the breeze teasing tendrils from the tight knot on the back of her head, hands on the retaining wall, expression distant as she stared at the sea, hoping it would regurgitate its dead.

It never did, at least not as living creatures. Only as mangled, bloated bodies, bruised-gray and recognizable only by clothing or the ring that managed to cling to a bent and broken finger. Her father had never washed ashore. He disappeared in 1932. Some said he left the coast looking for work, and others swore he had run from Addy's mother and her dark, evil ways.

But his boat had come ashore, its hull cracked, its rudder and anchor gone, and her father's favorite coat tied to the wheel. The water had been high that day.

Other fishermen had drowned, richer ones, who had gone out on larger boats. The fact that Addy's father washed over surprised no one, least of all Addy's mother. She had cursed him for disappearing so soon, but in the same breath she had said to Addy that her father would return.

The craziness had started then. The lessons from the Book, the services in a religion that had never been part of a church, the daily trips to the Churn.

Addy had hated it all.

A branch brushed against Addy's robe, pricking her thigh. She pushed the branch away, the needles sharp against her palm, and was about to go back inside when something caught her gaze.

A man walked around the cliff. From this height he was tiny, more a bird's-eye view of a man than a man himself. Still she could make out a few details.

His black hair was plastered against his skull, his clothing wet and pasted against his body as if he had been in a downpour and failed to dry off. He walked with his head down, hands shoved in the pockets of his pants, his shoulders huddled forward as if to protect himself against an unseen threat. His walk had no real purpose, yet he wasn't ambling as some did on the beach. He almost appeared to be pacing, or walking as she had once seen Spence do, walking and staring at the beach instead of crying.

Spence. The man on the beach reminded her of Spence.

Spence who died fifty years ago.

Because of her.

A shiver that had nothing to do with the wind ran down her back. She turned her back on the sea, the beach, the man, and hurried toward her mother's transformed house.

3

BILLY HADN'T BEEN INSIDE the Senior Center since Campbell Anderson retired from the weekly poker game. Campbell's arthritis had grown so bad that he could no longer hold the cards, and with his retirement went the only person who could outplay Billy. Campbell kept the game interesting; he and Billy would often have unspoken pacts to lose for a month or two so that the others would be able to collect their share of the penny pots. But Billy didn't want to keep up the ruse on his own, and the conversation had never been very stimulating. So he saw his friends on Seniors' Night at Pier 101 in the winter and on the beach on hazy summer mornings.

He had never been to the Senior Center for a funeral.

Someone had tied black balloons to the wooden handicap railing that led up the concrete steps. A notice on the door reminded those who didn't know that the rec area would be closed for a private gathering. Although he wondered how Olivia's funeral could be private. She had lived in Dory Cove all her life. The locals—even a number of the weekenders—had known her. Only the tourists had no idea of the tragedy Dory Cove had suffered. And the tourists would have no need to enter the Senior Center's recreation area.

Evelyn had told him to bring food. Food was her answer to everything. It was a wonder she hadn't ballooned to twice her original weight.

He had considered stopping at the Safeway at the north end of the Cove and taking a deli plate, but everyone would have seen through the ruse. The town knew that Billy Malone never cooked. He had his breakfast at Ruthie's on Timber Street, his lunches at the Pier, and his dinners with whatever friend would take him. Billy Malone had other uses in Dory Cove. He was surprised that Addy hadn't come to him with some legal question. He knew that Olivia's will was twisty—all her bitterness, her longing, and her unfulfilled dreams were in that document—but Addy had said nothing to him. Perhaps she hadn't read it yet.

The Center looked different this morning, darker, somber, as if some of the joy had left its walls. He usually loved this place. It had once been the old high school gym. The wooden floor had become uneven over time—a hazard to elderly feet—and the sea wind had formed dry rot on the west face, but the ancient folded-up bleachers and the nonregulation basketball hoops spoke of a hope that all the seniors had, that their ancient bodies would be given new life, that they would get one more chance at a slam dunk, one more opportunity to run the length of the court and back without wheezing.

A few years ago Abel Rodgers had proposed redecorating the interior, putting in tile floors and removing the bleachers, but for once Billy, who normally supported sensible measures, opposed this one. He believed the hope was more important than even flooring, the memories etched into the fading tournament banners worth the risk of broken bones. Youth was not something people should cover over with sensible solutions, but a part of life, a part that was never entirely outgrown.

The Center's familiar scents of mothballs and boiled cabbage were now overlaid with the rich smell of food. The women had set up buffet tables beside the folded-up bleachers on the right wall, and from the door Billy could guess at the entrees: baked ham, twice-baked potatoes, green bean casserole. The list went on: the average church supper, the Friday-night bingo fare, the special-occasion potluck dinners. Only this time Olivia's cranberry nut bread wouldn't be among the tea cakes, her tuna casserole with its carefully apportioned bread crumbs in its usual green bowl wouldn't be between the potato dishes and Ruthie's wild-rice stuffing.

A small pang touched his heart. He and Olivia had made their peace long ago. Even though he had never liked her, he knew he would miss her. She had been a part of the Cove since he arrived.

He moved into the throng of early arrivals, the Funeral Goers, he called them, for their love of eulogies, even those given for people the Funeral Goers didn't know. He greeted each by name, then went to the kitchen door and offered his services to the Center staff. They sent him out to put up more metal folding chairs. The chairs were stacked beneath the basketball hoop on the far wall. When he picked up the first, his back complained. The metal was cold to the touch. He hadn't been this kind of useful in years. He was doing it to avoid watching the door, waiting for the moment when Addy arrived.

The huge ceilings in the Center made the conversations disappear. He heard the sound of voices but couldn't pick out tones or words. Yet the snap of the chairs, the ringing of the metal legs against the wooden floors, the groans he uttered each time his back twinged, seemed unbelievably loud to him. He worked until there were no more chairs to unfold and then he returned to the center of the gym floor.

The crowd had grown. He saw Charlie Winter making his careful way across the rutted wood. Evelyn was adjusting the desserts on the buffet table so that hers had a prominent place.

Addy hadn't yet arrived.

A woman in her forties, a member of the Center staff, was arranging flowers on tables near the door. Someone had set out a sign-up book so that the family would know who attended. Pictures of Olivia were scattered around the room. Most were of the Olivia the town had just known, the outspoken elderly woman who spent her Wednesdays at the Center, who splurged with her granddaughter for lunches at the Inn on Churn Beach, who made her careful way to the beach on warm summer evenings so that she could watch the sunset.

Only a few photographs were of the Olivia he had met when he came to town, the worry-lined woman who had reached an early middle age raising a daughter on the remains of a fisherman's income. Olivia had done well for herself. By the time she died, she had turned that pittance into a small fortune.

Billy still didn't know how she had done it. When he asked on the day she had made out her will, Olivia had smiled at him. *Sometimes the gods give,* she had said, *and sometimes they take away.*

He had known the second. Had always known the second. What he had never fathomed was Olivia's deep faith in a god who lived in the Churn, a god who was part of a pantheon of nature gods, who seemed more real to her than the people of Dory Cove. He hadn't fathomed that nor Olivia's belief that they watched out for her welfare.

Nor her sense of betrayal on the day she died.

Someone had placed Zeke and Olivia's wedding picture near a painting of the sea. Billy paused over it. Addy had none of Olivia's look, or Zeke's for that matter. She had developed into her own woman, with no resemblance at all to her family. Lisa looked like Olivia, except for the rounded chin and the gazelle-thin neck. Zeke appeared to have been lost in the genetic maelstrom. Olivia's genes had dominated her family, just as she had done.

Except for Addy.

Addy had always managed to escape.

A small platform had been set up in front of the chairs, and on a podium beside it rested another picture of Olivia. The body remained at the funeral home.

Olivia had an aversion to anyplace known as a chapel—she felt that such buildings barred her gods—and so a service, even in as nondenominational a place as a funeral home chapel, seemed wrong.

Addy had planned this part of the service well.

He sighed and straightened. The twinge in his back had become a low ache. As he stood, he saw a man in his forties enter, glance around in a confused manner, and make his way to the flower table to look at the photographs. His dark, thinning hair accented his cheekbones and showed that Olivia's eyes had traveled to another generation. Behind the man, a woman slipped through the door. She, too, had Olivia's features and the faded look of early middle age. She had two children in tow, and for a moment Billy wondered if history had repeated itself, if she, like Olivia, had had to raise them alone. Then a man entered behind her, clearly a husband, and they conferred as they glanced around the room.

The first man and the woman were Addy's children by her first husband, Tyler or Taylor or some such. The man who had made her a war bride, impregnated her twice, and divorced her a year after he returned. Olivia had called Addy after that, offering to pay Addy's train fare and to help raise the children if Addy would return to Dory Cove. But nothing, not even the humiliation of a postwar divorce, could drag Addy back to the town she had abandoned.

Nothing except the death of her own mother.

"That photograph has always been my favorite." The voice beside him was soft, female. He knew, just from the content of the sentence, that the speaker was not Addy.

He was wearing his formal smile by the time he turned, and then the smile became genuine. Addy's daughter Lisa stood beside him, her eyes red-rimmed and her cheeks tear-streaked. With ringless fingers still untouched by age, she adjusted the photograph slightly, pushing it just a hairbreadth closer to the painting.

She had planned the service, not her mother. Addy had never been as sensitive to Olivia's needs.

"They do look happy, don't they," Billy said, although he wasn't sure if the word was right. Olivia's smile had a touch of victory to it. Zeke was the one who looked lovestruck, as if the woman beside him were the center of his entire world.

Lisa nodded. Her eyes were tearing again. "Grandma wanted ... to be buried on the sea-side of the cemetery, but Mom refuses. Is there anything I can do?"

Billy suppressed a sigh. She was nearly a member of Dory Cove. Just like the others, she went to him for free legal advice and thought nothing of it, not realizing the jeopardy she put him in, the careful way he had to couch his answers so that he would protect himself from a misheard remark becoming a malpractice suit. Some of his colleagues refused to give advice altogether, but these were his friends, his neighbors. Billy couldn't turn them away, not even the ones who shunned him.

"Did your grandmother buy a plot?" he asked, even though he knew the answer. He had begged Olivia when she had made out the will to make her funeral arrangements. Her face had flushed then with the anger she had been holding back all that afternoon, anger he hoped had been at Addy, not at him.

I want someone to throw me into the Churn, she had said.

No one can do that, Olivia, he had said. *It's illegal now.*

But it's part of my religion. Surely you can fight it on those grounds, can't you, Billy?

I could try, Olivia. Do you want me to?

Seems an awful expense for something so silly, she had said, and he had thought that the end of it until Lisa told him how Olivia had gotten so sick.

"Grammy didn't buy a plot," Lisa was saying. "I wanted her to, but the will was as far as she would go."

"Has Addy read the will?"

"Not yet," Lisa said. "She wouldn't even go into Grandma's bedroom until last night. I had a hell of a time with her in the kitchen. She seemed so relieved that Gram and I had modernized it."

The kitchen had always been Olivia's domain. In Billy's first year at Dory Cove, work as a stock and delivery boy was the only job he could find, and even then people had complained that he stole employment from good white folks. Mr. Parnell had never been able to fill the position before Billy arrived. Still, Mr. Parnell insisted that Billy go to the back door when he made deliveries so that no one saw him standing like a white man on the front steps. The first time he had gone to the back of Olivia's and rapped on the metal screen, she had let out a yelp that sent a shiver down his back.

I don't want any man coming to my back door except Addy's father, she had said. *You come around to the front next time.*

When he had told Mr. Parnell, Mr. Parnell had shaken his head and muttered how he no longer understood women. It took a few months before Billy understood himself.

"Mr. Malone?" Lisa said.

He smiled at her. "Just a memory," he said. "Olivia's death has done that to me. Kind of like she was an anchor holding down the past. Now that she's gone, everything's swirling and bubbling."

"For me too," Lisa said, but somehow he doubted it. He had had a lot of memories when he was in his thirties, but the world was still the same. The war touched Dory Cove—the fear of Japanese invasion ever present—but he hadn't enlisted. No, the changes hadn't overwhelmed him until the late sixties. Olivia had explained that to him too: *Keep what you want from the old, and face the rest with courage. The best we can do is hang on to ourselves.*

Her way of hanging on to herself had been to cling to her fantasy of Zeke's return. She would never have been able to handle it if he had actually arrived. No one could.

"About that plot," Lisa said, "can I do something?"

Billy frowned to regain the thread of the conversation. The cemetery, a plot overlooking the sea. "Aren't they burying Olivia this afternoon?"

"No graveside services. She hoped—" Lisa flushed.

"I know what she hoped," Billy said.

"She wasn't crazy," Lisa said, and he understood the rest of the sentence even though she didn't say it. Olivia wasn't crazy despite how she died. She had climbed down the rocky path leading from her house to the Churn, slipped, and caught pneumonia in the rain. No one would have found her, either, if it hadn't been for the young hiker who happened to be exploring the Churn that day. He got her to the hospital, where she lingered for two weeks before her body gave out.

"I know she wasn't crazy," Billy said. "It's hard to practice a religion the rest of the world has forgotten." If they ever knew it.

"Not everyone has forgotten," Lisa said.

Billy glanced at Evelyn. She was talking to a female member of the Center staff. "No," he said. "I suppose you're right."

Lisa didn't follow his gaze. "I arranged for the burial to wait a day. I wanted to see if I could bring Mom around."

Billy sighed. Lisa had Olivia's determination. No matter how hard he tried, he couldn't wrench the conversation away from the subject of Olivia's burial. And he knew what Lisa wanted of him. "I'll talk with Addy."

Lisa's smile was soft, sad, and radiant at the same time. "Would you? I would appreciate it."

He nodded and felt himself smile in return. He had vaguely hoped he wouldn't have to talk with Addy, that he could look at her, and remember her, from afar. But he had committed himself now. He would have to make the first overture.

Mae Nuyen approached Lisa, twisting a handkerchief in her swollen, wrinkled hands. She wore her black funeral frock, stained with punch along one side, and a black straw hat that was becoming unwound. Mae still lived alone, although she shouldn't be. The entire town looked after her. Olivia had in particular.

"Lisa, honey," Mae said in her quavering voice, and Billy used the moment to escape.

Lisa's half-sister and -brother were standing side by side, talking and nodding with Michael Dunstaff. The children held their father's hand a few feet away, looking solemn in their Sunday best. The Senior card players were gathered around Campbell, who was making one of his rare appearances, and Olivia's friends from Bingo Night were having a heated discussion near some of the older pictures.

Addy still hadn't arrived. The services couldn't start without her. Billy glanced at Lisa, still talking with Mae, and wished he had taken the time to ask why she had arrived without her mother. So typical of Addy to miss every important event in Olivia's life, including the eulogies.

Then the Center door swung open, and Addy stood in the frame. A square of sunshine cut through the artificial lighting, reminding Billy that there was a beautiful day outside these walls, a day in which tourists flew kites on the beach, and children ran, laughing, after the family dog.

Addy appeared to be steeling herself to face the crowd of her mother's friends, her old friends, her daughter's friends. He still wasn't used to the curls that topped her head, nor the simple elegance with which she dressed. Her black dress gathered at the waist and released into a full skirt that would have looked festive if she were dancing. But she was not. Her legs were still good. She carried a tiny black purse that matched her pumps. Her stylishness would count against her in Dory Cove; the people here cared more for the deceased than they did fashion.

No one greeted her. Charlie Winter, who sat near the door, pretended to adjust his cane. Several old-timers deliberately moved out of her way. Her children glanced over the heads of the people they were talking with, nodded at her, but did not rush to her side. Her granddaughter shouted, "Grandma!" but her son-in-law held the little girl back, preventing her from running to her grandmother.

Addy waggled her fingers at the girl, but continued toward the center of the room.

Conversation continued, a dull sound that got eaten by the high ceilings, but it almost seemed as if no one spoke. Certainly everyone was watching her. Some people had never seen Addy Hawthorne, had only heard of her in whispered conversations behind Olivia's back.

She weaved in and out of the uneven rows of chairs, searching. Finally she seemed to find what she was looking for. Her gaze appeared to lock on Billy's. His heart leapt. No one who had lived in Dory Cove during the Depression acknowledged Billy Malone first. No one.

But she didn't smile, and after a moment he realized she wasn't looking at him, but at Lisa. Mae's plaintive voice paused mid-sentence, and like everyone else in the Center, she watched Addy.

Addy's shoes clicked on the wood, the purposeful sound of a woman who used feminine clothing as a tool of power. She stopped in front of Lisa without even appearing to notice Mac or Billy.

"You could have started without me," she said softly.

"It's a funeral, Mom."

Addy shrugged. Her words sounded cold, but the tightness of her face, the way she held her mouth, suggested that Addy Hawthorne wanted desperately to be somewhere else, that if she stayed in the Center much longer, she would break into loud, wailing sobs. Billy started to step forward, to say to Addy how sorry he was about her loss, to soften her arrival into the middle of Dory Cove society, when she reached around her daughter.

Addy ran a finger along the wooden frame around the seascape, then with a sharp, violent gesture, pulled it facedown. The slap echoed throughout the Center, and any conversation that hadn't stopped did.

"It's Grammy's funeral, Mom," Lisa said, her voice pleading. She hovered over the table as if she wasn't certain if she should pick up the painting or leave it lie.

There was a queer fluttering in Billy's stomach. His heart was pounding harder than usual. Lisa had asked him to get involved with the burial; this was probably the first step.

"Addy," he said, his voice so soft, he was certain no one else heard him. "Olivia loved the sea."

She whirled, and her skirt flared as he had known it would. "Billy Malone," she said, her blue eyes dry and hard. "I thought I'd read somewhere that you had gotten an education."

Billy's face grew hot. He was suddenly thankful for his color, thankful that his blush wouldn't show. He swallowed against the dryness in his throat. "Olivia would want the seascape."

"Olivia is dead." Addy's face was white, unnaturally white. He couldn't tell if she had become pale with anger or with grief.

"But we're here to remember her," Billy said.

"I'm sure we can remember her without the goddamn sea," Addy said.

"I don't believe we can," Billy said. He reached around Lisa and set the painting upright. "The sea was part of Olivia."

"Don't I know it," Addy said. "I don't need to be reminded."

"But some of us do." Billy had adopted his lawyer tone now, the one he used with unreasonable clients. "We're here for your mother, to remember her life, to celebrate who she was. Your mother was a mainstay of this community, and her love of the sea was part of that. If you find something you don't like, you can grit your teeth, smile, and pretend it doesn't bother you. Or you can leave."

He wasn't certain if it was Lisa who gasped or the entire room. The look Addy shot him was pure hatred.

"She was my mother."

"It would do you good to remember that," Billy said.

4

CHARLIE WINTER used his plastic fork to push Lucinda's green bean casserole away from his three slices of ham. Evelyn had given him too much food, as usual, and most of it was vegetables, things he would never ever eat. Fortunately she had brought a second Chinet plate filled with desserts to compensate.

He was sitting as close to the door as he could get. After he had said his public good-bye to Olivia, recounting the time after the war when she had brought him a dinner and saved him from himself, he did not return to his original seat. He had walked to the tiny sign-in table near the door. Evelyn later confided that she had expected him to walk out. He should have too. He had said his personal good-byes to Olivia the night before while he stared at her sunken face. He couldn't believe that she had died. She had always seemed powerful to him, more powerful than anything.

What he hadn't said during his eulogy was that the day she had brought him dinner, she had found his body in his living room, but his mind had been in the Pacific, his gun trained on a young Japanese soldier who was about to kill him. Olivia had cracked a rib trying to bring Charlie to the present.

After that, he had never understood how anyone could think her malicious or evil.

Especially Addy. Olivia had given everything to Addy, and Addy had paid her back by leaving and then by creating a scene at Olivia's memorial. Just like Addy to forget this funeral was not about her. Amazing that fifty years could go by without the girl learning a damn thing. She was as selfish as she had always been.

Good thing Billy confronted her. Charlie hadn't even wanted to talk to her. But she had spoiled the funeral for her family. Lisa, at least, would want to remember her grandmother in a special way. The others probably would too.

He picked at the store-bought white bread Carolyn Murphy had brought—a woman with that many kids should've at least learned to bake—and winced when his fingers slid into the melting packet of butter that Evelyn had placed below the bread. He missed Olivia's cranberry nut bread. He always gave Evelyn instructions to get him two slices, and she always brought three. He had half hoped that Addy would bring the tea bread, but she had come in clutching only her purse.

Selfish again.

She sat alone in the rows of folding chairs, hunched over her plate, eating daintily, trying to keep the food off her expensive dress. Her granddaughter had sat beside her for a while, until the little girl got bored and rejoined her family.

Addy wasn't making points with anyone on this day.

Her eulogy was embarrassingly short. She probably wouldn't have made a statement at all if Father Callahan hadn't asked her to go first. He had taken the situation under control after the blowup. Someone had to. Better someone with experience.

Charlie pulled the fat off the slice of roast beef that Evelyn had given him and ate it. The doc had warned him about cholesterol for years, but Charlie didn't care. If he went out, he would at least have gone out enjoying his meals. He didn't have anyone to worry about him. Unlike Addy, who had an entire family without Olivia, he had no children, no woman, no parents. He had been alone since his parents died after the war.

Addy's son stopped at the table. He was lean and angular, even though he had to be nearing fifty. His hair was balding on the crown. His eyes were red with suppressed tears.

"Would you mind if I took the book?" he said, his baritone so soft that Charlie almost couldn't hear it. "I think maybe it'll pull Mother out of her shell."

"I don't care," Charlie said.

The son, Marty, Martin Andrew Taylor—Charlie remembered because Olivia was upset that Addy hadn't named him for Zeke— shot Charlie an odd glance, as if something in Charlie's tone had disturbed him. The boy had no right to judge Charlie. As far as Charlie was concerned, they were all as bad as Addy. All except Lisa, the young, pretty one, the one who had visited Olivia every week for the last fifteen years.

She had sat in the front as close to the podium as she could get. And when it came time for her to speak, she had struggled so hard against tears that her words were almost unintelligible. Evelyn said that Lisa had planned Olivia's funeral, that Lisa had begged her mother to come, that Lisa had tried to make everything right.

Addy had refused to come when Olivia was sick, had almost refused to come to bury her mother, until she was told that nothing could proceed without her. Lisa had been beside herself, Evelyn said, with anger, with tears, with frustration.

Almost made Charlie glad he had no family. When he died, the state got his stuff, someone would hold an auction, and no one would bother to have a feast in the gymnasium where he had learned to play basketball at the age of six.

The son took the book, and the pen as if he thought Charlie would steal it, and walked behind the folding chairs toward his mother. Addy crouched closer to her plate, her shoulders down. When her son sat beside her, she looked at him as if she didn't recognize him. He held out the book and she grinned, shook her head, then returned to eating. The son sat beside her for a while, watching her eat, then he stood and walked toward the back of the room where his sister and her family ate at one of the buffet tables. He carried the book with him.

Lisa wound her way around the chairs, avoiding her mother, stopping to speak with the members of the poker group and the Friday Night Bingo club. When she finally got to Charlie, he was ready for her. He held out the thin, clear plastic cup, punch still lining its bottom, and said, "Mind getting me more?"

Her smile was genuine. "Not at all." She took the cup from him and walked to the table.

He never understood how a girl like her failed to get married. She had the looks, the brains, and the compassion. Some guy should have snapped her up long ago.

She came back carrying two glasses. She set them both on the table, then grabbed one of the folding chairs and placed it beside his. He sighed. He had thought the drink trick would get rid of her. It usually worked with Evelyn.

"Mom said last night she knew you."

Charlie shrugged. "Long time ago."

"She said you were friends."

"She don't know what friendship is." Charlie took his punch glass and sipped. Then he pushed aside his plate with the green beans and creamed peas untouched.

Lisa looked down at her hands. "I'm sorry," she said. "It's just Grammy never talked about Mom much."

"I can see why," Charlie said. He pulled the dessert plate closer. Evelyn's chocolate marshmallow cake, Ruthie's strawberry pie, four chocolate chip cookies from the bakery, and a German chocolate cake whose origins he didn't recognize.

None went with punch made from 7UP, Kool-Aid, and ginger ale.

"Would you rather have coffee?" Lisa asked.

He glanced at her. Evelyn would have asked to make him feel guilty. But Lisa seemed genuinely concerned. She had been that way with Olivia, too, helping her remodel the house, taking her out to eat, making sure she was comfortable as her heart gave slowly stopped working.

Evelyn should have learned that genuine look because it worked. He felt as if he were being rude. But that didn't stop him from asking for the coffee. "If you don't mind," he said, wondering where he had ever learned those polite words.

She took his dinner plate, scraped the food remains into one garbage can, and put the plate in another. Then she went to the big silver coffee urn, took one of the large chipped mugs, and filled it. When she finished, she turned to him and waved a hand over the cream and sugar. He shook his head. He would have enough sugar with dessert.

Actually he should have been helping her. No one in her family seemed to care. Sure, the brother looked as if he had been crying, but Charlie couldn't remember the last time the guy had visited Olivia. And he had left the arrangements to Lisa, just like his sister had. Then there was Addy, who was still hunched over her plate like a hooker begging God for forgiveness.

"No cream or sugar?" Lisa asked as she sat.

He took the mug from her. The heat hadn't entirely worked its way through the ceramic. "That's right." He held his plate out to her. "Want a cookie?"

She grinned. It created small lines around her eyes. Even she was getting older. Somewhere near forty, if memory served him, although she looked like she had just gotten out of college.

"Sure." She took the smallest one.

"You can have two," he said.

She shook her head.

He picked up the largest cookie and took a large bite. Crumbs spilled down his shirt and onto his best suit. He brushed them away. "So what," he said, trying not to sound as reluctant as he felt, "do you want to know about Addy?"

"Why she hates this place," Lisa said.

Charlie coughed, slapped his chest, and then sipped the punch. The mixture of tart and sweet puckered his lips. He had to take a drink of the too-hot coffee to compensate.

When the crisis had passed, he had an answer. It was the best he could do without warning. "Your grandmother wasn't the easiest woman back then. She had a lot to think about, like how to raise a girl without a father on very little money. Addy blamed the Cove, blamed the sea, for her father's death. It wasn't until—" Spence, he wanted to say, Spence who had helped her through that. But telling Lisa about Spence opened too many doors better left closed. "I think she might have got over it, except for that storm."

"The one where her boyfriend died."

He nodded, and took another bit of cookie. They had used syrup instead of sugar in the mix, and it made the cookie chewier than he liked. "You got to remember context, though. Her father drowned. Then the boy she thought she was going to marry drowned. She couldn't stay here after that."

Lisa took a delicate nibble of her own cookie, her gaze far away. She seemed satisfied with his answer. "You'd think," she said slowly, "that she'd get over it."

He shook his head. "Some things you don't get over."

She glanced at his legs before looking at his face. She thought he was talking about that. A man never forgot his injury, not when he had to deal with it moment to moment. But he hadn't actually been talking about his legs, or even the war. And the realization left him chilled.

"You think she'll sell Grammy's house?" Lisa asked.

He finished the cookie and wiped his mouth with the back of his hand. "You know her better than I do. I haven't talked to her in fifty years."

"Except last night."

"If you call that talking." He sipped coffee to clear his palate, then took a taste of the German chocolate. It had the flavor of store-bought. He pushed it aside.

Lisa patted his good knee and stood up. Then she made her way across the room again, stopping and talking briefly to everyone she knew. Olivia's heir apparent, a woman who had a kind word for everyone. Only Lisa didn't have Olivia's darkness.

Addy did.

5

EVELYN BRAND scooped the last piece of chocolate marshmallow cake out of the battered pan and grabbed a piece of Chinet. She put the cake on it, slid a napkin on the bottom, and placed a plastic fork on the side. Then she excused herself from her duties as unofficial hostess of this event and walked across the gym floor to Addy.

Others had tried to speak to her. Her little granddaughter had succeeded for a time, playing finger games with Addy, and laughing even though Addy didn't join her. Her son had tried, but Addy had clearly rebuked him. Evelyn had seen the decades-old pain on his face as he walked away. Everyone else had given Addy a wide berth. Billy had even left early, obviously appalled at calling attention to himself at Olivia's memorial.

Evelyn had no such qualms. She owed it to Olivia, just as she owed Olivia everything else.

Evelyn's sensible flat shoes caught on the uneven wood planks and she wished, for the hundredth time, that Billy would get over his sentimentalism. Abel Rodgers had been right when he tried to make the place over. He had thought he would have Billy on his side. But for once Billy was on the side of the old fogies.

He liked the memories he had of this place, although he had never gone to school in Dory Cove. He had been a janitor here before he got his education, and yet he didn't want it touched.

The crowd was thinning now. People had had their meals, and their conversations about Olivia. Those who had missed the viewing last night were going for a viewing this afternoon. There would be no graveside service, for which Evelyn was relieved. She wished it were possible for Olivia to be returned to the Churn, as was her wish, but it was too late for that.

If only Olivia had asked her for help instead of going to the Churn herself.

But Evelyn knew why Olivia hadn't. It required faith in Evelyn, faith that Evelyn believed as deeply as Olivia. And Evelyn never had. They both knew that.

She had tried. But Olivia's attitude toward Evelyn had contaminated Evelyn's beliefs. Olivia had always thought Evelyn second best, certainly not as talented or as important as Addy. Evelyn had thought that attitude would change over the years, but it never had.

For Olivia, Evelyn was a substitute. A marked substitute.

Addy sat alone, like a child who expected a spanking. Her loose curls were silver with touches of black. Her dress accented her hair. From the back, she looked like a woman of forty or less—she had the full figure of middle age, but that was the only thing that belied her apparent youth. It wasn't until a person saw her gently textured face, her lined neck and age-spotted hands, that the fact she was near seventy became apparent.

Seventy was old to be losing a parent. Evelyn had lost hers twenty years before.

She couldn't imagine having her mother around now. It seemed almost unnatural—a woman needed time to head her clan. Addy might not have that time.

Evelyn entered Addy's row and stopped one chair away. Evelyn held the plate and waited until Addy noticed her. It took a full minute before Addy looked up.

"Did you come to tell me what an ass I made of myself?" Addy asked.

"Actually," Evelyn said, "I brought you the last piece of cake."

To her surprise, Addy smiled and set her half-finished plate aside. She hadn't touched the meat or the twice-baked potatoes, but all of the vegetables were gone, even Agnes's horrible creamed peas. She took the plate Evelyn offered her and patted the chair beside her.

Evelyn sat at the edge of the chair, uncertain whether she was going to relax into the moment or not. She had, in the interchange, lost control of the situation, but she wasn't certain how.

Addy cut a piece of cake with her plastic fork. The frosting splintered, revealing the marshmallow beneath. She ate, swallowed, and nodded as if she agreed with the taste or it agreed with her.

"I don't know why this place brings out the worse in me," she said. "I wasn't going to come back, but Lisa insisted."

Evelyn resisted the urge to glance around the room. Addy had never confided in her, not in the time she lived in Dory Cove, nor after she had left. "Perhaps it's not the place. Perhaps it's Olivia."

Addy shook her head. "I'd love to blame Mom, but she had nothing to do with Spence."

She half gasped in the middle of the last word, as if she hadn't expected to say it. Evelyn's memory flashed on Spence, not on his face, which she could only remember vaguely now, but on the warmth of his hand when he had touched her cheek two days before he died.

"Evelyn." Addy's voice was soft. "Is the beach near Mom's house still private?"

"Beaches are never private in Oregon," Evelyn said automatically. She had to answer that question routinely when she helped out at the Tourist Information Center. Tourists always wanted to know how far they could walk. Evelyn would patiently explain that the state owned the beaches. Anyone could walk.

"I know that," Addy said. "That's not what I mean. Is it still hard to get to? Don't tourists usually avoid it?"

"Usually," Evelyn said. The beach was more accurately described as a small cove. To get to it from the north, a person had to climb over a series of ever-slicker rocks. To get to it from the east, a person had to trespass and slide down the cliff face that eroded on Olivia's land. The only way to easily walk on the beach was to walk around the Devil's Churn, follow the carved footpath down the side of the lava rock, and jump to the sand below. It was a young person's journey. If Evelyn tried it now, she would break bones. It was amazing that Olivia had gone as far as she had. "Why? Did something happen?"

Addy cut another piece of cake, but did not eat it. "I saw a man walking along the water's edge this morning."

Evelyn waited for more, but Addy remained quiet. After a moment she stabbed the piece of cake and ate it. Evelyn wasn't quite certain what to make of the revelation. "Did he threaten you in some way?"

Addy shook her head. "He didn't even see me."

"Then what—"

"Grandma!" The little girl barreled into Addy's leg. Addy had to hold the chair in front of her to keep her balance. "Daddy says we get to stay at Great-Grandma's house."

A man stood at the end of the row, looking chagrined. Addy didn't look at him. Instead she set the cake plate down and pulled the little girl onto her lap.

"Evelyn," Addy said. "This is my granddaughter, Tiffany Taylor-Simmons. Tiffany, this is my old friend, Mrs. Brand."

"Tiffany," Evelyn said, smiling at the girl. Tiffany grinned back, clearly lacking the shyness that Evelyn remembered in the young Addy.

"You coming to Great-Grandma's house?" Tiffany said. "Daddy says it's right by the sea."

The man made his way toward Addy. "I'm sorry," he said softly. "But somehow she heard that your mother's house was by the sea and she decided we'd go."

"It's all right, Bruce," Addy said. "She may as well stay at the house once in her life. We probably should get some pictures, too, before we sell it."

"You're going to sell?" Evelyn breathed. Zeke had built the house. Addy herself had been born there. Evelyn couldn't conceive of selling something with that much history.

Addy played with her granddaughter's thin blonde hair, adjusting the barrette and combing the tresses with her hands. "In a few years it'll fall into the sea. Then it'll do us no good at all. Better to let someone else take it now, and enjoy it for a few years."

"There might be a way to save it, Addy," her son-in-law said.

"Let someone else find the way," Addy said.

"Would you think of selling it into the family?"

"No." Addy's tone was so firm, the little girl looked up at her in surprise.

"How come you're so sad, Grandma?" Tiffany asked.

Addy put her arms around Tiffany and pulled her close. Addy buried her face in the girl's hair and closed her eyes. Evelyn hadn't seen any sign of affection from Addy in the days she had been back. This was startling, even to her relatives.

Tiffany looked to her father in surprise. Her father nodded, a small, thin smile on his face.

Tiffany patted Addy's hand, giving comfort as best a child could. "It's okay, Grandma," she said. "I love you."

As if those words could make everything all better. Tiffany spoke with enough sincerity. Addy opened her eyes, and her gaze met Evelyn's. And in that moment, a wave of jealousy swept through Evelyn, deep and fine, as startling as Addy's hug.

Addy had run from her responsibilities, had left Dory Cove and her mother, and still she had a child to hug, and family to support her through a crisis. Evelyn had done everything right, and she was alone.

Like Olivia had been.

Except Olivia had had Lisa. Evelyn wouldn't even have that.

"I love you too, baby," Addy said. She pulled away just enough so that she could look the little girl in the face. Addy smoothed back Tiffany's bangs. "I'm sad, honey, because Great-Grandma died."

"But we didn't know her," Tiffany said.

Evelyn clasped her hands in her lap. So much Olivia had missed because Addy had run away. She had missed this child, and her brother. She had only had Lisa, who, in her own way, was as needy as Olivia.

"I knew her," Addy said. "She was my mother."

"Your mommy is dead?"

Addy nodded.

Tiffany brought a hand up and put it on Addy's cheek, her small face solemn. "That would make me sad too."

Addy's nose got red and her eyes filled with tears, but they didn't fall. Instead she leaned over and kissed her granddaughter on the head. "I love you, Tiff."

"I love you too, Grandma," Tiffany said. Then she looked over Addy's shoulder. "You going to eat that cake?"

Addy half laughed, half sobbed, then sat up, wiping the back of her right hand over her cheek. "No. You can have it."

"Great!" Tiffany climbed off her grandmother's lap and reached for the cake.

"What do you say?" The son-in-law's voice made Evelyn jump. She had forgotten he was there.

"Thanks," Tiffany said, her mouth already full of cake. She ate with her hands, the perfect little barbarian princess, finishing Evelyn's cake with the same look of rapture Olivia had always had. Bits were passed on, pieces scattered to each generation. The person never returned whole, but in a moment here and a moment there.

"I'm going to miss Olivia," Evelyn said. "Who'd've thought so back when we were kids, huh?"

Addy smiled. She didn't look at Evelyn, but continued watching her granddaughter eat. "You two could always talk. I never could. Not after Dad died. It was all too much for me, the religious stuff, the magic, the green glow. Remember that?"

Too well. Evelyn shuddered and thought of the man who had climbed on the ocean's flat green surface the night before. She had to swallow before she spoke. "I think that was how Olivia coped."

"Probably," Addy said. "That was how she stayed."

Evelyn frowned. Perhaps she was reading the wistfulness into Addy's tone. Had Addy wanted to stay in Dory Cove, but saw no choice about leaving?

Tiffany wiped her mouth, smearing chocolate all over her lips. Her stained arm brushed dangerously close to her full taffeta skirt. Her father caught her hand. "I think we should get cleaned up."

"No," Tiffany said. "I wanna stay with Grandma."

"You'll see me later," Addy said. Then she leaned closer to her granddaughter. "I think you should lick your lips. You'll get more chocolate that way."

Tiffany giggled. Her father took that moment to scoop her up in his arms, and carried her toward her mother.

"She seems like a charming child," Evelyn said.

Addy nodded. "She is."

"You're lucky to have her."

Addy gave Evelyn an appraising glance. "Yes," she said. "I am."

"For a minute I didn't think you'd tell her about Olivia."

Addy shrugged. "She needs to know. It's my fault she never got to spend much time with her great-grandmother. She should at least understand that people will mourn Mom."

"Will you mourn her?" Evelyn asked.

Addy's jaw set and her gaze grew far away. For a moment Evelyn thought she wasn't going to answer. Then Addy took a deep breath. "My mother had more strength than anyone I've ever met. She watched the sea take my father away, but she chose to remain beside it. She sold his business and parlayed the money into a sum large enough to raise me and still have enough left over for herself. Enough to carry her through fifty years. She never once said an unkind word to me. She never once blamed me for leaving. She always came to visit, and she never complained."

Evelyn's fingers had turned cold. People were leaving the Center. It wasn't as warm as it had been. "Why didn't you say that earlier?"

Addy made a tiny, almost imperceptible shake of her head. "I did what people expected of me. Everyone in Dory Cove thinks I abandoned my mother and that I was a horrible child. Mom did nothing to dissuade them."

"I thought you said she never said an unkind word."

"She never did," Addy said. "But there are things you can do to make your opinions known, even without speaking them. Mother always let people bad-mouth me. Her way was to remain quiet on the things she agreed with."

"She talked about you a lot," Evelyn said.

Addy turned. The frown lines around her eyes appeared deeper. "Did she?"

Evelyn nodded. "She kept us all informed about what was happening in your life."

"Did she ever say she was proud of me?"

Evelyn glanced down at her hands. What was there to be proud of? Once divorced, once widowed under bad circumstances, unwilling to do her familial duties. No, Olivia had never said she was proud of Addy, although she had fairly burst with pride each time she mentioned Lisa.

Addy's mouth twisted into a bitter smile. "She didn't, did she? I went through more hell than she could ever conceive of, and she saw it all as failure. And you wonder why I didn't speak kindly of her when Father Callahan made me go up front."

"You weren't unkind," Evelyn said. "You didn't say much at all."

"Served her right, too. You reap what you sow, Evelyn." Addy pushed herself out of her chair, picked up her food plate, and carried it to the garbage.

Evelyn's chill had grown deeper. She made herself stand and brush the crumbs off her skirt.

You reap what you sow.

She certainly hoped not.

6

ADDY TURNED the rental car into the steep narrow driveway and parked in the garage, which looked as if it had been added during the war. Marty, Lisa, and Loni and Bruce with Tiffany and Jason were all coming back to the house. If Addy had realized this would happen, she would have done the breakfast dishes straightened her room upstairs.

Then she smiled at herself. Who would punish her? Her mother was dead.

The house brought it all back, the insecurities, the loneliness, the deep-seated dread that she lived with a crazy woman, a woman whose obsession would turn to something darker, something even more terrifying. On the day Spence died, when Addy had come home, rain-drenched and shaken, in shock and chilled nearly to death, her mother had taken her coat, then led her to the kitchen stove.

As she brewed some coffee, she took out the Book and placed it on the kitchen table. The Storm had died off after Spence disappeared under the waves, and the sky was a reddish blue that suggested twilight wasn't long off.

Her mother took out the votive candles, lit them, and said a small prayer over them, a prayer that Addy had never heard before, one to the gods of the deep.

Then her mother had asked, oh so casually, "Did you see him drown?"
Tears had filled Addy's eyes. She had nodded.

"You could have saved him, you know," her mother had said. "The Churn would never hurt you. All you had to do was reach in—"

"Then we both would have died," Addy had said.

"You belong there, Adelaide," her mother had said softly. "As much as you do here."

Addy hadn't answered. She had accepted the coffee without a word, gone upstairs, changed, packed her suitcase, and gone to Billy Malone's because she knew no one would look for her there. The next day Billy had taken her to the train in Yachats, and she left Dory Cove for good.

The car smelled like ham. The leftover food at the service was, by American tradition, hers. It went with the casseroles that the good ladies of Dory Cove had brought her for the last two days. Lisa had made her take each with a smile and a kind word. The refrigerator was full. Addy had been about to dump one casserole when Lisa stopped her and reminded her that the local garbagemen would notice if she threw everything away.

Addy hated living this close, losing all her privacy. She wanted to go back to Chicago, where she could disappear into the city if she needed to, sit in a restaurant where no one knew her, and read. Lisa didn't understand that need for privacy. To Lisa, the closeness of Dory Cove was something like heaven. If Lisa hadn't had to work, she would live here. As it was, she lived as close as she could manage, about an hour away over the Coastal Mountain range.

Addy got out, opened the back passenger door, and struggled with an armload of food. Something wet and cold trailed along her left breast. The dress was silk; if she spilled part of a casserole on it, she had ruined it. Not that it mattered. She would never wear the dress again.

She walked the narrow path between the house and the garage and let herself in the back door. After all her years in cities, she was no longer used to a place that she didn't have to lock. Neither she nor Lisa had a key; Lisa believed that none existed.

Addy set the food on the dining room table and went out for another load, when Marty's car pulled up. He drove a green Mazda, about six years old. It wasn't new, wasn't old enough to be considered passé either. Just out of fashion enough to suggest that Marty wasn't as successful as he could be, that his divorce had left him poorer rather than richer.

Addy understood that one.

"Hey, Mom," he said as he got out of the car. "Need help?"

"Didn't they give you any food?"

"I think I look too mean. No one even talked to me." He winked. Her son had never been mean. It had been Loni who wanted to pull the wings off flies.

Addy laughed. It felt good, bubbling from her. This town couldn't crush her spirit, even if it did make her act like her teenage self. "Well, then, help me unload my car. I already spilled that god-awful fake Oriental casserole on my dress."

"Actually," Marty said as he came into the garage with her, "my favorite was the creamed peas and pearl onions. I haven't seen anything like that since you dragged us to church dinners for free meals."

A pang shot through Addy's heart. She had thought he was too young to remember that. When Drew had left her with two children under five, no money, and no job, she had had to survive somehow. She watched the papers for church potluck suppers and had taken the children to them. Often she went to two and three services on Sunday mornings because she felt so guilty for eating the free food. The connection served in other ways. One of the ministers noticed her plight and hired her as a church secretary, a poorly paying job that at least kept a roof over her head and clothes on her children's backs. Sometimes, when she thought about it, she believed she hadn't loved her second husband at all. She had merely married him to escape an increasingly desperate situation.

"Mom?" Marty said. "Didn't mean to make you uncomfortable."

She shook her head. "The past seems real close today," she said.

He took more half-eaten casseroles out of the back of her rental car and handed her a few. "No desserts?" he said.

"Given the choice of food there, what would you eat?" she asked.

He laughed in return.

She had missed her son. He had moved to Seattle straight out of college and got a job with Boeing. He had married a year later, and waited to have children until the time was right. Apparently the time never was, and after Cindy left him, he had nothing but the job. Now, he said, there were rumors of layoffs throughout the plant, and he worried that he would have nothing at all.

He had almost been unable to come. He had a job interview with a computer firm in Silicon Valley the day before that he couldn't afford to miss. He had left the interview and driven straight through. She could see the exhaustion in the bags under his eyes, the slowness of his step. She had worked so hard; God should have at least been kind to her children.

She took two more casseroles inside. As she set them down, she heard the purr of Bruce and Loni's status symbol pull into the driveway. They had rented a car, too, but of course, they had gone for the most expensive model they could find.

Addy shook her head. She knew that Loni got the attitude from her, but for Addy it had been different. It had been a point of pride to have nice things. It had been proof that even though she was poor, she could still provide for her family.

She had used the same psychology today, overdressing, showing Dory Cove that she didn't need them.

It would have worked, too, if sentimental Lisa hadn't put that seascape up so close to the picture of Addy's father.

The front screen door slammed.

"Gram!!" Tiffany's voice held all the excitement a six-year-old's could. "I saw the ocean!"

"You did not," her brother Jason said in his most serious tone. "That was the sky."

And then they were upon her, all energy and joy. It should have felt inappropriate, but it didn't. It felt right on this day of death.

"Sometimes," Addy said as gently as she could, "you can't tell the sea from the sky."

"Told ya!" Tiffany said.

"It was the sky," Jason mumbled. He was a somber little boy who had none of Tiffany's enthusiasm. She somehow overcame her parents' fascination with fine things. Jason was oppressed by it. Whenever he wore his dress clothes, he moved like a mannequin. Once Addy had taken him to buy an expensive pair of tennis shoes—the kind Loni had told her to get—and he had asked for a second pair, a cheap pair that he could cover in mud.

"It was probably both," Addy said. "You want to see where I grew up?"

"You grew up here?" Tiffany said. "Right by the water."

"Right by," Addy said. "I was born in that bedroom over there."

"Wow," Jason said with the proper awe. "This place is *old*."

Addy grinned. She supposed it was.

"Now, kids," Loni said from the door. "Be nice to your grandmother."

"They are," Addy said softly. She put a hand on the back of each of their heads and propelled them forward. She showed them her mother's bedroom first and explained that in the Olden Days babies were born at home. ("I was born at home," Tiffany said. "You were not," Jason said. "You were born in some icky hospital.")

She waved a hand at the kitchen—they would see that soon enough—and opened the door that led to the enclosed steps. The children found everything fascinating, from the runner along the stairs ("When this place was built," Addy said, "Only rich people had carpet") to the little attic rooms under the eaves.

Tiffany bounced on Addy's bed and looked out the window at the sea.

"Do you think the ocean is scary?" Tiffany asked. "Mom says that I gotta be careful near it. She says it could eat me."

Score one for Loni. "It's scary," Addy said. She didn't want her grandchildren anywhere near that water.

"I saw people on the beach," Jason said. "It can't be that scary."

"Your great-grandfather died in the sea," Addy said. "And he knew it as well as I know you. The sea is tricky. Sometimes it's nice and sometimes it's mean. You never turn your back on it."

"Because it might hurt you?" Jason asked.

Addy nodded.

"Like Jason," Tiffany said, already bored with the window. She opened drawers in the cabinets, then ran down the stairs and yelled from the base, "How come there's a door here?"

Addy took Jason's hand. He didn't pull away. He was getting old enough that she had to be careful when and where she paid attention to him.

"Because," Addy said as she started down the stairs, Jason beside her, "when I was growing up, we had to keep the upstairs cold. We closed the door so that no heat would come up here."

Tiffany played with the glass knob, then turned it and swung the door out. "How come it's not cold now?"

Addy didn't want to take the time to explain the vagaries of central heating. "Because I like it better this way."

"Me, too," Jason said.

They turned left, into the kitchen, and Addy stopped, her heart in her throat.

They were all in that room, all the people who were important to her, her children and her grandchildren. In the room she hated, overlooking the sea.

Loni had put one of the aprons hanging from a peg around her dove-gray dress. She was storing casseroles in Tupperware bowls, then setting the dishes aside. Lisa had run water and soap into the sink, ignoring the dishwasher beside her. Marty had grabbed a bottle of sweet sherry from the pantry and was pouring a glass.

"Doesn't she have anything better around here?"

"Mogen David," Addy said.

Marty shook his head. "I said 'better.'"

"I don't think we should drink today," Loni said primly.

"Why not?" Addy asked. "Mother would have."

Her mother drank every day. One glass of sweet sherry on weekdays, a glass of wine on Sunday. Once, when she came to Chicago, Addy had bought an expensive red and poured that for her mother, but her mother had complained.

She wanted what she was used to, what she had had every Sunday for as long as Addy could remember.

"Mom," Lisa said.

Addy didn't even face her youngest child. "That's the second time today you've used that tone with me, Lisa. I'm still a capable adult. I do know what I'm doing."

"Couldn't tell from this afternoon," Lisa muttered.

Addy glanced over her shoulder, the anger that had been bubbling all day threatening to overflow. "What?"

"What were you doing with that painting? It was so childish." Lisa had her shoes off. Her dress ran to mid-calf. In her nylon feet she looked like a little girl playing dress-up.

Addy could hear her mother's voice as clearly as if she were still alive. *Count to ten, Addy, before you respond in anger.* But she couldn't. She turned all the way around and gripped the high-backed wooden chair in front of her.

"I was childish," Addy said softly. "That painting had no place at my mother's funeral."

"But she painted it," Lisa said.

Addy nodded. "Have you looked in the attic? There are forty, maybe a hundred, more where that came from. Some even have your grandfather on them, walking back to her on a green glow. It was her sickness, Lisa. That's what you were paying homage to. Her sickness."

Lisa jutted out her chin, a gesture she had learned from Addy. "Funny," Lisa said. "I thought I was honoring her art."

They stared at each other. The others continued performing their tasks, backs stiff, movements rigid. From the dining room, Jason's voice carried in a stage whisper. "See?" he said. "They always fight."

Loni set down the casserole she was scraping. "Out of the mouth of babes," she said.

"What do you know of it?" Addy snapped. "What do any of you know of it? To you she was just a sweet old woman with stories and a love of the sea. She mellowed. When you were born, Loni, she refused to travel to

Chicago to see you. Or you, Marty. She was ready by the time you were born, Lisa. By then she figured eighteen years had gone by, missing a day or two wouldn't matter. But after my father died, she never let the sea out of her sight. As long as there was sunlight or the possibility of sunlight, my mother watched the waves. I remember her standing in the garden, clutching a handful of weeds and staring at the sea while Mr. Parnell from the grocery stood behind her, almost yelling because he was trying so hard to get her attention. I had brought him. I wanted to sell him vegetables so that we had a little extra money. But she didn't listen. She never listened when she was close to the sea. She never listened at all."

Addy's breathing was harsh. A lump in her throat made it difficult to talk. She swallowed once, twice, three times, but it didn't go away.

"You can't hate her forever, Mom," Lisa said.

"I didn't hate her," Addy said. "Maybe if I'd hated her, it wouldn't have mattered so much."

Lisa looked down. Loni picked up the bowl and started scraping again as if Addy had said nothing. Addy turned to Marty. He was studying the bottle of sherry in his hands.

She ran her fingers through her curls. The kitchen was hot, as hot as it got in the old days when the fire was stoked and bread was in the oven.

"I'll be back," she said. She started toward the front door when she remembered that she was parked in. The only way out was to the garden.

And the sea.

She pushed past Lisa, walked around the table, and opened the door. The wind was fresh, as always, smelling of the sea. The salt sprayed her face. Ahead of her the sea disappeared into the electric blue sky.

The door slammed behind her, the rattle of a screen door against its frame. No one had followed her out. No one would beg her to return, to pay attention to them, to help them. Her children were fiercely independent. Loni was as self-centered as her father had been, Marty preoccupied with the changes in his life.

Lisa tried, but she had never understood Addy. From the day she could speak, she had allied herself with her grandmother, and the alliance remained. Olivia, the old woman, had a warmth that Olivia the mother never had, and Addy couldn't forgive her for that.

Except for the broken stone walkway, the garden had reverted to its wild self.

Addy almost liked the cluster of wind-blown shrubs, the scraggly grass, the sand poking its way through the meager soil. It was so much better than the perfect rows cordoned off with little white rope bought at Winter's Feed and Seed.

The wind uprooted the garden, and her mother cursed. The birds raided the garden, and her mother cursed. The sand defeated the garden, and her mother cursed. The garden had become central to their lives because her mother needed something to do with her hands while her gaze focused on the sea.

Addy walked to the edge of the shrubs, her heels catching on the broken stones. No sign of the man she had seen that morning. Even his footprints had been covered over by the waves. The beach looked smooth, new, as new as it had been on the day it had been created.

At sea, a sailboat bobbed without its sail, its mast so far away that it looked like a pencil scratch on a perfect blue canvas. From that distance they could not see her, only the shore. She remembered that from the days her father took her fishing. The sea had reached up to her, caressing her, and she thought she had seen a man beneath the waves. He had smiled at her, and she had smiled back.

She had leaned over the side to touch him, when her father grabbed her waist and pulled her to the center of the boat.

He had never taken her to sea again.

Nearly sixty years had passed since that day, and she could still remember it as clearly as breakfast that morning. She hadn't been lying when she said to Marty that the past seemed close. It seemed closer than usual. These days she tried to spend her time in the present.

But Dory Cove wasn't allowing that. She had thought to escape her past by holding the memorial in the Senior Center, little suspecting that the Senior Center was her old high school gymnasium. Her mother had hated organized religion—its vision of the afterlife held no place for her strange beliefs—and so going to a church wouldn't have been right, either.

Addy had decided against Dunstaff's for her own protection. Dunstaff's—the current owner's grandfather—had buried her father, and she still remembered the service.

Dunstaff's had been down the block then, in a building that no longer existed.

It smelled of dying flowers and formaldehyde, a combination that made her sneeze. Her grandmother Natty, her father's mother, brought her to the service.

Gram Natty had arrived at the house to discover Addy's mother sitting in the living room, glowering. When Natty arrived, Addy's mother had told her to get out, that nothing of Zeke belonged in the house. Natty had ignored her and then had taken Addy outside, saying that her mother would be all right in time, that time was a great healer.

Addy had worn new patent leather shoes that were one size too small. They pinched her feet. Already her mother's aversion to the church was known, and Dunstaff's had agreed to hold the service in their chapel. The coffin was closed because there was no body. Her mother had refused to come into the chapel, saying it had nothing of the gods. When Natty had finally confronted her, saying that no matter what her relationship to Zeke, she still owed something to Addy, her mother had smiled.

I don't owe Addy a thing, her mother had said.

You owe her comfort. Her father is dead, Natty had said.

Her father will never die, her mother had said, and stalked out of the building.

She never went inside Dunstaff's again.

"Excuse me." A male voice rose with the wind. Addy turned, expecting to see Bruce or Marty. What she did see made her clutch the shrub behind her for support.

A man stood at the edge of the remaining retainer wall. His hair was wind-blown and black, so black that its highlights shone blue in the sunlight. A curl fell over his forehead, something he had always hated and had never been able to control. His lips were full and almost feminine, his eyes big and blue, his skin untouched by the passage of time. He wore a blue-and-white pullover shirt that tucked into his dungarees with the front-button fly. On his feet he had scuffed penny loafers without socks.

The clothing was salt-encrusted, and the shoes still had the appearance of damp. His hand clutched the stone wall, his knuckles white with the pressure of his fingers.

Addy swallowed. The past was so real, she was hallucinating it now. "Spence?" she asked.

He didn't move. The wind teased the curl on his forehead. "What happened here?" he asked. "Did the storm eat all of the cliff?"

She had never forgotten his voice. Sometimes she thought she heard it in restaurants, low and warm, smooth like Bing Crosby's had been, with a touch of the rogue, almost as if he had swallowed a mouthful of stones and they rubbed against the deepest timbers of his range.

When she didn't answer, he frowned. "I'm looking for Addy Hawthorne," he said.

She squeezed the shrub, its prickly needles biting into her palm. "You found her," Addy said, even though she hadn't answered to Addy Hawthorne in over four decades.

"Is she inside?" He glanced at the kitchen wall, then took a step back as if it startled him. For an hallucination, he seemed real enough.

Addy shook her head, deciding to play along. Better this quiet conversation than the screams her mother used to send across the garden in the first year after her father's death. "I'm Addy Hawthorne."

"You—?" He took a step inside the wall, then saw the scraggly grass, the misshapen shrubs, the broken stones. He ran a hand through his hair, a gesture she thought she had forgotten, but as familiar to her as the smell of the sea, then he peered at her. "Addy?"

She nodded. "Can I help you?"

"Addy?" He came closer inside the wall. The sides of his loafers were covered with sand. A grass stain marred the knee of his dungarees. He must have climbed up the cliff face, along the route where the old path to the beach used to be.

The route where her mother had fallen and taken ill.

"What happened here, Addy?" he asked.

As he grew closer, she realized he brought the smell of the sea with him. His clothes reeked of brine. A lightness filled her stomach, the first buzz of an adrenaline rush. "Who are you?" she asked. "Who are you to come into my garden and ask questions? Who are you?"

"Spence. Spence Chadwick," he said, his voice breaking like waves on a beach. "My God, Addy. Something happened here, didn't it? Something awful."

She tried to back away, but the shrub's needles pricked through her skirt.

Maybe this was what her mother had seen. Maybe this was what had driven her crazy that summer so many years ago.

"You can't be Spence," Addy whispered. "Spence is dead."

He shook his head. His eyes were wider and they mirrored her fright. "I'm not dead, Addy. What happened here? Please—"

"You're dead!" she screamed. "You're dead. Go away! You can't make me like her! You can't!"

"Addy—"

"Get away! Get out of here! Stay away from me!"

He reached out to her as the screen door slammed. Marty stood on the stoop, followed by Bruce and Loni. Loni pushed one of the children back.

Addy slapped at the man's hand. "Get away," she said again, softer now, afraid to let her children see her as a hysterical woman, screaming at nothing.

"You heard my mother," Marty said. "Get out of here, or we'll call the police."

Addy raised her head toward Marty. They saw the man too. He glanced over his shoulder, his eyes wild, his jaw working. He turned back to her.

"Addy," he said, as if he expected her to intercede for him, as if he expected something more from her than she was willing to give.

"I don't like jokes like this," she said. "You can tell whoever sent you that this isn't funny. And if you come back here, I swear I'll have you arrested so fast you won't have time to call your friend to giggle. Is that clear?"

Marty came down the steps, with Bruce behind him. She had never noticed before what big men they were. They towered over Spence—the man, the visitor, the stranger.

He glanced at them, then at her, then back at them. He made a soft, whimpering cry, like a puppy afraid it was going to get hit, then he turned and ran around the house.

Addy remained in her position, needles sticking her hands and the backs of her thighs. The lightness was gone, replaced by a burning in her chest, as if she had smoked too many cigarettes way too fast.

"Mom, are you all right?" Marty asked.

"Do you know that man?" Bruce asked.

"God, that was scary," Loni said from the door, her hand splayed at the base of her throat.

He had looked no more than twenty. She had heard of people having doubles; she had seen how common it was in families. Lisa had the look of Addy's mother, enough to fool a person after fifty years. But Spence had had no children. Spence had had no siblings.

Spence had been dead a long, long time.

Marty put his hands on Addy's arms and pulled her forward. She leaned against his chest. His shirt smelled of laundry soap and the leather from his coat.

She wanted to cry, but couldn't. The tears had gathered in her throat, making speech impossible.

"Who do you think he was?" Bruce asked.

"I don't know, but he seemed to know Mom," Marty said. She heard his voice and felt it rumble through his chest. He put a hand on her back and patted her as if she were the child. "You okay to go in, Mom?"

She nodded. She couldn't explain this to them. They would think she was making it up. They would think that she imagined the resemblance.

"Do you think he was here for Mom?" Loni said. "Or for something of Grandma's?"

"There's those brokers," Bruce said, "the ones who try to buy antiques off the family for cheap. I think we should call the police."

Addy let Martin lead her into the house. She welcomed the strength of his arm on her back. Tiffany huddled just behind the door, her forefinger in her mouth.

Jason stood by the stove, ready to hide if he needed to.

"You knew him, didn't you, Mom?" Lisa said. She had watched through the windows, staring out to sea the way her grandmother used to do. Her hands were shaking.

Addy nodded. No matter what her mind told her, her heart was convinced she had just spoken with Spencer Chadwick, her first love, a man younger than her children, a man who had been dead for fifty years.

7

T HE POLICE were leaving by the time Billy Malone arrived at Olivia's house. Evelyn had heard the report on her police scanner and had called him. She had planned to go up later, to see how Addy was doing. He decided to go right away, figuring this would be a good opportunity to talk with Addy about the burial plot.

Besides, he wanted to see her again. He wanted to apologize. He shouldn't have spoken to her that way at the memorial service.

The police had parked their single squad car at the base of the driveway. Billy parked behind them, his only luxury, his black Saab, looking out of place on this residential street full of trucks and well-made family sedans.

The officers apparently recognized his car because they waited, hands on door latches, and watched him park. He recognized them, too, Patrick FitzGerald and Jonah Huffman, two of the best, the kind who understand that tourists have different values, the kind who talk to kids and warn them before placing them in handcuffs or roughing them up.

They were also two of the more intelligent officers, men who understood subtleties. Jonah had often explained how important the little things were to Billy, on their monthly drives to the Oregon NAACP meetings in Portland.

"Someone call you?" Fitz asked. No preamble, no greeting. They were on a job, doing business, and the local attorney shows up out of the blue.

Billy rarely did criminal work, although he had training in it. There just wasn't much call for anything more than the occasional petty-theft plea bargain, the seasonal trespass of vagrants into summer homes, the routine teenage vandalism. His appearance probably did look odd to the police.

"No one called," Billy said as he got out of the car. The twinge in his back had grown to a full-blown spasm and he had to move slowly. "Evelyn Brand heard the report on the police scanner and was worried. I am the emissary sent to make certain all is right at the Hawthornes."

A slight mistruth, but not an important one.

"Damn shame," Fitz said, "coming on the heels of a funeral." He got into the car, apparently having said his piece. Jonah continued leaning on the car roof, his massive forearms looking even bigger against the metal.

"Off the record," he said.

Billy nodded. He hated it when Jonah talked off the record. Jonah went for hunches, for feelings, for impressions that were often right but even more often couldn't be proved.

"There any money in the Hawthorne estate?"

Money? The question startled Billy. He had never thought of Olivia having money. But she did. A lot of money, not counting the house that Californians would probably spend about $200,000 on, not realizing that it was about to slip into the sea. Then there were the antiques.

Billy shrugged. "I suppose there's money," he said. "But not the kind that's readily apparent. Why?"

Jonah shook his head. "Just a theory." He put his chin on his arms, which made him look like a wistful child who had overgrown his classmates. "This isn't a straightforward trespass."

Billy straightened and put a hand on the small of his own back, giving himself support. He shut the car door and, for the first time in a while, locked it. "What is it, then?"

"You ever hear of a guy named Spencer Chadwick?"

Billy froze. "He and Addy were engaged once."

"He's dead, right? Drowned?"

"In the storm of '39." Billy was amazed he could speak the words.

"And didn't her mom have something about drowned men coming back from the sea?"

"Her mother always believed her father would return that way."

Jonah slapped the car hood, the thump echoing off the small knolls around them. "Thougtht so! You hear that, Fitz?"

"I heard," Fitz said through the open window. "Still makes no sense. It was just a prank, Jonah. Let it go."

Billy pushed hard on his back. The pain had flared. He had never felt more like an old man than he did at this moment. "You'd better tell me what's going on."

"Some kid shows up, saying he's Spence Chadwick. He cornered Adelaide in the garden and spooked her real bad. Her son called us. He was real concerned."

Spence. Despite himself, Billy raised his head and looked toward the Churn. In fifty years he had not returned to the Churn, to the place where Spence died, even though he lived only a few miles away.

"I bet he was concerned," Billy said.

"So I figure maybe there's money. They're trying to drive their mother bats and split up the fortune."

It wouldn't work. The fortune, such as it was, was already split. But Billy, as Olivia's attorney, couldn't tell the police that. Yet.

"Those grandkids have no idea how much money there is," Fitz said. Now Billy understood the question. Fitz had been trying to get Jonah off this tangent and back to the real direction the case was taking.

"It seems to me a good way to do it, the thing that she always hated about her mother."

"You know how hard it is to find a look-alike?" Fitz said.

"Doesn't have to be a real look-alike. Who can remember how someone looked after he's been dead fifty years?"

"I can," Billy said quietly. He still saw Spence's face in his dreams, eyes wide and terror-filled, hand outstretched as he waited in the middle of the Churn for the next wave to crash in and crush him.

Jonah frowned at him, and Fitz leaned his head out the window. They were both in their thirties; they had no idea what it was like to live over twice that long. He would allow that to be their explanation. They didn't need any more.

A chill had settled in his bones. He didn't need any more either. Not so close to Olivia's death. Not when he could still picture her, smiling at him and saying softly, *Addy never believed me, Billy, but if she had acted that day, we could have brought Spence back. Sometimes I think she still can.*

Billy nodded at the police, acknowledging that his comment had silence them. "If I were you," he said, "I'd chalk it up to trespass, write the report, and leave it. If it becomes anything more than that, you have a file."

"I still think it's mighty strange," Jonah said.

"It is strange," Billy said. "It's very strange." Too strange. He would think about it later.

"I thought I'd seen everything in this town too," Fitz said. He put his head back in the car and started it. The engine had a slight knock. "Get in, Jonah. I'm sure we could find some tourists taking One-oh-one at seventy-five if we really tried."

"Such excitement in my life," Jonah said as he ducked into the car. "See ya, Billy."

Billy waved at them as he limped past the car. The walk uphill would be no good for his back. After he saw Addy, he would go home, take an Advil, and place his trusty ice pack between his spine and the couch. That and a little mindless television would help put the day behind him.

Olivia's driveway had crumbled twice in the years he had been in Dory Cove. The first time, the cheap blacktop the contractor had used revealed itself to be a stone-and-gravel mixture improperly made. The second time was after the big storm in '63, the one that had destroyed half of Florence before moving inland. Its winds had battered Dory Cove too—although nothing like the storm of '39—and the heavy rains eroded both sides of the knoll that the Hawthorne house sat on. The repair had been a good one, but it had been twenty-six years before. Small cracks now webbed the concrete like spiders in broken glass.

Cars filled Olivia's driveway. He was glad he hadn't tried to drive up. Lisa's red Datsun was parked precariously on the hill, gripping only by its emergency brake. He hoped he was far enough back to avoid impact if that brake let go.

He walked up the front steps and knocked as he opened the door. That had been his habit with Olivia and he saw no reason to change it now. The little girl shrieked as he entered. Her mother, who had been coming to the door, shushed her.

"Can I help you, Mr.—?"

"Malone," he said. "Where's Addy?"

"She's not up for visitors," Addy's daughter said.

"She'll see me."

"Billy." Lisa was standing in front of the door leading upstairs. She fidgeted with her gold necklace with her right hand. "Mom's pretty shook."

"I'd be too if I just saw a dead man," Billy said.

"We're trying not to refer to him that way," the other daughter said. She held out her hand to her daughter. The little girl went over to her and hid her face in her mother's thigh. So different from the child who had played exuberantly through Olivia's memorial service. "I think it would be better if you return tomorrow."

"Is she in the kitchen?" Billy asked Lisa.

Lisa nodded.

He walked past the older daughter and touched Lisa's arm as he passed, showing a confidence he didn't feel. Inside he was trembling, although his hands were steady. He had felt like this during the bar exam, during his first few days in court, during the days when people routinely ignored him and called him boy.

The sunlight streamed into the kitchen, bathing everything in a bright light. Addy sat at the kitchen table, her son hovering behind her. Her grandson peeked out of the breakfast nook at Billy, and her son-in-law stood by the window, gazing out to sea.

Addy's hands were wrapped around a cup of coffee, and she hunched, as she had done at the funeral after she had fought with him.

"Adelaide," Billy said.

At her name she turned. For a moment she didn't seem to recognize him. Then a single tear spilled out of her right eye and down her cheek. It dripped off her chin and left a wet splotch on the silk of her dress.

"Would you leave us, please?" he said to the other people in the room.

"I think Mom needs her family right now," the son said.

"It's all right," Lisa said. She was standing just behind Billy. "Billy Malone is the attorney in Dory Cove. He knew Mom a long time ago."

The son put his hand on his mother's. Possessive. The favored child. Billy had seen it before in families broken up young. The oldest child became the adult and the one most trusted by the parent.

"Do you want me to stay, Mom?"

Addy shook her head. She hadn't broken gaze with Billy. "I'll be all right." Her voice was soft, not the strident voice of the morning. A voice with no fight left in it.

"Come on," Lisa said.

The son-in-law turned away from the window, grabbed the grand-son's hand, and led him from the room. The son frowned at Billy, as if warning him to be careful. Lisa touched his arm in return, a gesture that showed she trusted him.

Billy waited until their footsteps had disappeared into the front room before joining Addy at the table.

She was still a beautiful woman, more beautiful now, if truth be told, than she had been as a teenager. The lines had softened her face, and the silver curls suited her.

"I'm sorry about this morning," she said.

He shook his head. "I'm the one who should apologize. I shouldn't have said those things. I knew that the seascape would set you off. I just forgot is all. Fifty years is a long time, Addy."

"I know," she whispered. Then, too late, she swiped at the wet trail leading down her cheek. "Guess I'm seeing everyone from my past."

She let out a shaky laugh. He caught her hand. Her fingers were bony and brittle. She was too thin for a woman her age.

"You want to tell me about it?"

"He looked like Spence, Billy." She pulled her hand from his, twisted her fingers around an imaginary wedding ring, a habit that she must have had for decades. "I thought that before he said his name. I thought he was an hallucination until Marty saw him. I was acting like he was made up out of my brain." She slid her fingers into her hair, leaned forward, and closed her eyes. "My God, Billy. I thought I was becoming my mother. I thought..."

Her voice trailed off and she shook her head. He could see the effort she was making. She was trying to hold back tears.

"You're not like Olivia, Addy. Never have been. Always too grounded in reality."

She laughed again. It was a brittle sound. "New Ageisms from you, Billy? I thought you were above trends."

He ignored the sarcasm. He remembered when it was once her best and only defense. "Addy," he said, leaning forward so that she could see him through that mop of hair. "Someone wanted you to think you were like Olivia. Someone wanted to mess with your mind. Someone who had to know about Spence, about Olivia's obsession, about the return from the sea."

Slowly she brought her head up. Her eyes were dry. She swallowed so hard, he could see her throat work. "You, Billy?"

"Why would I do that, Addy?" he asked quietly. "I know much better ways."

Color filled her cheeks and she leaned back as if he had slapped her. "I'm sorry," she said. Her eyes filled with tears again, but this time they didn't fall. "I'm sorry."

"Don't apologize. I'm as likely as the next person. There's a lot of people in Dory Cove who know when you left, a lot of people who knew about Olivia."

She wiped at the corner of each eye, delicately, and then he saw the lenses floating in them. Age had touched Addy Hawthorne in more ways than her silver hair and her delicately etched skin. His bifocals were tucked in the pocket of his suitcoat. He only wore them for reading.

"He smelled of the sea," she said. "I saw salt on his clothes. And the details were right. The penny loafers, no socks. That loose curl."

Billy remembered them. Only he remembered the curl plastered to Spence's forehead by the sea.

"How much of his resemblance were those details? How much did you see that you expected to see?"

She shook her head. "I didn't expect Spence. Mother, maybe, but not Spence. Although"— she frowned as if a memory were coming to her— "I thought I saw him this morning. Someone was walking on the beach, and I thought he looked like Spence."

"Which put Spence in your mind."

"And made me more susceptible to believing the boy when he came up the walk." The strength seemed to flow back into her, and with it anger. This was the Addy he knew. Her eyes flashed. "I hate this town," she muttered.

She stood, glanced at the windows, then reached over and latched the back door, turning the deadbolt as if it were the best security system money could buy.

She paused, both hands on the door, her back to Billy. "Why would anyone do this?" she said.

"Jonah suggested money."

The brittle laugh again. He wondered where she'd learned it. She hadn't done it when she lived in Dory Cove. "Money." She shook her head and pushed away from the door. "I saw the will, Billy. I read it this morning before I came to the Senior Center. She never said anything, but it was so clear how much she hated me."

"She didn't hate you, Addy."

"No, I suppose not." She poured herself a cup of coffee, then held the glass coffeepot out to him in mute question. He shook his head. She nodded, added sugar, and stirred. The spoon scraped against the ceramic mug, a comforting sound. "Mothers aren't supposed to hate their children, are they?"

"Addy, she was bitter. She thought you left her too."

Addy shrugged. "I did leave her. And she was right. I would have sold the house. Lisa will hold on to it until the sea steals it."

"I don't think anyone would begrudge you a token from your mother's estate." Billy said.

Addy wrapped her hands around the mug and shook her head. "I don't want any part of this place. I know she did it to punish me, but when she died, I thought I would get it all, and I panicked about that, I really did. I probably would have sold it, divided that and the remaining money among the kids, and let it go."

She took a sip, winced at the heat, and set the mug back down. "I think she divided everything fairly too. Although I don't know what the older ones will say about Lisa getting the house."

"Let me worry about that."

Addy nodded. "All right."

The sun was setting over the ocean. Force of habit made Billy raise his head and stare into the orange light. Every afternoon he spent in this kitchen, he would silently watch the sunset with Olivia. *Did it glow? Was there a glow?* She would ask as her eyesight failed. And each time, he would deny it. She would sigh and shake her head. *Probably just as well,* she would say in her last year of life. *What would he do with an old woman like me?*

What indeed?

He glanced at Addy. She was studying the stove as if it held the secrets of the universe, avoiding the sunset.

"You never answered me," she said when she noticed him looking at her. "Why do you think someone did this?"

"Maybe they did this because you left," he said. "A lot of people were unhappy for a long time after you left."

"I wasn't that important."

"Yes, you were," he said.

She opened her mouth, about to say something, when he amended, "To Olivia, you were."

Addy shook her head. Her relationship with Olivia would always be stuck now, stuck in the place they had left it fifty years before. Nothing could change that. And Addy didn't seem to realize it.

"Maybe it wasn't because I left," she said. "Maybe it was because I came back."

"Why would anyone want to keep you out of Dory Cove?"

She shrugged. "You tell me."

"The storm," he said. "The storm of '39. Olivia once said you caused it."

She pushed away from the table so hard that the coffee sloshed out of her mug. Some splashed her dress, but she didn't seem to notice. "The Storm. It always comes back to the Storm. There's been a world war, a police action, and Vietnam, ten presidents, and a whole lifetime since then. Children and grandchildren have been born. Why would anyone care about 1939?"

"Because you do," Billy said.

She sighed, grabbed a paper towel, and swiped at her dress. Then she tossed another towel on the table, and Billy wiped up the coffee. "I didn't cause any Storm. If anyone did, Mother did." Addy took a deep breath. "I left because Spence died."

"I know," Billy said.

"And because Mother asked me if I had seen him die. She said I could have pulled him out."

"You couldn't have, Addy, believe me."

"She seemed to think I could. She said the Churn would recognize me."

"I know," Billy said. "You told me when you left. I remember."

She scooped up the paper towels. "So why do you keep asking?"

"Those were the things that made you leave," he said. "I want to know what kept you away."

Addy walked to the window and put her hands on the glass. She pressed her nose against the pane and stared as the sun sank below the horizon. There, in the growing dusk, she looked just like Olivia.

"I was afraid," she said. "What if I caused it all? What if the Storm was tied to me? And what if I could have saved Spence? Maybe I would have tried to bring him back. Maybe I would have been just like her. I would have stood here every night of my life and waited for Spence to come back."

Billy gasped. The sound was involuntary, the sharpness of a pain he thought he had forgotten rising in his breast. "You married twice, Addy. Neither man was Spence."

"Have you looked at Marty?" Her face was entirely in shadow now. No green glow had crossed it. As he watched, a yellow square appeared on the lawn. Someone upstairs had turned on a light. "I mean really looked at him?"

"No," Billy said.

"He looks just like his father. Only it's hard to tell because he's older now. But I remember the day I realized what I had done. Marty had turned thirteen and he had his growth spurt. And suddenly when he moved a certain way or laughed a certain way, I saw Spence."

"Spence?"

She nodded.

"He's Spence's son?"

"No. He was born three years after Spence died. But his father looked like Spence. And his stepfather too."

She sighed and flicked on the light beside the door. Billy blinked in the brightness.

"I have the same obsession," she said. "It just manifested itself in a different way."

"You lived your own life," Billy said.

"Maybe," Addy said. "And maybe Mother did too. Maybe we just don't know it."

He frowned, thinking of Olivia alone in this house for five decades. He saw her at the Center, and at Safeway, and on his frequent visits. She and Lisa attended local events, and she took long walks on the beach. But he had never inquired about what she did with her mind, how she thought about life, what she expected. It was almost as if he didn't want to know.

Addy rejoined him at the table. She took an extra paper towel and wiped the sides and bottom of her mug. Then she sipped the coffee. "Have you ever wondered," she said, "if Mother was right?"

"Addy." He had been afraid of this from the moment he heard the police report. The strain of returning to Dory Cove. The death of her mother, the reunion of her children. The fifty-year anniversary of the Storm.

"I mean it," Addy said. "I used to lie awake at night in this house and wonder what I would do if my father returned. Would he be a ghost? A ghoul? A creature made of seawater? Or a flesh-and-blood man?"

"Some people think your father ran off."

"I know," Addy said. "It was possible. It was the Depression. He lived with Mother. That would be enough to drive anyone away."

"He could have returned in that case, a flesh-and-blood man."

"I suppose," Addy said. "But we'll never know, will we? My father never came back. Spence did."

"Someone posing as Spence."

"If we could find him, we would know who hired him."

"Good point," Billy said. "I'll talk to Jonah and Fitz."

Addy nodded. "Wouldn't it be ironic if Mother's crazy beliefs had truth to them?" she said.

"I don't see how it would make any difference," Billy said.

"Oh, it makes a lot of difference," Addy said. "Because if they did, then I saw Spence this afternoon."

"Let it go, Adelaide."

"And if I did, imagine what he's going through right now."

Billy hadn't wanted to imagine that. He hadn't wanted to believe that anyone could come back from the dead, whether Olivia preached resurrection or Addy did.

"God," he said, "if that had been Spence, he would only be nineteen years old."

"And scared," Addy whispered.

"And alone."

They looked at each other across the table, a glance like the ones they had shared when she arrived at his shack, her suitcase in her left hand.

"I'll make sure they try to find him," Billy said.

Her smile was small, but genuine. "It would put all our minds at rest if they did."

8

CHARLIE WINTER had just sat down to a dinner of two-minute eggs and toast when he heard a thud on the side of his house. He cursed, set down his spoon, and pushed away from the table, toppling a pile of magazines he had stacked on the corner. They landed with a series of thuds, drowning out any noise from outside. He cursed again, grabbed his cane—as much for a weapon as anything else—and kicked aside some empty boxes with his good leg so that he could open the back door.

The sunlight had the overheated orange quality it always had in the late afternoon, the sensation of something being too ripe, of overstaying its welcome.

When Charlie had been a boy, the back door overlooked a long marsh that led to the sandy beach. Now that marsh had been divided into condominiums that never completely sold, and he had to watch between the tall reddish buildings.

Probably one of the kids over here, snooping through his stuff.

He'd put a stop to that. He'd do his tough-old-man routine and the kid would never come again.

He stood on the stoop and looked for movement. Nothing. The wooden crates that he had once kept as mementos but that were now rotting reminders of how much time had passed appeared to have been moved. He squinted at them, almost making out the words Winter's Feed and Seed, the store as dead as his parents, as long gone as his leg. He should really get the village to take away the crates. He had no use for them, and they only served as homes for mice and opossum and all other kinds of dirty things. But somehow he felt that getting rid of the crates was the final betrayal. He still had the building, but any memory of what it had once been would be completely gone.

Carefully he walked down the concrete steps onto the gravel. Then he made his slow way to the crates. As a child he had done this often for his father, looking for the hobo too shy or too hungry to beg for a handout. Now Charlie made the trek alone, thumping his cane as hard as he could so that a recalcitrant teenager would be terrified and run away.

When he reached the scattered crates, he heard no shuffling at all. He expected to. His arrival usually terrified mice or gulls digging for trash that had spilled out of the nearby cans. The lack of noise startled him more than noise would. By now the local teens would have been halfway to the condominiums.

"I see you," he said, filling his voice with all the courage he did not feel. "Get out."

A filthy hand emerged, followed by another. The fingers were extended to show that the person carried no weapons.

"All the way out," Charlie said. His heart was pounding so hard that he could hear it in his ears. He braced his feet in the gravel and picked up his cane, holding it over his chest, ready to let it free if the intruder so much as smiled at him wrong.

Slowly the arms appeared, wearing a salt-covered pullover. The left wrist had a watch old enough to be an antique, and it had stopped a few minutes short of nine. The watch's face was cracked, sending a warning bell through Charlie's memory, one he couldn't afford to heed at the moment.

Then a body unfolded itself into a masculine shape, a teenager as he had expected. A tangled mop of black hair hid the boy's face. He tossed his head, and the hair fell back, revealing skin that looked ruddy in the dying light, big blue eyes, and lips as full as a girl's.

Charlie didn't gasp. He was too much of a soldier for that, but it took him a moment to realize he had been holding his breath. Trick of the light. Trick of memory. Olivia's funeral had him too far in the past. He had had enough flashbacks to know that sometimes phantoms were only in his mind.

"What do you want?" He reverted to his lieutenant's voice, one he hadn't used since the Pacific.

"I was looking for Winter's Feed and Seed," the boy said.

"Nice try," Charlie said. "But that's written on the crates you were hiding in."

"I *was*." The boy sounded close to tears. "My God, I don't know what's happened to this place. My house is gone, and nothing looks the same. I thought Old Man Winter was here, and maybe I could get some food."

"I'm Old Man Winter," Charlie said. "And I can point you to St. Mary's. They give out free meals."

"You're not Old Man Winter," the boy said. "I *know* him. He doesn't have a cane, and he's not as old as you. If he knew you were being mean to me, he'd fire you."

A shiver ran down Charlie's back. His father would have fired an employee who turned away a hungry boy. This had to be a stress flashback, but it was an odd one. He usually had them about the war.

"Listen, boy, I don't know who put you up to this, but Winter's Feed and Seed has been out of business since the 1940s. It's my home now. I keep the crates as a kind of commemorative."

"The 1940s," the boy said, his voice small. "This isn't 1939, is it?"

Charlie laughed. Now he understood where the flashback came from. It had come from seeing Addy. "No," he said. "This is 1989." He put his cane down and waited for the boy to disappear. Acknowledging the present always put the past in its place.

The sun was almost down. The ruddy look had left the boy's face. His mouth opened and closed and opened again. "1989?" he whispered.

Charlie was holding his breath, still waiting for the boy to disappear. The boy didn't move. "1989," Charlie said again. "George Bush is president.

Dan Quayle is vice president. The Germans are our allies and we have a trade agreement with Japan. It's been forty-four years since V-J Day, and I am sixty-seven years old."

He was saying his mantra, the one that had always brought him out before, the one the man at the Vets' Center had taught him almost fifteen years before.

The boy remained.

Then the boy shook his head. "Mind if I put my arms down?" he asked in a subdued tone.

It didn't look as if the boy was going to hurt him, although Charlie kept his grip on his cane. "All right."

The boy let his arms fall to his side. He took a deep breath and looked at the condos. Their shadow had grown in the dying rays of the sun. In a moment his face would be in darkness.

Charlie blinked and looked at the boy. The resemblance was startling. Perhaps that, and Addy, started the memories. Perhaps they had had a conversation that Charlie hadn't understood. He felt a flush grow in his neck. Perhaps he had seemed like a crazy old man. It wouldn't be the first time he answered questions only he had heard.

"You say I can get a free meal at the Catholic church?" the boy asked. "Is that still on—where is that?"

"Right near the Senior Center on 101," Charlie said. The answer was by rote.

"You walk out to the highway and turn left. Follow the sidewalk and you can't miss it."

The boy smiled, but it was a perfunctory and preoccupied look. "Thanks," he said. He ran a hand through his hair, stepped over the crates, and walked toward the side of the building.

He seemed real enough, and hungry enough. And he—or the projection Charlie had made him into—had been right. His father would never have turned away a starving man.

"Look," Charlie said. "I got some food inside and some warm clothes and a comfortable couch. St. Mary's can't give you a roof over your head."

The boy stopped. He ran his hand through his hair again. Then he dipped his head, turned, and came back. "You don't mind?" he asked, standing in the shadow of the condominiums.

"I don't mind," Charlie said, even though it was half a lie. He hadn't had anyone in his house since Nixon was president. His privacy was very important to him. But the memory of his father's generosity, and the boy's resemblance to a young man that Charlie had once admired, would have caused him many sleepless nights.

He set the cane on the gravel and limped toward the stoop. When he realized the boy hadn't caught up with him, he turned and glanced over his shoulder. The boy was watching him walk.

"What happened to you?" the boy asked.

"Stepped on a land mine in '44," Charlie said. "Lucky to have this much mobility."

He was still amazed at how easily those sentences came out. For years he had merely growled, "The war," in response to that question. It was only when "the war" sparked a question in return—"Which war?"—that he had to learn a phrase that shut people up.

The boy still wasn't following him.

"You coming?" Charlie asked.

"Oh," the boy said. "Yeah." He half walked, half ran until he caught up. He smelled of the sea: brine and fish oils and seaweed. He must have been sleeping outside for several nights.

The boy stood on the stoop and pushed the door open for Charlie. Charlie nodded his thanks. The inside of the house felt too warm, almost stifling, after the coolness of the growing twilight. The boy followed him in, pulling the door closed behind him. Charlie flicked on the light, revealing his uneaten meal and the magazines scattered all over the floor.

"I interrupted your dinner," the boy said. He licked his lips as if he couldn't contain his hunger.

"Not much to miss," Charlie said. "I was being lazy. Now that you're here, I'll make something good."

"Do you mind if I have the egg?" the boy asked.

Charlie looked at him. The boy was thin, but not quite scraggly. "When was the last time you ate?"

The boy frowned, blinked, and then his frown grew deeper. "I don't know," he said. There was an edge of distress in his voice that Charlie recognized. He had heard it in the base hospital before a guy would lose himself to a screaming jag.

"That's all right," Charlie said. "Eat some egg, and you'll feel better. Then you get into the shower while I cook."

"You have a shower bath?" the boy asked in wonderment. He already had his hand on the egg cup and was tapping it with the spoon.

Charlie froze at the phrase. He hadn't heard it in years, maybe decades. *Shower bath.* "Yes," he said. "Just down the hall." He was tempted to ask if the boy had ever used one.

The boy was eating the egg with gusto, even though it was cold. Boys of that age always at a lot, though. That was no indicator of how long it had been since he had a real meal. Within minutes he had finished the eggs and the toast.

"Still want dinner?" Charlie asked with amusement.

"If it's not too much trouble."

"It's not."

The boy wiped his mouth with the back of his hand. He should have grinned at that point, but if anything, his solemnity had grown. "You said you had some clothes. I know I'm imposing, but I would like to get out of these. They're covered with salt."

Charlie nodded. "In the hallway that leads to the bathroom there is a long drawer. It's full of clothes. Take what you want. I'll get you some shoes after dinner."

"Thanks," the boy said. Then he looked over his shoulder. "The shower bath is down this hall?"

"Yes," Charlie said. He didn't want to walk it with the boy, didn't want to see the piles of laundry scattered by the bedroom door, the tilted paintings, the dirty dishes still on the bedside table, waiting for him to get up enough energy to clean them. "It won't be too long until dinner."

"All right," the boy said. He headed down the hall. Charlie heard the squeak of the drawer as it opened. A few moments later it shut, followed by the sound of the bathroom door closing.

The kitchen smelled of fish. Charlie wiped a hand over his nose. It was good that the boy was taking a shower. Charlie wouldn't have been able to eat next to him.

Charlie cleared the egg dishes off the table, rinsed a skillet, and opened the refrigerator. He had some hamburger in there and a jar of Newman's Own spaghetti sauce. He always kept noodles around too—the meal was quick and easy, another staple of his long and uninteresting life.

Until now.

The boy looked too much like Spence. Even when Charlie was seeing clearly.

And although Charlie knew he was in 1989, he'd still heard the boy say things like *shower bath* and ask questions about things he should know.

The shower hadn't started running yet. If a nineteen-year-old from 1939 arrived fifty years in the future, how long would it take him to figure out a modern shower?

Charlie pulled the hamburger out of the refrigerator, refusing to think about it. He didn't dare think about it. He had his own ghosts and hallucinations. He suffered what the 'Nam vets called post-traumatic stress disorder, a term he used to hate but had learned to call his own. He had thought he could defeat those demons. But this seemed an unusual manifestation of them.

He had never had anything against Spence. Spence had been two years older—a lifetime to a seventeen-year-old boy. Charlie had admired Spence. In fact Spence had inspired Charlie to join up, indirectly. Charlie had always used Spence as his model, and until that mine hit, Spence had been his measure of behavior. Would Spence have joined up in December of 1941? Of course. Would Spence have volunteered for dangerous duty? Of course. Would Spence have led his men across that field? Of course.

Of course.

Of course.

Of course Charlie didn't know, because Spence had died two years before he even had a chance to join up. Perhaps the demons that guarded Charlie's imagination were sending him Spence now as a type of torture. The boy that Charlie saw looked like the boy he remembered, only heartbreakingly young, at the beginning of his life, a boy who played at courage but who really had no idea what it meant. Charlie's role model, the one who had led him across the Pacific and back, was slender, frightened, and young enough to be his grandson.

The shower turned on. Charlie heard the hiss through the kitchen pipes, and he smiled. Spence—or whatever his name was—would be all right.

The question was whether Charlie would.

9

EVELYN BRAND had heard the gossip before Lisa arrived. That made conversation easier. It had also given Evelyn time to react, time to reflect on what needed to be done.

She had fresh coffee in the pot and had made cinnamon rolls. She and Lisa had had this date for days. If Addy was going to be any trouble over the new burial site for her mother, Evelyn was supposed to talk to her. It was appropriate to bury Olivia facing the sea. Everyone knew that. Only Addy's stubbornness would prevent it.

But things had changed now. Evelyn had been awake all night. In addition to the cinnamon rolls, she had baked cookies, brownies, and a blackberry jam pie she would give to Charlie if she ever got the chance. She kept expecting a knock on her door, but none came. Only Billy, who'd called after he left Addy to ask if Evelyn knew anyone who would harass her. Billy believed that the boy who claimed to be Spence was a prankster.

Evelyn wasn't so sure. She could still see the man lifting himself out of the ocean, stepping onto the path of light. If only she hadn't been such a coward. If only she had continued looking through the binoculars, then she would have known if he had walked to the Churn. Addy had said she had seen a strange man walking on the beach. What if that had been Spence, disoriented, frightened, still filled with his last memories of falling into the Devil's Churn and smashing up against the lava rock, reaching out to hands that could never pull him ashore.

Olivia would have chided her. By failing to watch him emerge, Evelyn had turned her back on the magic.

Again.

But she hadn't been born to it like Addy, and she didn't love it like Olivia.

Evelyn had felt guilty each time she used it. The cost had been too great, to her, to others. Olivia's magic required sacrifices, the kind Evelyn could never make.

Evelyn had made that clear when Olivia had tried to resurrect Evelyn's son.

Evelyn had stopped her, and Olivia had accused her of being afraid.

She had been afraid, afraid that her son would return, a monster from the deep who looked like a boy but was a boy no longer. Olivia's rituals did not guarantee humanity. If anything, Olivia's magic stole humanity from its practitioners. Olivia, in the years before she died, only played at compassion to retain her power in other people's lives.

Evelyn never wanted lose her compassion.

She sat at her kitchen table, a cup of coffee before her. The house smelled warm and sweet, homey smells, smells that reassured. A layer of morning fog hovered over the ocean, like a cloud brought to earth, and covered the beaches and the hotels. Her house was just high enough to see the sun above the fog. She was in the light while the rest of Dory Cove was in the dark.

A car pulled into the driveway and stopped, its engine ticking. Evelyn straightened in her chair. She was listening now to each movement outside, ready to jump up when the doorbell rang, but not to move too quickly. She didn't want to seem too eager. But she did want to see how Addy was doing, whether Addy still believed that the boy had been Spence.

And if he was, what then? What would he be? And would he search for Evelyn too? They had been confidants just before he died. But Evelyn had moved from her parents' house decades ago. Spence would never have been able to find her.

Even her last name was different.

A single car door slammed, followed by sharp, firm footsteps on the sidewalk.

A single set of steps. How odd. Lisa had said she would call if they couldn't make it, and it was nearly nine. Perhaps Evelyn had another visitor.

She held her breath. Spence wouldn't drive here. But Billy might. Billy might ask more of those embarrassing questions about the people in Dory Cove, the ones who held grudges against Addy, the ones who would try to hurt her. Billy was a fine one to ask. He pretended his past didn't exist, that he had been a part of this community from the beginning, but he had always been struggling to belong.

And Addy's return was a vivid reminder of that.

Her visitor ignored the doorbell and knocked, three firm raps that echoed in the silent house. Evelyn let out her breath and stood so quickly, she nearly toppled her chair. She was nervous, and her lack of sleep made it worse. Dory Cove had always been a strange place to live, but no stranger than the last few days.

Or perhaps it was just the quiet events mixing with the events of the past.

Sometimes the past was more vivid to her than the future.

It only took her a moment to cross the kitchen and head for the door, but in that time the person knocked again.

"Coming," Evelyn said.

She hurried through the narrow hallway to the square entry her husband had insisted on building. She had a coat tree and an antique table in that entry, the table standing below an oval mirror she had bought at a garage sale. A bouquet of lilacs stood to one side, tasteful yet full of spring. As she pulled open the door, she was surprised to see Addy alone.

"I thought Lisa would be with you," Evelyn said.

"I need to talk to you without Lisa," Addy said.

Evelyn stood away from the door so that Addy could come in. Addy looked spectacular, too gorgeous for a nearly seventy-year-old woman who had just lost her mother and had had a scare the day before. She wore a black and gray sweater that brought out the black highlights in her hair, and gray slacks that accented her slenderness. Her shoes were black, too, flats that made her only a few inches taller than Evelyn.

Addy followed Evelyn through the hallway into the kitchen. The scents of baking seemed even stronger than they had a moment ago. Evelyn turned to gauge the effects on Addy and frowned.

Addy stood next to the island, her hand resting on the tile, staring at the windows. For a moment, in the bright daylight, she looked like Olivia.

"How do you do this?" Addy asked. "How can you stare at the sea every day?"

Most people envied Evelyn's view. If they asked at all, they asked how she had managed to afford a place like this, and she would tell them about the ways she and her husband had sacrificed, the changes they had made in the house, the plans they had forgone.

"I like the sea," Evelyn said.

"Even after Spence?" Addy asked.

Evelyn shrugged. "You can't blame the sea for being itself."

She went into the kitchen and hovered near the coffeemaker. "I have fresh cinnamon rolls. You want one with a cup of coffee?"

That broke the spell. Addy turned to her gratefully. "I would love one. I haven't had breakfast yet."

Evelyn poured coffee into her Oregon Coast mugs, knowing her desire to force the ocean on Addy was perverse, but giving into it anyway. She put the large cinnamon rolls on plates, then lathered butter on each. Frosting dripped off the sides, not yet hardened. The insides of the rolls were still warm.

Then the two women sat together at the kitchen table as if they had done so every week of their lives.

"Why didn't you want Lisa to join us?" Evelyn asked.

Addy sighed. "She trusts you. She likes all of Mother's friends, but you seem to be someone she trusts more than the others."

Evelyn nodded, waiting. Lisa had been anticipating the fight over Olivia's grave for two weeks now, ever since it had become clear that Olivia was going to die and Addy would have to handle the estate.

"Did Mother talk to you about the will?"

Evelyn started. She had not expected a discussion about the will. She had heard that some of the provisions were unusual—Olivia had hinted at that—but she didn't know what they were. To cover her surprise, she took a sip of coffee. It was hot, but the beans were fresh, just the way she liked them. "She simply said that some people wouldn't like it."

"She meant me, obviously." Addy picked up her fork and cut into the cinnamon roll. A bit of steam curled out of the center. They were hotter than Evelyn had thought. "But not for the reasons she thinks. She made me executor, but she only left me a token fee for my work. To cover my time, is how she put it.

I don't mind that. I never expected anything from Mother. Frankly, I'm surprised she had an estate at all. I thought she would have gone into a nursing home years ago."

"Olivia had ways of keeping herself healthy," Evelyn said softly.

Addy frowned at her, but didn't ask. Evelyn was grateful for that. She didn't want to talk about all those years she had substituted for Addy, all those years of training, of religious discussions, of spells.

"She left the house to Lisa, which didn't bother me that much. It sits on a sand cliff. The ocean will eat it sooner or later. The sensible thing is for Lisa to sell, but she won't. She's talking about selling her house in Salem and using the money to build a seawall."

Despite the warmth of the mug in her hands, Evelyn turned cold. The house had to die. It had lived beyond its time. Olivia was dead. The god she had built it for would never walk its floors. To leave the house would be criminal.

Uninhabited, it would invite all sorts of dark magic to the Cove. Even if Lisa lived there, she wouldn't be strong enough to keep all the forces out. Olivia hadn't been, and she had been the strongest of all of them.

Olivia should have explained that to Lisa.

"A sea wall would cost a fortune. She would need permits from the state, and a contractor, and then she would have to build a huge concrete structure just to make the thing work." Evelyn set her mug down. Her hands were shaking. She put them in her lap to hide them from Addy.

"That's what I told her, but apparently her house was appraised at over one hundred thousand dollars. Since she wouldn't have to buy a new house, she wouldn't need the money. She could use the cash for the seawall, and live off her savings until she found a way to tide herself over in Dory Cove."

Evelyn let out a slow breath. Olivia had wanted to keep the house away from Addy because she had known that Addy would sell it. There was no telling what the new owners would do, Olivia would say. They would remodel or shore up the basement.

Or build a seawall.

"You want me to talk to her?" Evelyn asked.

"Please," Addy said. "She says Mother gave her the house because she understood its value to the family."

"I don't know if she'll listen to me," Evelyn said. She had never given Lisa advice. She had always been Lisa's ear, clarifying family history, helping her convince Olivia of the changes that needed to be made. In some ways Evelyn had fulfilled the duties of motherhood—the good duties—without having to undertake any of the bad.

"She'll listen to you more than she'll listen to me," Addy said. She scraped the frosting off the side of the roll and placed it on the side of her plate. "I even bargained Mother's gravesite. I told Lisa that if she sold the house, I would bury Mother in Paris if Lisa told me to."

The chill that had risen earlier grew deeper. Following Olivia's wishes had been important to Lisa, once. "And she said no?"

"She said I was mixing issues, that one had nothing to do with the other.

Mother had left the house to her so that I wouldn't sell it."

"That's true, Addy," Evelyn said.

Addy raised her eyes toward the ceiling and sighed loudly. "How can it be that my mother still controls my life even though she's dead?"

Evelyn set her mug down. "Your mother never controlled your life, Addy. You've been gone since you were nineteen years old. If you saw your mother once a year, you saw her a lot."

Addy brought her head down. "My mother controlled my life," she said. "I lived on the prairie so that I wouldn't have to see the ocean. I married men I didn't love because I didn't want to be alone and obsessed the rest of my days. I made my children go to good Christian churches so that they would learn a real religion, one that taught about love instead of power and hatred. I worked even though the ideal woman remained at home like a spider in the nest, wrapping her web around anything that ventured into her domain. Everything I did was a reaction against my mother."

"Including your desire to sell her house. Your desire to bury her away from the sea," Evelyn said.

Addy nodded. "Even that."

"Olivia knew. That's why she gave the house to Lisa."

"Then why are you so shocked that Lisa wants to keep it?"

Evelyn took a deep breath. She wasn't certain how to explain. She glanced at the ocean. The fog was lifting off it. She could see patches of blue mixed with the cloud.

"Your mother," she said slowly, "belonged to an ancient and natural religion."

"I know," Addy snapped. "All that mystical bullshit about spiritual places and strange powers and how they would unite to bring my father back."

"There's more to it than that," Evelyn said. She took another sip of her coffee. The liquid was getting cold and bitter. "Your parents built that house according to your mother's precepts. It faced west, the direction of truth. It had an unblocked ocean breeze so that she could smell the scent of the gods. It was made of Douglas fir taken from the nearby cliffs. Every part of that house, even the remodel comes from that small section of coast."

"From the Churn," Addy said.

Evelyn nodded.

"Except the glass."

"No, even the glass. There are glass blowers in Lincoln City. They used the sand that Olivia brought them to make the panes for the new windows."

"And the old windows?"

"Your mother made those herself."

Addy scooped up the frosting and ate it off her fork as if she were trying to stab herself. She winced and took a quick sip of coffee, then bowed her head. "I don't understand what this has to do with Lisa."

"Your mother built that house to be as much of the natural order as she could.

It is a part of that cliff like the shrubs are part of that cliff. If Lisa builds a seawall, she ruins that order."

"If she builds a seawall," Addy said, "she also protects the house."

Evelyn nodded. "But all things decay, even houses. If Lisa builds a seawall, she prevents the erosion of the cliff face; she prevents the inevitable destruction of the house."

"That house was everything to Mother. She gave the house to Lisa so that Lisa would continue the family homestead."

Evelyn froze, her hands on the mug. Addy really hadn't spoken to her mother much. "Your mother did want the house to disappear after she left. Her power filled it. Without her, the house would become power without guidance. You studied the Book with her. Power without guidance could be bent at a whim. Any energy inside would be dangerous. That's why she wanted the house to go to someone who understood. She must have thought Lisa did."

"But Lisa didn't."

"Or Lisa is ignoring her." Evelyn's mouth was dry. She was dizzy from lack of sleep. "I'll talk to her. I'll remind her."

Addy shook her head. "It does no good to keep the house and let it decay. I always found Mother's talk of her magical powers ridiculous. It's nice to know that Lisa did too. Lisa wants to hang on because of the memories, and if she is going to keep it, she should protect it. That's only common sense, Evelyn. But she should sell. She'll get more money out of it now, and be able to find a good home on the coast if that's what she wants. Someone will buy it from her. If you're going to argue that she keep the house and not improve it, I don't want you near her."

"You came over here to ask me to talk to your daughter," Evelyn said.

Addy nodded. "But only if you talk sense."

"Addy," Evelyn said. "Your sense may not be mine."

"You believe all that stuff my mother said, don't you?"

Evelyn licked the sugar off her lips. She didn't know how to respond.

"Obviously," Addy said. She stood. "Thanks for the coffee and the roll."

"You're not finished," Evelyn said.

"Oh, I think I am." Addy smiled at her, a thin, cramped little smile that held back more than it showed. "I can let myself out."

She walked toward the door. As she headed toward the hall, Evelyn said, "Addy, we were friends once."

Addy peeked her head back inside. "You know," she said, "I said that to Charlie Winter two nights ago. He reminded me what it was like around here. We were never friends, Evelyn. We just grew up together."

Evelyn caught her breath. Addy disappeared, her footsteps echoing in the hallway. The front door slammed, then Addy's footsteps rang on the concrete, growing progressively fainter. Evelyn stood as she heard the car drive away.

No matter what Addy said, Evelyn would talk with Lisa. Her grandmother had given her a charge. The girl should follow it, not try some crazy scheme on her own. Evelyn could almost see Lisa in the kitchen of that house, waiting for her grandmother to return.

But Olivia hadn't died in the ocean, despite her attempt to do so. No god could give her back because no god had stolen her. Lisa had to know that. If she didn't know that, she hadn't listened to her grandmother.

She hadn't learned.

And that terrified Evelyn most of all.

10

B Y THE TIME Addy reached Highway 101, the fog had lifted. The
sky was pale blue, the sunlight thin, as if it were still being filtered
on its way to the earth. Dory Cove looked busy, although tourist
season hadn't yet begun. Half a dozen campers passed as Addy sat at the
stop sign below Evelyn's house. She had almost decided to turn right, go
the opposite way from her mother's house, when an opening appeared
in traffic.

Her mouth still tasted of the butter frosting Evelyn had used on the
rolls, and there was an odd knot in the middle of her shoulder blades.
Addy felt as if everything in Dory Cove were slightly skewed. If she were
to call her friends back in Chicago to tell them about her last few days
and the arguments she had been having, they would have asked after
her mental health. If she convinced them she was fine, they would have
wondered what sort of odd place she had grown up in. In some ways it
was as if time had not touched the Cove, as if the weirdness that she had
felt as a child had not changed at all, although the buildings were different, the stores were newer, and the franchises had moved in.

As she approached Dunstaff's, she saw Lisa's car in the lot. Addy
ground her teeth, then forced herself to stop. The dentist had already
warned her about that habit, saying her back teeth were now little more
than nubs. If she continued, she would need crowns and, he implied,

giving an elderly woman crowns would be a silly expense. She knew he wanted to talk her into dentures, a thought she was not yet willing to face.

The knot between her shoulder blades had grown. It hadn't taken Lisa long to act on Olivia's wishes. Sometimes it seemed as if Lisa had been Olivia's child, not Addy's.

Olivia had acted that way from the beginning. She had arrived at the hospital at the moment of Lisa's birth, had cared for Lisa in those early weeks, and had protected Lisa with a fierceness that scared Addy. They had had a closeness that Addy and Lisa would never have. And Addy didn't know how to combat that. She hoped Lisa would be as solicitous of her one day, although she doubted it. Addy's desires had never figured into their relationship.

She pulled into the parking lot and parked beside her daughter's car. She should probably stay away. She had lost ground that morning, offering the only thing she controlled—Olivia's burial place—like a bargaining chip to her daughter.

But Addy wasn't willing to give up. She wanted Lisa to sell the house; if she caught the girl, in public, she might be able to convince Lisa to do just that.

Addy's flats worked better on the gravel than her heels had two nights before. She half ran toward the steps, took them quickly, and pulled open the heavy metal door to Dunstaff's.

The funeral home was silent. No need for sentimental music today. The hour of mourning had passed. Her mother's coffin no longer sat in the vestibule, and the tiny chapel was dark.

Michael Dunstaff's wife, Mary, came out of the office. She wore a dark blue dress that was too tight around the hips, shoes that had been fashionable five years before, and her hair in a cap of curls that would have looked more appropriate on a woman twice her age. She approached all the clients of Dunstaff's with an air of agitation as if she were afraid they would judge her for marrying a funeral director.

"Mrs. Rustin," Mary said. "Can I help you?"

"I'm here to see your husband," Addy said. Her words were clipped, her manner authoritative. She only used this mode when she was very, very angry. She hadn't realized how angry she was until this moment.

"I'm afraid he's in a private meeting," Mary said.

Addy nodded. Then she smiled. People who had been on the receiving end of that smile often told her it was not pleasant. "A private meeting?" she asked. "With my daughter? Discussing my mother? I'm the executor of the will, Mary. If Mr. Dunstaff speaks with anyone privately, it should be me."

Mary Dunstaff had the grace to flush. She couldn't lie for her husband. She knew who Addy and Lisa were. "Come with me," Mary said softly.

She led Addy to the back office. The office had also been designed to be tasteful, a comfortable, soothing room, almost like the secretary's office in a large church. A place a person in need wouldn't mind waiting. Lisa sat on a brown chair with wooden arms. She was leaning forward, looking at papers on Dunstaff's mahogany desk.

Dunstaff looked up at his wife. Addy could see the rebuke on his face, but also knew that he would never yell at his wife in front of others. It would destroy his soothing persona.

"Mrs. Rustin," he said. "Your daughter and I were just discussing your decision to place your mother in a resting-place close to the ocean."

"My daughter is not the official representative of my family, Michael," Addy said, deliberately using his first name. She wanted him in a one-down position. "If anyone would have the right to speak for me, it would be my eldest, my son Marty. But I am in good health. I need no one to speak for me, and I have not yet made a decision about my mother."

Dunstaff took his hands off the paper as if it burned him. "Forgive me, Mrs. Rustin. Decisions can be difficult at times like these, and family relationships always differ. The matter is delicate."

"You're right," Addy said. "The matter is quite delicate." Lisa still leaned forward. She had a challenging look that Addy had not seen since Lisa was thirteen and testing the strength of the rules Addy had imposed. "Lisa, wait for me in the vestibule."

"Mother—"

"I said wait for me." Addy kept her tone firm. She had learned that it took only one sentence to make her children react as if they were six again. Lisa stood up, adjusted her sweater, grabbed her purse, and left the room.

Dunstaff stood too. He was a short man who was beginning to become pudgy. His suit was well tailored, though, unlike his wife's dress, and his tie was silk. "Forgive me, Mrs. Rustin—"

Addy looked at Mary. "You'll excuse us?" she asked.

Mary nodded, and closed the door.

Addy waited until Mary was gone before continuing. "Michael, I know that those ocean plots are four times more expensive than the plots in the back. I love the concept of an ocean-view burial space, but even if the dead could see, it would be difficult to do so through the most expensive coffin you have and six feet of dirt, wouldn't it?"

"Mrs. Rustin, now, if you're suggesting—"

"I am not suggesting a damn thing, Michael. I am stating that you are taking advantage of my tangled family relationships. My daughter was close to her grandmother, and her emotions are volatile right now. She can't make a good decision. I will ask you again, and this time you will be straight with me. Did my mother ever pick a burial plot?"

"She indicated—"

"Did my mother come into your office, put her finger on that piece of paper, and put up cash for a burial plot?"

"No cash, but—"

"Did my mother come to your office? Did you ever show her that piece of paper?"

Dunstaff looked down. "No."

"Then you only have my daughter's word, don't you?"

"Do you disbelieve your own daughter, Mrs. Rustin?"

"Is that a professional question, *Mr.* Dunstaff?"

He didn't move.

Addy adjusted her purse on her shoulder. "I think we can come to an understanding, Michael, that will keep me satisfied. I will buy one of your 'view' plots for the same price as one of your non-view plots. Then everyone will be happy. You will get a chance to place my mother to rest in an expensive coffin. My daughter will get her view, and I will pay the price I want to pay."

"Mrs. Rustin," Dunstaff said. "I'm afraid I can't give you the view plot for the same price as the other."

She crossed her arms. "And why is that, Michael? Because view plots cost more to dig? Because gravediggers charge more per hour? Because the soil is different every six feet on that knoll? Or because you can command a higher price from that area by conning grieving people like my daughter?"

"Mrs. Rustin." His voice had taken a pleading quality. "I do not con people."

She smiled, the same smile she had used on his wife. "No, I don't suppose you do. A man with a monopoly can get away with anything. Where's your nearest competition? Yachats? I think I'll talk to them."

"You used the coffin, Mrs. Rustin." The pleading had left his voice. He straightened and she saw the man beneath the smarmy exterior.

"I did not use the coffin, Michael. You conned my daughter—who has no authority in this matter—into choosing it."

"But you approved it," he said.

"Have I signed any documents? It seems to me that we were going to wait until the matter of the gravesite was settled. My daughter even put down the deposit so that things could move forward in case I didn't arrive in time. I did not give her permission to do that. In fact, I believe you told her that was customary. You used that same word with me two days ago."

"Mrs. Rustin—"

"Michael," she said firmly. "Give me a view plot at my price and I will pay you cash this morning."

He stared at her. His eyes were small and intelligent. She could almost see him turning the options over in his brain. She knew she had him. She had known she had him from the moment she had seen the expensive coffin two days before.

Funeral home directors were very sensitive to claims they were ripping off the survivors. Dunstaff, for all his hatred of the job he inherited, felt the same way.

"I suppose you want the site that Lisa picked out, the one overlooking the Devil's Churn?"

The room spun. The anger she had been using as a weapon reached back and slapped her. She nearly yelled at him, until she realized that was exactly what he wanted. The moment she got emotional, he would have won.

"Yes," she said as calmly as she could. "That's fine."

He glared at her. "If you'll be so kind as to wait with your daughter while I fill out the agreement."

"I'll wait in here, thank you," Addy said.

She sat down in the chair Lisa had been in and watched as Dunstaff filled out every line of his little agreement. The frosting turned sour in her mouth. She hated small towns. Even Dunstaff, who had never met her, knew the story of the Devil's Churn, and knew it well enough to use it against her. She would be glad when all the details were done, her mother's possessions discovered and disbursed, and she could return to Chicago, a happy orphan at the ripe old age of sixty-nine.

He finished filling in the fine print and turned the contract toward her. She read it carefully, crossing out the hidden costs that he tried to stick in to cover his losses, and then signed it. Then she took out her checkbook and wrote him a check for a sum she thought was still twice as large as it should have been.

"I'm sure a business such as yours is used to out-of-town checks," she said as she handed him her check to forestall his next argument.

"Most people use a credit card," he said.

"Lucky for you, then, that I have enough money in the bank to afford this," she said, and smiled. She stood, took her copy of the contract, and put it in her purse.

Then she shook his hand. "Let me know when the burial will be. My mother didn't want a graveside service, but I think we should watch as she makes her final passage, don't you?"

His gaze flicked away from hers. He was sneaky. He had not meant to put her mother in a view plot, figuring Addy would never visit and Lisa would blame the site on her mother. But now he had no choice. "That's fine, Mrs. Rustin. We'll have the gravesite prepared by tomorrow afternoon. Shall we say two?"

"Two would be lovely," Addy said. She pulled her fingers from his and left the office, resisting the urge to wipe her hand on her slacks.

Lisa was pacing the vestibule, a brochure folded in her hand. Mary Dunstaff was nowhere in sight. Still, Addy wasn't going to give Michael Dunstaff the satisfaction of a scene in his funeral parlor.

She grabbed her daughter's arm and propelled her outside, as she used to do when Lisa was loud in church. "You moved quickly, didn't you?"

"You said it was all right." Lisa's voice rose, just as it used to when she broke curfew.

"I said I was considering the new location. I never said it was all right. Then you said that we were discussing two separate topics, and wouldn't let me relate the grave site to the house. I thought that closed the matter."

Lisa wrenched her arm free and walked down the steps. "You never understood Grandma, did you, Mother?"

"You're the second person to accuse me of that today," Addy said. "I understood her well enough. I never liked her much, but I understood her."

"Did you? Everyone has a secret life. Did you have any idea what hers was?"

"I didn't care," Addy said, "as long as she stayed away from mine."

"That was easy enough, wasn't it? With you clear across the country."

Addy followed Lisa down the steps. Lisa walked quickly across the gravel parking lot, so quickly that Addy had trouble keeping up.

"Is that what this is about?" Addy asked. "You think I neglected your grandmother?"

"I think you deliberately hurt her, over and over again," Lisa said. "This grave thing is just one more way to get back at her for something I'll bet she didn't even know she did."

"This grave thing," Addy said slowly. "This grave thing was between you and me. And Dunstaff, who was cheating you."

"He was not!"

"Then explain how I managed to get the same plot of land for one-fourth the price."

Lisa whirled. Her pin-curls bobbed against her cheeks. She looked four years old and furious. "You got the ocean view?"

Addy nodded.

"But I thought you didn't want it."

"You were right," Addy said. "What I want doesn't matter. It is what Mother wanted. She killed herself trying to get to that Churn, and since we can't cremate her, this is the next best thing."

"You did that for Grandma?"

Addy nodded. "People seem to forget that she was my mother. I did love her."

"That's what you say, but I had seen no evidence of it. Until now." Lisa brushed her hair away from her face.

"You can't measure a person's love by whether or not they're going to do what you want," Addy said.

Lisa didn't move. She didn't say a word. She just stared at Addy as if she couldn't believe her mother had said that.

The breeze came off the ocean, carrying with it the same scent of brine she had smelled on the impostor the day before. She shuddered. She hoped the police caught him. "You don't measure love that way, do you, Lisa?"

"Why shouldn't I?" Lisa said. "You do."

"No, I don't," Addy said.

"You didn't like how your mother behaved, so you never visited her."

"I saw her."

"On your terms. You never came to her home. That broke her heart."

"I couldn't come back here," Addy said. "I'm having trouble being here even now."

"Because your boyfriend died?"

The words hung between them. Addy looked around her. From this angle, Dory Cove could have been any coastal town. The sea breeze, the tourist cars, the tiny storefronts off the highway. It was the Churn that made everything different.

The Churn governed life in Dory Cove.

Addy bit her lower lip, then realized she was doing it and stopped. "Spence's death is part of it, like Dad's death is part of it. Mother's strange behavior, that's part of it too. And the Churn…" she shuddered as she said that "…and Billy and all the history. They're all part of how I feel about the Cove and why I hate it here. This place steals people's souls, Lisa."

"That's dramatic," Lisa said. "And convenient."

Addy shrugged. "It's true."

"It's an exaggeration from a nineteen-year-old's perspective filtered through too many years in church."

Addy's heart was pounding hard. Somehow she had to make Lisa understand.

"Dory Cove used to be Devil's Cove. The name changed about the time I was born, when the railroad was being built through this section of coast, and when the stage went from Florence to Astoria. Tourism was starting, and people were afraid to stop in a place called Devil's Cove. It was right beside Devil's Churn, near the Devil's Elbow. The story was that the Devil used to live in this section of the Coast, and anyone who fell into the Churn fell all the way to hell."

Her voice quavered as she spoke that old rumor.

"You believe that?" Lisa asked.

Addy shrugged, belying all those nightmares of Spence trapped in a burning hell at the bottom of the sea. "I grew up with it. I've lived a lot of places, honey, and they all have their stories, but none of them have recurring tales of the dead rising up. Outside of tornado country, none of them experience instant storms like we get here. There was no warning for the Storm of '39. There'd been a storm just like it in 1889 and there is supposed to be another this year. A storm that just appeared, destroyed everything in its path, and then disappeared."

"We have tornadoes in Oregon."

"These were considered hurricanes."

"Weather prediction has changed."

Addy smiled. Her modern daughter. "Yes," Addy said. "Science can predict everything."

"You sound like you don't believe that."

"I don't," Addy said. "I lived through the Storm of '39. It hit only in the Churn and the Cove. Everywhere else in the state that day had sunshine and record warm temperatures. Not a cloud in the sky, except here. Just like the one fifty years before. Do you know what the Indians called the Cove?"

"They called the Willamette Valley the Valley of Sickness," Lisa said, clearly using her knowledge as a shield against any argument her mother would make, "and later we learned that was because of the marsh and the mold allergies."

"They called it the Place of Death. There are no Indian ruins here. No tribes stayed in this section of coastline. They warned Cook away, and they warned Lewis and Clark away. The fifty-year Storm has been part of this area's history since white men first discovered the place. The Cove is cursed, Lisa. It has been from the beginning."

"Are you telling me the Devil lives on the Oregon Coast?" Lisa spoke with contempt. A wind had come up, and it blew her hair forward, obscuring her eyes.

Addy bit her lower lip. She looked away from her daughter, toward the ocean, toward the open expanse of sky and water. The feeling inside her was too strong to explain. She knew if she walked to the water's edge and stared long enough, she would see that male face again, the one that had nearly drawn her into the deep. Even now she could feel the sea's pull. It would take her into its cold heart whether she wanted to go or not. That, more than anything, kept her away.

"I don't know what we're fighting about," Addy said. The wind caught her words and whipped them away. For a moment, she thought that Lisa didn't hear her.

"We're fighting about the way you treated Grammy."

Straight, firm, to the point. Lisa had absorbed everything that was her grandmother, down to the attitude about Addy. *You are wrong. You're a bad person, and you are wrong.*

Addy pushed curls off her right cheek and turned toward her daughter. Lisa had let her hair tangle, its Louise Brooks bob now looking like a jumbled mess. A strand had caught on her lip, and she didn't seem to notice. Only her eyes were visible: dark, glittery, judgmental.

"I treated my mother as best I could," Addy said. "She's lucky she had you."

"Don't make this into something about you," Lisa said. "This is about how your selfishness hurt someone."

Addy took in a deep breath, nearly gagging on the salty taste in the air. The wind stilled for a moment, but on the ocean the waves were high. Another gust would come, Addy was sure of that.

She took a step closer to her daughter. "Are we talking about the way I treated my mother? Or are we talking about the way I treated you?"

Lisa bit her lower lip, then tugged the strand of hair away. Her eyes had narrowed. "You didn't *treat* me, Mother. You were never there. Loni raised me. Loni and Marty."

A gust hit Addy in the face. Pieces of gravel stung her cheeks, her eyes, and the pain brought tears. She raised a hand, shielding herself, even though she knew her mother had put these ideas in Lisa's head. Her mother had made Lisa feel like Addy didn't love her. The only way to get through, then, was to remind Lisa who she was, not who her grandmother wanted her to be.

"Girls your age fought for independence," Addy said. "Girls your age celebrate the right to work. How come you're angry at me for working?"

"It's not the same, Mother."

"It's exactly the same," Addy said. "I gave you what I could. I was there until you were nine. Then I had to work. Your father left us with no money."

"My father?" Lisa sounded shrill. "My father *died*, Mother. My father left me too. You never thought of that. Just like you don't think that anyone

95

loved Grammy. You didn't, so of course we didn't either. Well, I did. I loved Grammy, and I loved Dad, and you killed them."

The gust died on the last part of her sentence, making the accusation echo in the silence. Addy put a hand to her throat. A lump had grown there, a lump that felt twice the size of her Adam's Apple. "Your father died in Memphis. I was in Chicago."

"And Grammy died here. But they died because of you. Because you didn't love them enough. Because you drove them away. I worked so hard to show Grammy that someone loved her. She didn't think anyone did."

Addy had heard that from her own mother enough to know that Lisa wasn't lying. Addy's mother had believed that no one loved her. But Addy was also old enough to know that her mother's belief was based in part on her father's early death, and on her mother's attitude, from that moment on, that no one could ever love her.

"You're stronger than I was," Addy said. "I couldn't convince her of anything."

Lisa did not answer. She stared at Addy as if she had never seen her before. "You said you loved her. You treated her like shit."

Addy couldn't take any more. Her eyes were burning from the wind, the salt, and the gravel. Her shoulders ached, and she couldn't swallow without feeling that lump. She walked to her daughter's side and met her gaze, adult to adult. "I treated my mother like shit?" Addy asked. "You mean like you treat me?"

Lisa's mouth moved for a moment, as if she were trying to find words. Then she said, "You have no right to talk to me like that."

"Why not, Lisa?" Addy asked. "Because I was never there for you? Because I didn't treat you the way you wanted to be treated? Because you're not sure if I love you?"

Lisa had gone pale. The wind was dying down, but clouds were moving in. They gathered like troops on the horizon. "Yes," she whispered.

"Isn't that funny?" Addy said. "That's how I felt about my mother. Maybe that's the way of mothers and daughters, Lisa. Maybe it all gets repaired between grandmothers and granddaughters. Have you ever thought of that?"

"It sounds like an excuse," Lisa said, but her eyes had an odd tightness to them as if she were holding back tears.

"Maybe," Addy said. "But if it is, tell me why I can't talk to Loni, but Tiffany and I get along just fine."

"Because you make an effort with Tiffany."

"And my mother made an effort with you." The lump remained in Addy's throat, but it was smaller now.

Lisa's shoulders had hunched forward, and she was slouching. The wind had become a breeze, but it had a chill that it had lacked a few moments before.

Goose bumps stood out on Lisa's arms.

"For the record," Addy said, softening her tone, "I was there for you. I put a roof over your head and food in your mouth after your father abandoned all of us. I did the work of two parents, and sometimes that meant leaving you physically to take care of your needs. I treated you like a child, a little girl who needed guidance and discipline and warmth. There were days when I couldn't be nice, and there were days when you couldn't be nice, and I've done a lot I regret, but I've done a lot I'm proud of too. I'm proud of the fact that you gave to your grandmother. I'd like to think that you learned some of that capacity for love from me. Because that's the thing you don't understand, Lisa, no matter what I do. I love you. I have from the moment I knew you were coming, and I always will."

Lisa's lower lip trembled. "You don't act like you love me," she said, her voice as small as it had been when she first made that accusation, at the age of three.

The lump was back. Addy caught her breath. Her heart ached, as if it had been sucker-punched. Her whole life people had accused her of not loving them.

Donald had said that the night before he died, when he had called her collect from Memphis. *Maybe if you loved me, doll, I'd feel like that godforsaken house was home.* Her mother had made the same accusation each time they spoke. *If you loved me, you'd come to me.* And now her daughter, her precious youngest daughter, the child she had tried to win but never could, was saying the same thing.

Addy shrugged. She didn't have any more words. She put a hand on Lisa's cheek. Lisa's skin was cold and raw from the wind. "You'll always be my baby," Addy said, and walked away.

11

THE WIND kicked up as Billy left Ruthie's. The smell of the diner stuck to his suit, as it always did for the first two hours of the morning. The lingering taste of strong coffee and Ruthie's blue plate special reminded him that he should feel more wide-awake than he did. But his eyes were gritty, as if he hadn't slept at all, and there was a fog on his mind that not even the windswept sunlight could fix.

He had arrived at the diner late because he didn't want to participate in the breakfast conversation. Half a dozen men gathered in Ruthie's after the breakfast rush to drink coffee and reminisce. This morning, he guessed, they would have gossiped about the funeral, and some of them might even have mentioned the sighting of Spencer Chadwick.

Old men believed in ghosts. They lived with thousands of them—regrets, dead loved ones, the women never kissed. Every morning, the conversation at Ruthie's Diner circled around the ghosts. Billy had been afraid that this morning someone would actually step into the circle and begin the discussion he had dreaded all his life.

He hoped the police found the intruder. He hoped that someone had been playing a joke on Addy. He didn't like to think of the alternative.

Now his was the only car remaining in the lot. The Saab looked out of place on the gravel drive next to the square building with the caked windows and peeling paint. Ruthie deliberately kept her place looking run-down and unappealing on the outside because, she claimed, the tourists never gave her a second glance. The diner was for locals only: its look advertised that as well as its location on the east side of 101, pushed up against the knolls that eventually became the Coastal Mountain range. The only things the diner had going for it were Ruthie's cooking which, she said, she couldn't do for a crowd, and for the privacy it gave the regulars.

The wind whipped the edges of his sports coat, flipping them and slapping them against his side. Sand and dust from the road blew past him, blasting his car and making him wince. The weather always changed here—something he liked about the coast and had missed when he lived in the valley. He squinted, and saw storm clouds on the horizon.

A chill ran through him. The regulars had been talking about the storm since the first of the year. They talked about it in the same hushed tones Californians reserved for the Big One, the earthquake that would take out Los Angeles, maybe even make the whole state slide into the ocean. In Dory Cove, the Big One was a storm like the one that killed Spencer Chadwick and fifteen others, a live thing that returned to wreak death and destruction every fifty years.

Portland meteorologists had come to study the storm. A few national weather experts had picked up on the storm too. The fact that it had hit in the month of August every fifty years since the late eighteenth century made it a natural for weather experts. The fact that the storm struck the coast only in the Churn and Dory Cove made it a target for psychics, tabloids, and miscellaneous occult freaks.

Some of them were in town, he knew, but they would get tired of waiting. The storm always arrived in August, but exactly what day no one knew.

Although the way the patterns were matching the ones in his memory meant the storm would arrive soon.

Billy didn't like to think about it, any more than he liked to think about the fault line that ran along two hundred miles of the coast.

He sighed and walked toward his car. The black paint absorbed the sunlight, much as the clouds were about to do. Then, without consciously thinking about it, he glanced over his car, down 101, past his office, and at Dunstaff's.

For a moment he thought the two women standing on the gravel were an illusion, a product of his own tortured mind. Olivia and Addy, fighting as they always had. Then he realized he was seeing Addy—an older Addy—fighting with her own daughter, with Lisa. Their movements were sharp, their body language clearly filled with anger. He could even guess what they were fighting about: Olivia's final resting place. He shook his head as he opened the car door. Olivia would be dust before they had this conflict settled.

"Billy!" The voice belonged to Ruthie. She had a tone that duplicated his long-dead mother's, a tone that brooked no disagreement. He turned.

Ruthie stood at the edge of the lot, holding the diner's screen door with one hand. The wind rattled the glass. She was in her mid-forties, willowy and graceful, her hands twice as old as she was from all their work in dough and hot water.

"Telephone."

He sighed again. Maybe he should change his schedule, vary his routine enough so that the whole town couldn't find him when they were looking. But, knowing his habits, he would make the trip to the new restaurants into a routine—Ruthie's on Monday, the bakery on Tuesday, the Dune Rock Cafe on Wednesday—and people would find him again.

"Who is it?" he asked.

"Evelyn."

Ruthie amazed him. She always managed to say Evelyn's name without distaste, even though she detested Evelyn for reasons she would not name. Ruthie was a returnie, a townie who had left for college swearing she would never come back, only to find that she couldn't live away from the ocean for very long.

He pushed the car door closed and walked back to the diner, moving slowly in the vain hope that Evelyn would hang up. She had gotten him to see Addy the day before, and that more than anything had resulted in his tiredness. He had spent two hours sitting in the dark, nursing a beer, as old memories played in his head, memories he had thought long buried.

They hadn't been. He had known that the moment he saw Addy. But he had pretended all along.

The diner smelled of Ruthie's strong coffee, bread, and cinnamon. Beneath it all was the constant odor of ancient grease and of the vinegar that Ruthie used to wipe the tables. Coffee cups remained on the big round table in the corner, but his breakfast dishes were gone. He walked behind the cash register as if he owned the place and picked up the black handset, his fingers slipping on its plastic surface.

"Evelyn," he said, not wanting to go through the preliminaries.

"Did you see the clouds?" she asked.

"They'll blow over." He kept his voice calm. He didn't know how he had become the touchstone for all of Evelyn's irrational fears.

"It's coming, Billy. I can feel it."

"What's the weather say?" he asked.

"They didn't predict that last one."

He knew that. He hadn't forgotten that storm. He never would. "What's it say?"

There was a long silence on the other end of the line. Then Evelyn's voice returned, soft, as if she knew what his response would be even before she spoke.

"Scattered showers."

He nodded and braced himself against the chipped countertop. "Evelyn, you can't call me every time there's clouds."

"It's coming, Billy. I'm not making this up."

"Someday we'll have a bad storm, Ev. It happens."

"Not like the last one."

Never like the last one. But he said nothing.

"Billy?"

"I'm here, Ev."

"You think I'm silly, don't you?"

He closed his eyes. When he was silent, she begged for reassurance. When he disagreed with her, she tried to convince him. When he agreed, she got angry and accused him of making matters worse.

"I just don't understand why you worry so much about something you can't control."

Her silence lasted longer this time. Ruthie watched from the edge of the counter, a dish towel in her hand. The cinnamon smell had grown stronger.

Through the window, he saw a small sand swirl kicked up by the wind.

"What if I told you I can control this?" Evelyn said.

"I would ask you why you're calling me."

"I think we should go to the Churn, Billy."

He turned his back so that Ruthie couldn't see his face. "You know I don't go there."

"I think if we go, we can stop all of this from happening."

"All of what, Evelyn?"

"The tragedy." Her voice shook. He could hear the vibrato through the static in the line.

"There is no tragedy," he said, "except in your own mind."

Ruthie twisted the towel around her fingers. A shuddery gasp filtered through the phone.

"You're cruel, Billy," Evelyn said.

"No," he said. "I'm not. I'm tired. You've been doom-crying since you heard Addy was coming back, Evelyn. Does she frighten you?"

"She left, and things got quiet here," Evelyn said.

"So you blame her for Spence's death? Addy left after it, after none of her friends would help her." None of her *white* friends, he added, but only in his mind. He never brought up race. Ever. Like the others here, he pretended that race issues didn't exist. Life was easier that way, and the slights were small enough—in comparison—that he had the luxury to do so.

"I would have helped her," Evelyn said.

He almost laughed. Evelyn had hated Addy in those days, and even though Evelyn appeared to have buried the memory, Billy hadn't.

Ruthie had come up beside him. How many conversations had she overheard like this one?

"I need the phone," Ruthie said. "Can't tie it up this long."

She spoke just loud enough that her voice carried into the speaker.

"Don't think I don't know what she's doing," Evelyn said. "She doesn't want anyone to talk to you."

"It's a business phone, Evelyn," Billy said. His voice was soft. "I'll call you when I get to the office." Then he placed the handset on its cradle.

"Why don't you tell her to go away?" Ruthie asked. She had tucked the towel into the waistband of her apron. With one work-wrinkled hand she brushed back her hair, tucking the loose strands behind her ear.

The counter dug into his hip. He couldn't explain to Ruthie the strange bonds between the older people in this town. She was young enough to be his daughter, and the generational difference told here. She could remember the fifties—a child's memories, like his of the twenties—but the true reality of the time she had been born didn't filter into her. She was a woman of the sixties, a woman accustomed to her own strength, to being her own boss, to living her own life, free of men. A white woman raised in the north who had black friends, who may have had a black lover, who believed in her heart that all people were created equal. The texture of his relationships with the white members of his generation was impossible to explain. The insults, the expectations, the lower-class status were so subtle that Ruthie, with her good liberal heart in the right place, would accuse him of being oversensitive, of being unable to let the past go.

He pushed away from the counter. "Evelyn's been part of my life for more than fifty years," he said. "I think I can tolerate her for a few more."

Ruthie shook her head. "You're more tolerant than I could ever be. I'm not sure that woman should live alone. She's crazy, if you ask me."

"She's always been this way, and she raised children and contributed to the community. It just seems crazy now because she's old. Before, people called her unusual, and before that they called her independent."

Ruthie studied him for a moment. Lines had formed around her eyes in the years he had known her. They gave her a look of wisdom that more than made up for her loss of youthful beauty. "Hit a nerve, did I?"

"No," Billy said. "I've been defending Evelyn as long as I've known her. I just get tired of it sometimes."

Ruthie said nothing. Her silence made him defensive. He didn't know how his relationship with Evelyn had developed, but somehow he had become her confidant, her lackey, her confessor. She never did any of those things for him—she never so much as brought him soup when he was sick like she did the older white men in town—but he'd come to accept that as Evelyn, as part of an ancient pattern too comfortable, too familiar, to break.

"You going to come in late tomorrow too?" Ruthie asked.

He smiled. She saw through him so easily. "Probably," he said. "I don't believe in dredging up past hurts."

"Sometimes talking about the past is the best way to lay it to rest," Ruthie said.

"I'm not sure I want to lay it to rest," he said.

"Then it'll stop haunting you."

He made his way around the counter and back to the diner's door without answering her. She was still a young woman, still had years to live before she understood.

He liked his ghosts.

He would be lonely without them.

12

CHARLIE AWOKE to the sound of skittering rats. He hunched, pain throbbing through his legs. The sun hadn't risen yet, but the cot felt softer than usual. The ward was quiet—the other men had to be sleeping. He couldn't hear the roar of planes overhead either, just the rustling and clanging as the rats made their way closer. His breath was coming rapidly. He couldn't run. His right leg was gone, even though he didn't quite believe it, could still feel it, pain surging through it as the pain surged through the left.

He gripped the blanket in his fist and wondered when they had replaced the coarse army wool with a soft homemade quilt. Maybe his mother had sent it from home. A sorrow he didn't realize he felt moved into his chest and mixed with the fear. His mother. He wanted to go home.

A door banged, and he frowned. Banging doors weren't possible in MASH tents. He blinked his eyes open. The darkness wasn't as thick as he thought. Light filtered through miniblinds, and a Mickey Mouse night-light cut through the gloom. A stack of magazines rested beside Mickey, and one was turned up with a computer-generated sign taped to its front.

It's 1989 and the War is Over!!!!!!!

The terror slithered from his chest through his mouth and, as he exhaled, out of his body. He had made that sign at Kinko's the last time he was in Portland. He had placed it over the crude handmade sign he had scrawled late one night just after a terrible flashback. The magazine beneath it was a 1985 copy of *Time*, reminding the country of the fortieth anniversary of the bombing of Hiroshima.

He had bought the Mickey Mouse night-light ten years before when he went to Disneyland with a group from the Vets' Center, and he had bought the miniblinds with his latest disability check because he hated the way the light filtered through the worn curtains his mother had made years before.

His grandmother had made the quilt bunched in his hand the year he was born. If he got out of bed, his foot would touch a carpet installed in 1970 with cigarette holes from those desperate years before he got professional help.

He was home; he was safe; and he was sixty-seven years old.

But he could still hear the rats rustling outside his door.

He swallowed hard and pushed up on one elbow. In the bad years, every time he had had a flashback, he had been convinced that one day he would never emerge from them. He would be stuck in that oppressive heat forever, lying in a pool of his own blood, listening to the medics debate if he would live long enough to make it to camp. His counselors had said the flashbacks would get shorter, and they had. But with that change came a new fear: the flashbacks would get shorter, but parts of them would linger into the present, like tears in wallpaper that revealed the paint behind. Eventually all the wallpaper would peel away, and the past would surround him. He would never break free.

The rats banged pots in the kitchen.

He frowned. They were bold rats, but in the Pacific everything was bold, even the flies. Especially the flies.

He should be thankful the rats came and not the flies.

He swung his left leg and the stump of the right off the bed, then grabbed his crutches. This difficult awakening shouldn't surprise him, not after the extended hallucination the night before. The longer the night wore on, the more the teenager looked and acted like Spence. The more present Spence became, the more Charlie knew he was imagining everything. But he didn't fight that hallucination. For once, a visitor from his past was benign.

Charlie had believed enough in the hallucination to sleep in his shorts instead of sleeping nude. They felt odd now, twisted around his waist. That feeling as well as the sound had brought back the hospital tent.

And the dark.

He always slipped to the past in the dark.

He pulled open the door and hobbled into the hallway. The air still smelled of his dinner the night before: bacon, eggs, and toast. He must have set the light timer he had attached to the coffeemaker because he also caught the odor of fresh Colombian. His stomach rumbled. Maybe he would take himself to Ruthie's, sit with the Senior Center crowd, and gossip so that he could have eggs. He didn't feel like cooking after his night.

The bacon was making his mouth water. He stepped into the living room, saw blankets folded on the couch, a pillow placed carefully beneath them.

He hadn't had bacon last night. He had made spaghetti for himself and the boy. And if he hadn't done that, he had had two-minute eggs. He had been about to eat when he had heard the rustling from outdoors.

Rustling.

Blankets.

Bacon.

Charlie shivered. He wished he had brought a robe.

"Hey, I didn't wake you, did I?"

The voice was young and familiar. He had invited a visitor in last night, a boy who reminded him of Spence, a boy who had tugged on charity Charlie thought he had lost in the war.

The boy was standing in front of the stove, a spatula in his right hand. He had his back to Charlie. "I was trying to be quiet, but it was hard. I couldn't find your pots and then it took me a while to figure out the stove. Pretty fancy stuff. Glad you left the instructions on that coffee thing. I'd've never figured that out on my own."

Charlie's head whirled. He felt dizzy and disoriented. He had expected the boy to be gone like the rats and the cot, a product of his splintered imagination.

Instead the boy remained, looking more like Spence than ever.

"I'll be right back," Charlie said, his tone sharper than he had planned. He turned and left the living room as quickly as he could, given the limitations of crutches. Once inside his bedroom, he closed the door and sat on the bed. The crutches clattered beside him. He put a hand over his face, his heart beating as rapidly as when he woke into a flashback.

The wallpaper was peeling around him. His mantras weren't working any more. If he could kick the magazine away from Mickey Mouse, he would. But he couldn't. He would have to go back into the living room and fight the visions on his own.

Carefully he strapped on his leg, then he dressed and grabbed his cane. He hobbled out to find the boy sliding eggs onto the plates.

"It's amazing what a little food and sleep will do," the boy said. "I feel a lot better than I did yesterday."

He looked better too. The shadows beneath his eyes were gone. His hair looked clean, and although the clothes he chose were too big for him, they made him appear more like a boy of the eighties than a boy of the thirties.

"You didn't have to make breakfast," Charlie said. He had trouble keeping the resentment from his voice. Having a visitor was difficult enough; allowing the visitor to rummage through his kitchen and touch his stuff made him very nervous.

"Least I could do," the boy said. "You're the only one who would help me."

Charlie swallowed. The fluttery feeling remained in his chest. He remembered the feeling from the war. Four years that feeling had gone everywhere with him.

It returned with the visions and sometimes, when it left, he felt bereft, as if a friend had abandoned him.

The boy had straightened the kitchen. He had done the dishes and left them to dry in the rack. The table was clear, too, except for a plate piled with bacon, another covered with toast, and a third heaped with scrambled eggs. Coffee steamed from two mugs, and beside Charlie's plate sat the creamer full of milk and the bowl full of sugar.

Charlie took the egg platter and helped himself. He had no words yet. He wasn't certain if he would accept the hallucination into his life or not.

The boy sat down, put half the bacon on his plate, and left the rest for Charlie.

Then he took the egg platter when Charlie handed it to him and filled the rest of his plate with eggs. The boy ate the toast off the communal plate, drank a full glass of orange juice, and shoveled in the eggs. He ate like a teenager. He moved like a teenager. He had to be a teenager.

Charlie picked up a piece of bacon and bit it. The bacon was underdone, a bit chewy but good. He always picked it up special at the butcher's, preferring fresh meat to supermarket-wrapped. The boy had cooked breakfast. In all his years, Charlie had never had an hallucination that was nourishing.

"Who're your parents, son?" Charlie asked.

The boy stopped eating. He raised his head and frowned at Charlie. "Why?"

The fluttery feeling grew. Charlie covered it with another bite of bacon. "Because you look like someone I knew once. Figure I might know your folks."

The boy pushed his plate away. The curl had fallen over his forehead, obscuring his right eye. "You know my folks," he said softly.

Charlie made himself swallow the bacon. Then he took a bite of egg, trying to make believe this was a normal breakfast conversation. "I do?"

"Yes!" The boy shoved his chair back and retreated to the counter. "Can we stop pretending now? Everything's so goddamn weird and I—"

His voice broke and he stopped talking. He brought his right arm up and covered his face with it, like a pulp-magazine sketch of a man in trouble. But the arm only remained there for a moment. When he brought it down again, his eyes were red, his lower lip trembled, but no tears stained his face.

"And you what?" Charlie asked. He had learned a long time ago. Give the past no mercy. No mercy at all.

"And I don't know what to do," the boy whispered.

Whatever Charlie had expected the boy to say, it wasn't that. Flashbacks had always controlled Charlie. He had learned to escape them, but never to guide them. With his right hand he took another forkful of breakfast. He clenched his left in his lap. If he accepted this moment as real, did that make him crazy? And if it was real, did denying it make him inhumane?

The conundrum was too much for him. The boy was watching him as if everything depended on this moment.

"Sit down and finish your breakfast," Charlie said. "Things are clearer on a full stomach."

The boy hesitated. Charlie nodded at the chair, like his father used to do, and the boy sat. They ate together, the boy so quickly that the food disappeared in a matter of minutes, Charlie taking his time.

When Charlie had finished, he leaned back in his chair, sipped his coffee, and stared at the boy. "You aren't going to go away, are you?"

The boy's eyes grew wide. His face was lean with high cheekbones and that angular thinness that came only with youth. "I will if you want me to."

"And where would you go?"

He shrugged one shoulder. "You said the church gives handouts. Maybe there. No one else seems willing to help me."

It had been Charlie's experience that flashbacks, when challenged, disappeared as if they had never been. But the breakfast was eaten, the blankets remained on the couch, and the boy remained solid, no matter how many questions Charlie asked.

"I'll help you," Charlie said, "if you level with me."

"I'll level with you." The boy swallowed so hard, his Adam's apple bobbed. "But you won't believe me."

"Try me," Charlie said.

The boy got up and poured himself more coffee. Then he brought the mug back to the table, sat down, and sipped before he spoke. The movements seemed to calm him.

"My parents," he said, "are Frank and Irma Chadwick. They live—lived—at 6434 Lilac Way. But the house is gone. Someone put a motel there—"

"The Surf and Sand," Charlie said. "Built in 1953."

The boy closed his mouth. He took a piece of toast, slathered marionberry jam on it, and then pushed the toast away. "You know who I am, don't you?"

"Tell me," Charlie said.

"I'm Spencer Chadwick. And this is some weird dream, right? I hit my head when I fell. The last thing I remember is Billy yelling and water getting up my nose and the rocks—" His voice had the edge it had had the night before. A few more sentences and the boy would be screaming. "—and I went under and I couldn't breathe and I hit—"

Charlie reached across the table and grabbed the boy's hand. The boy yanked his hand away, knocking his plate on the floor. The plate exploded when it hit the tile, the sound as loud as a mortar shell. The boy jumped, but stopped speaking.

The rising terror was broken.

"Panicking isn't going to get you through this," Charlie said. "Believe me, I know."

The boy's hand had been warm in his. Never in his life had Charlie been able to hallucinate touch. Concentrating on the feelings in his hands had always opened a door to the present, the way the quilt had that morning. The boy was real, and he knew things no one but Spence could know.

Only Charlie, Billy, Addy, and Evelyn knew who had been at the Churn that day. And the four survivors had sworn not to talk about it.

Charlie leaned forward. He had learned in the war that the only way to deal with an irrational situation was to remain calm. Fear built on itself and made matters worse. The calm man was the man who survived.

"I'm Charlie Winter," he said. "By rights, you should be two years older than me."

"I know," the boy said. His voice quivered. Charlie had been about to ask the boy his story, but it would be better if the boy didn't talk yet. The panic was still too close.

"There's been a lot of changes since you disappeared. The whole world is different."

"I seen that, just here in this kitchen," the boy said. He glanced at the floor. "Sorry about your plate."

Manners. Charlie had always said his generation knew manners. He had been right. He grinned. "That's all right," he said. "I meant for that to happen."

The boy brought his head up quickly. "You did?"

Charlie nodded. "You were about to get the heebie-jeebies on me, and I can't abide the heebie-jeebies. Not that you're not entitled. You are. Somehow you lost fifty years."

"I don't know where they went," the boy said.

Charlie stared at him. "You don't remember what happened to you?"

"I remember—sinking—and then I was gone a long time. Like I was asleep. But no dreams." He shuddered. "No dreams."

"How'd you get here?"

He raised his eyes. They were wide, confused, the way Charlie had seen a hundred times in boys who had survived battles when all their friends had died. "I pulled myself out. I—it was green and I—"

His voice was rising again. Charlie squeezed the boy's fingers. "It's okay," he said. "You don't have to talk about it now."

The boy made a shaky sigh. He swallowed, then asked, "You believe me, don't you?" His tone implied he didn't believe the situation himself.

Charlie took the remaining piece of toast and the marionberry jam. "Actually," he said as he spread the jam on the toast, being careful not to look at the boy, "I have been thinking that you're a figment of my imagination. A ghost. But I know a bunch of tricks for making figments go away, and you haven't, so I decided to treat you as real."

"Does that mean you believe me, or not?" The odd note was back in the boy's voice.

Charlie set his toast down. In his life he had seen men explode before his very eyes, Japanese soldiers charge into enemy lines with no way of defending themselves, and men with a graze to the arm keel over dead. He lived in a world that had created concentration camps and atomic weapons, a world with televisions and microwave ovens, a world with pacemakers and cures for polio. He had struggled with more phantoms than most people, and still managed to live day to day. A man who had a life like his had to give the unbelievable a chance every once in a while. It kept the demons at bay.

"Yeah," Charlie said. "I guess that means I believe you."

This time the boy did tear up. He wiped at his eyes with the heel of his hands, his fingers trembling. Charlie waited, half expecting, half dreading the hysteria that he knew the boy was holding back.

The boy took a deep breath and brought his hands down. Then he met Charlie's gaze. The boy's eyes were red, frightened, and large, revealing all that he tried to keep hidden, but he managed to hold himself together.

Just as Charlie would have expected Spence to do.

The old admiration rose, the admiration that made the young Charlie Winter follow Spence all over Dory Cove, the admiration that had made Charlie spy on Spence. The admiration that had led Charlie to the Devil's Churn on that fateful afternoon in 1939.

"What do we do now?" Spence asked.

Charlie shrugged. "I've never known anyone who waited fifty years to come back from the dead."

"You mean you know others who came back?" Spence asked. Charlie noted that he didn't use the word *dead*.

"A few," Charlie said. "But they'd only been dead a minute or two. Even then the doctors all called it a miracle."

"You think I'm a miracle?" Spence asked.

Charlie's left fist was clenched so hard, it ached. "I sure hope so," he said. He didn't want to think Spence could be anything else.

13

THE WIND had died down, the storm clouds had blown over, and the sun was out, but Evelyn's disquiet wouldn't leave her. The Storm hadn't come this morning, and it might not arrive tomorrow, but it would come. She knew that as clearly as she knew her own name.

Her terror was a live thing. She had to find a way to tame it. She had spent another sleepless night thinking, wishing Olivia were still alive so that they could talk.

But Olivia was dead. Only Evelyn was left. This time, Evelyn knew how to stop the Storm, and unlike Olivia she would. The Churn didn't need to feed itself. It took a few tourists every year. That would be enough.

It had to be.

She was driving south on 101 behind a Winnebago with California plates. The clock on the dash read 1:15, and the radio agreed. She was in her own car, hands tightly clinging to the wheel as she negotiated the winding curves near Olivia's house. She almost stopped, would have if she thought she could have a look at the Book. Instead, she had to make the packet from memory.

A calming packet. It was the best she could do. Perhaps if she gave the Churn the gift of calmness, the Storm would stay away.

She had to try, even though she was as afraid of the Churn as Billy was. Maybe more so because she knew what it could do.

The Winnebago struggled up the hill. Evelyn settled back into the drive. There was no place to pass on this stretch of 101. She would have to follow the mobile home all the way to the Churn. The drive to Olivia's was the last section of habitable real estate on this section of coastline. From the house's south side on, lava cliffs rose. Pine trees jutted out of the thin soil, some barely clinging to the cliff face by their roots.

A tiny path went from Olivia's to the Churn, but Evelyn hadn't been on that path in fifty years, not since Spence died. Although she hadn'y abandoned the Churn as Billy, Addy, and Charlie had, she always entered by the front. All these years she had swallowed her fear. Olivia had taken her there, had forced her into look into the depths.

Face your fear, Olivia had told her, but Evelyn really hadn't faced it until now.

Over the highway the pine trees loomed, creating a false night. The Winnebago blundered forward, apparently oblivious to the darkness. Evelyn slid farther back, preferring to have this part of the road to herself. There was magic at the Churn, and she could feel it even here, a few miles away.

Shortly after Spence's death, the state of Oregon made the Devil's Churn into a state park. They paved a parking lot, added a rest building, and maintained paths to the Churn itself. Evelyn remembered the debates leading to the change. Olivia had spearheaded a committee from the Cove that lobbied against the state park.

Olivia had been afraid that the state would ruin the wild magic of the Churn. Her efforts had caused a compromise. The parking lot, hiking trail, and rest area would be maintained, but the planned information building and the guided tours of the central coast—tours that would have included the Churn—were scrapped.

A single sign warned of the Churn ahead. The sign did not explain what the Devil's Churn was nor did it give any explicit directions. The Winnebago lumbered past the entrance sign and continued down 101. Evelyn turned into the wide parking lot alone.

Her Ford Escort was the only car in the upper half of the lot. She sat for a moment, her forehead resting on the steering wheel, as she waited for her heart rate to slow.

She would have to be careful this time. If she fell, no one would know. The Churn was dangerous for the young and agile. If she made a mistake—any mistake—it would be deadly.

She sighed, sat up, and stared through the windshield. Another car was parked in the lower lot beside a map of the Churn that had been erected in the mid-sixties. The car was in shadow. From her vantage, it appeared to be a newer-model Japanese car, but she couldn't be sure. It looked empty. She hoped that the occupant had driven to the Churn as a starting-off point for a hike along the Coast. There was a secluded beach that could be reached by walking around the Churn to the southeast face. A lot of hikers preferred that trail for its difficulty.

She didn't want to see anyone at the Churn. She needed to be alone here.

Evelyn grabbed her bag of herbs and got out of the car. If she ever had a real conversation with the powers, she would remind them that she was nearly seventy years old. Her bones were brittle, and she had arthritis in her left hip. She shouldn't be walking a trail that was treacherous to a person in her thirties.

But she had no real choice. Not with the Storm coming, and Addy seeing a man claiming to be Spence. Billy wasn't going to help Evelyn, even though the powers had always pointed to him, and Addy would never come to the Churn again. They were the only ones who had been at the Churn that day; Evelyn was the only one who would return.

She tied the bag of herbs to her belt and walked carefully along the sloped trail.

In the seventies the state had redone the parking area, covering it and the trail with blacktop. The blacktop was splitting now. Even though it was protected up here by the trees, weather had worn the blacktop away.

The rest rooms were behind her, a small square building made of cinderblock.

Flies clung to the mesh near the ceiling, and the entire area gave off a faint odor of urine and disinfectant. Evelyn hurried away from it, following the log fence until it took her to her favorite tree.

A huge oak twisted its way toward the sky. Some kindly planner had circled the trail around the oak's roots, leaving the oak as a majestic center to one of the most primitive areas of coastline left in the Northwest.

The oak's bark was so heavy and gnarled that it appeared to turn a face to the road. Every time she passed the oak, she half expected it to talk with her. Its branches hung low, and in the summer, with the weight of leaves, the branches often brushed her hair. When she had been younger, she would climb the oak and hide in its branches, watching visitors go in and out of the Churn.

But she hadn't done that since Olivia reminded her that a tree was a living being and didn't need a person climbing through its branches without permission. Olivia's rebuke had worked, but even now, decades later, Evelyn still felt as if the face in the oak were watching her with a bit of longing, a bit of hope, and a bit of disappointment.

She wanted to tell it that she couldn't climb anymore, that she would love to sit in its branches now that Olivia was dead, but she couldn't. Someone had parked a car on the west side of the parking lot, and Evelyn couldn't bear it if that someone approached the oak as she was apologizing to it.

The log fence ended as the trail turned toward the oak. Evelyn let go of the wood with reluctance. The fence would start up again when she reached the edge of the cliff. Until then she would have to trust her balance and the sureness of her step.

She watched her feet as she walked around the oak, unwilling to look at its face as she passed, glad that it was still spring so that the branches wouldn't brush her hair like a spurned but still hopeful lover.

The she heard the Churn booming below her. She could feel it through the ground, the power of the ocean as it slammed into the huge chasm carved over hundreds of years. The Devil's Churn wasn't listed in the Oregon guidebooks.

The authors of the books on Oregon place-names didn't mention the Churn, either, although they wrote of the Devil's Elbow. Dory Cove only got a passing mention as a renamed town, but its original name never got into the books either. Evelyn's mother always said the Devil's Churn got its name because it looked like a giant butter churn when viewed from above, but Evelyn never saw the resemblance.

She always thought the Devil's Churn and the Devil's Cove were named because the Devil owned them.

Olivia didn't believe in the Devil. She said the Churn got its name because of the people who lived in it, powerful, beautiful people with strong human bodies, gills, and tails. Evelyn had never seen them. If Olivia hadn't been so certain, Evelyn would have said she made them up.

Beyond the oak the path sloped. The trees thinned, and over the edge of the long cliff she could see the ocean touching the sky. The sky was pale without the clouds, and the ocean a blue-gray. She could barely make out the tiny shape of a ship traveling along the horizon.

In the seventies, after a series of mishaps, the state erected a wooden fence on the edge of the cliff face. Olivia had fought that, too, arguing that it would make the cliff face appear safer than it was. She had been right. The face was eroding underneath. One day the fence and the path would slide to the rocks below, taking some unsuspecting tourist with them.

But her public argument was not her true reason for opposing the change. Olivia opposed all changes in the Churn, claiming they diminished the area's magic.

Evelyn's legs were already aching and she still had to travel most of the distance. The cliff was about 150 feet above sea level, and the path wound its way down. She walked alone on the cracked blacktop, tiny plants brushing against her, tiny flowers blooming amidst the green.

The booms of the water making its way into the Churn sounded louder here, completely drowning out the gentle *shush-shush* of the ocean. When she reached the halfway point, cold spray traveling on the breeze tickled her face. Fear made her lightheaded. She always wanted to turn back at this point, but never did.

Except the day that Spence died.

She stopped at the large piece of driftwood someone had carved into a bench, and sat down. The strains of the last few days were beginning to tell on her. She would miss Olivia, too, perhaps more than Olivia's own family would, and she had not allowed herself to think on it. Olivia's death had also brought home a fact that Evelyn had been able to ignore through the death of her own parents: she was getting old. Although there were older people in Dory Cove, most of them were retirees and almost unknown to her. Olivia took with her a large segment of Evelyn's past.

A particularly loud boom sent spray spattering along the path. Evelyn leaned over. Through the meager protection of the rails, she could see the water frothing in the Churn. On storm or high-wind days, as this morning had been, the water in the Churn always had a soapy look to it. The activity was so great, the bubbles built on each other and coated the lava rocks until the next wave came in.

Sometimes that wave sent foam flying, and some of it landed in the tide pools at the center of the rocks. She hadn't seen that yet today, but she knew she would.

She knew the Churn was waiting, just as it always had.

She leaned back and stared at the path. So easy to climb back to the car, to forget the fear that had led her here.

Such a simple thing to go into the Churn, Olivia had said the day after Spence died. *Such a simple thing and you failed to do it.*

Those words came back each time Evelyn thought of retreating. Yet she remembered that day. She had awakened to a warm summer morning, the kind rare on the Oregon Coast. The weather forecasters had predicted unusual warmth—temperatures into the nineties—and she had actually pulled out her bathing suit. In those days, she relished the chill ocean on a hot day.

But she had never touched the ocean.

And she hadn't touched it since.

She got up. The memory was strong, too strong to sit with. She had just started working with Olivia, had just learned about the history of the Storm. The first time a white man had heard of the storms had been when Robert Gray reached Astoria via the Columbia River in 1792, three years after the Storm had gutted the coastline. He had attributed the freak occurrence to superstition. She knew it to be truth.

One of the first things Olivia had taught her was the Storm, and how it always came when the Churn needed a sacrifice.

Over the years she had suspected that Olivia had meant the sacrifice to be Evelyn.

Certainly not Addy. Despite what Addy thought, Olivia loved her. She would never have sacrificed her precious daughter. When Olivia had learned that Addy had been at the Churn that day, she had berated Evelyn. Then she had tried to talk Evelyn into going to the Churn, into offering herself in exchange for Spence.

Evelyn tried hard to forget that day. She finally came to peace with it by convincing herself that Olivia was speaking out of grief, grief over the loss of Addy.

But sometimes Olivia would look at Evelyn with a cool, malevolent gaze, and Evelyn would remember.

She had stopped coming to the Churn with Olivia when she realized that Olivia was making her walk farther and farther toward the edge on the lava rocks.

Evelyn gave up the magic and the religion shortly thereafter.

Until now.

She sighed and clutched the wooden rail as she made her way down the slope.

The steepness bothered her more on the way down than it did on the way up. She was always afraid she would slip, afraid she would fall across the rail and land on her back on the lava rock below. Her grip tightened on the weather-smoothed wood and she slowed as she walked.

The tide was coming in. The water exploded into the large crevice cut in the rocks. She could see the spray now, fanning fifty feet above the crevice, strong enough to suck the unwary into water below.

Falling into the Churn was an ugly way to die. The water was too deep and it moved too rapidly for a man to gain purchase. The edges of the rock, worn smooth, were impossible to grasp. No one could lean over the edge of the Churn and reach down to an extended arm. The distance was too far, the perch too precarious. Any attempt to save a man drowning in the Devil's Churn would result in another death.

Even now she could hear Spencer's screams.

The path ended at the top of a flight of stairs carved into the cliff side. The stairs had survived the weather better. They were protected from the winds, and rarely felt the touch of the water. But the steps also showed how very dangerous the Churn was.

The Churn was in a nook carved out of the cliff side. Lava rock spiked the ground around the crevice for a hundred feet on all sides. The crevice was huge.

A ship could enter its mouth and not scrape the sides. The crevice continued for the length of a football field, growing increasing narrow, until it ended in a small crack, small enough for a man to step across, on its eastern side. A small, innocent little crack that had been known to lure people into the Churn's depths by its very simplicity. The lava rock wound around the back side of the Churn and onto the northern face of the nook. From there a thin trail led over the cliff and ended just outside of Olivia's house—a two-mile hike over rough terrain.

The sound of the water smashing against the rocks was deafening. The booms echoed in the small space, reflecting and magnifying the power so that each smash became a physical event, accompanied by spray and the smell of brine.

The stairs were dry, as was the lava rock surrounding it. Mud coated the rocks, though, showing that on the stormiest days, not even the most surefooted should venture down the steps. Evelyn often thought the Churn the most dangerous place in Oregon. If the wind were to come up, a person standing on the steps would get swept out to sea.

If the Storm were to come up.

She rubbed her hands over her arms, feeling goose bumps. The air had a chill here, this close to the ocean. She glanced again at the sky. It was clear. No storm. Not yet. Not now.

She picked her way carefully down the steps, knowing that if she fell and broke a brittle bone, she would have to rescue herself from this place. The water crashed against the rocks with the regularity of a heartbeat. Its rhythm was both startling and reassuring. The thunderous sound was so overwhelming, she had trouble hearing herself think.

When she reached the bottom step, she paused. The water inside the Churn was always choppy. Sometimes the sea beyond was calmer. But the rocks broke the waves, making the waves pile on themselves until they created the large walls of water that swept people away.

The wind was blowing east, as it usually did here. She had a choice. She could walk to the mouth of the Churn and try to scatter the herbs over the larger body of water, hoping that none of the herbs would escape into the sea, or she could go to the crevice.

Olivia had always warned her to be certain.

Evelyn went to the crevice.

The walls of the cliff narrowed the farther east she went, and all of the rocks were slick. Wet lava rock looked black, almost a part of the ocean itself. The heavy morning wind had knocked a piece of driftwood the size of the bench onto the rocks. The driftwood was perched precariously over the frothing water. A large wave would knock it back into the Churn, where it would remain until the rocks smashed it to pieces.

She had to pick her way across the rocks, holding the sharp points and leaning toward the cliff face so that she would slip away from the water. Spray hit her constantly. The booming reverberated in the small space. Her hands were shaking.

If she had had a choice, she would not have come here alone.

She had come alone the day Spence died. She had been following him. She had seen him come down to the Churn from Olivia's house, and she had taken her father's car to what was then a turn-in. Later she had admitted to herself that she was courting humiliation. She wanted to ask him to pay attention to her instead of Addy. She would have made him a better wife. She loved him, loved the Cove, loved the ocean the way he did. Addy hated it all.

Evelyn had followed the footpath down to the top of the stairs, and had been standing there when the Churn stole Spence.

It had taken him a long time to die. Every time she thought he had slipped away, he would rise with a wave, skin flapping from cuts drained of blood, and scream for help. Billy had tried. He had gotten a piece of driftwood and used it as pole, but the waves shattered it. When he leaned over to yank Spence out himself, Addy had screamed and pulled Billy back.

Evelyn stopped near a dry patch of rocks and caught her breath. She walked five miles every day, and kept a garden, but her age still told. This kind of exertion was for a younger woman, a woman who wasn't afraid of breaking a bone each time she stubbed her toe. She looked toward the edge of the crevice. It was only a few feet away.

She climbed over a series of rocks almost as tall as she was. They were rounded on the top, flat from the pressure of the water. She crouched behind one and glanced back at sea, watching the waves to see if she could predict the large, dangerous ones.

Sometimes the waves with the most power broke on the Churn's mouth.

Sometimes they found their way through the center of the Churn, creating a wall of water that, for the second it was in the air, looked as smooth as glass.

Here the water had a different sound. The booming was accompanied by the splash of water against the rocks. Her shirt was drenched, but the herb packet was dry.

Damn Olivia and her rules. If she hadn't been so stern about the way things ought to be done, then Evelyn wouldn't be here now.

Damn herself. She could have backed away at any point, left this town, left the rules and the mysteries that Olivia had introduced her to. But she hadn't. She had never had the guts.

Or the ability to believe differently. She didn't believe in the Christian god, the god of the Hebrews. She didn't believe in Muhammad or Jesus or Moses. She wasn't Hindu or Buddhist. Even though, in the end, she denied the religion, she still believed. And her belief was limited to this range of coast. She believed, as Olivia had, that the earth had a power all its own, a power made manifest by the winds and the oceans and confirmed by the strange events in the summer of 1939.

She had the guts now. She had to. Someone had to try to stop the Storm.

Olivia had refused in 1939, and it had ruined all their lives. Evelyn couldn't carry that burden.

She wouldn't.

A huge wave splashed her with ice-cold water. She shivered behind the rock, then made herself stand. Nothing big appeared to be coming. This might be her best chance. She made herself walk to the edge of the Churn and quickly dumped the contents of the pouch into the water.

The herbs floated in the air, hovering in a soft wind. She clenched her fists, willing them to fall, and they finally did, like spray coming to earth, landing on the waves.

The foam disappeared instantly and for a moment the herbs floated on the restless surface. Then a roar from the mouth of the Churn startled her. She glanced at it, noted that the waves were small enough not to threaten her, and looked back at the water. It had turned the same greenish gray that she had seen a few nights ago. If the sunlight had hit it right, she would have said that the water glowed.

Something moved below. A hand, catching the herbs.

A hand.

Her heart pounded. Olivia's stories of sacrifice came back to her. Even now, with the Storm coming, Evelyn didn't want to be the sacrifice.

She scrambled away from the edge, nearly tripping on the lava rock. She glanced over her shoulder, but no one followed her. The water's surface was still calm.

And green.

She followed the cliff wall back to the stairs, forcing herself to walk slowly. She kept an eye on the Churn, half expecting to see a powerful human figure rise from the deep.

None did.

When she reached the bottom step, she rested. The water had calmed, at least for the moment, and the air had grown warmer. Sunlight had finally found the Churn and would send rays until sundown.

She was grateful for the light.

The sea crashed beyond her, the sound growing with each moment. Her heart was pounding faster than usual. She was still too close.

She stood abruptly and climbed the stairs, ignoring the stitch that was growing in her side and the way her breath was coming in sharp gasps. The air grew warmer the higher she climbed, and the fresh scent of wildflowers mingled with the sea.

Below, the booms grew. The spray felt like a fine mist. She grabbed the wooden banister like a lifeline and climbed to the bench. There she made herself sit, even though she wanted to run the rest of the way to her car.

A great way to stumble.

A great way to have a heart attack.

She didn't want to die, and she especially didn't want to die here, at the Churn, and have her body shattered against the rocks.

Like Spence's.

She raised her head and glanced north, in the direction of Olivia's house. Addy claimed she had seen Spence, a young Spence, and Billy thought someone was playing a prank. He had to be right. Evelyn had at first thought that Spence might have come back, but it wasn't until this moment that she remembered how battered he had been before he died, how he even lost the strength to scream, how his face had become a mass of pale flesh and broken bone before he finally slipped into the sea.

The wind came up and she shivered. Her blouse stuck to her back and bra. She would have a tough time explaining this to some passing tourist. The thought made her stand and carefully walk to the top of the trail.

The Churn sounded farther away here. She was glad to have it below and behind her. Part of her prayed the Storm would come because she knew deep down that once it did, she would never go to the Churn again.

The wind swirled around her. It wasn't a storm wind, like the morning's had been, but a playful evening breeze that was so common on the coast in the spring.

She paused when she reached the oak, grabbing its thick branches for support.

Black spots danced in front of her eyes. She had hurried up the last part of the trail too quickly and hadn't gotten enough air.

She made herself breathe slowly and regularly. The wind played with her hair, and the branches sighed around her as if the tree were happy for this slight attention. Here, away from the Churn, the air had a slightly foul stench, as if an animal had died nearby. The smell made her uneasy; spots or no spots, she would have to get home, away from the Churn and its memories of death.

She patted the tree trunk and walked to the parking lot, when the breeze touched her again. The smell was stronger. She looked around for carcasses on the ground. Someone probably hit a deer on 101 and dragged it off the road. But she found nothing.

Perhaps the breeze was toying with her. Anything could happen in this place.

She hadn't smelled the stench going in, but then the wind had had more purpose. Now it had a late-afternoon exuberance, as if its work for the day were done.

The stench got stronger as she made her way to her car. The parking lot was in shadow—trees loomed over it, and even the sunlight almost directly from the west couldn't penetrate. The breeze wasn't blowing from a particular direction as it had earlier. Perhaps she was smelling the rest room. That was probably the case. She hadn't used it in a long time and couldn't remember if it housed flush toilets or not.

But as she stepped over the concrete parking barriers, she realized that smell could only come from a decaying body. A shiver ran down her spine. Something made her turn—a movement, a flash of light, she would never be certain—and her gaze fell on the only other car in the lot.

It was not empty as she had originally thought. A man slumped over the steering wheel.

Her mouth was dry. Olivia's training pushed her forward. Anything that happened at the Churn had significance.

Anything at all.

Evelyn's steps slowed as she approached the car. The sunlight had found a hole in the leaves and was shining directly through the windshield. The man's face was hidden by the wheel, but the back of his head wasn't. His hair shone silver in the bright light except for the black, matted area, which she assumed was covered with dried blood.

She gagged at the stench.

She put a hand over her mouth and backed away, nearly tripping on the concrete blocks in her headlong rush to her own car. She had never seen him before, of that she was certain, just as she was certain she was the one who was supposed to find him, the one who had to report his death to the authorities, the one to start the next stage in motion.

She was the one because only she would note the slime trail leading up from the Churn, the long patch of rust that looked so out of place beside the door handle on his car, the saltwater marks on the driver's window.

She had seen the same thing fifty years ago, a week after Spence's death. A hobo, sprawled across the entrance to the Churn, his body covered with slime and seaweed, his drinking mug caked with salt, and a trail leading down to the Churn.

His skull had been crushed.

Olivia had said the experience marked Evelyn.

She backed her car out of the lot, her hands shaking.

She had been marked again.

14

ADDY SAT at her mother's dining room table, papers strewn around her. Her glasses had slid to the end of her nose and she had a headache building in the back of her skull. She blamed the headache on the lighting. The chandelier provided a thin, diffuse light that made the numbers on the pages look blurry.

Addy's calculator was solar-powered and temperamental. Soon she would be forced to get a lamp off a living room table to provide more light.

Loni and Lisa were in the kitchen, cooking, their soft voices soothing against the clank of pots and pans. Addy couldn't work in that kitchen. Even with its redesign, it was too reminiscent of the kitchen of her youth, too hot, too dark, and full of her mother's presence. Addy had studied in there as a girl because she had had nowhere else—her bedroom had been unheated—and she couldn't make herself work in there again.

Marty and Bruce were in the living room, trading pieces of the newspaper. The television remained off. It was a 1950s set complete with tubes. Marty had turned it on when he arrived to discover that her mother had not bothered ordering cable. The only channels she could receive were a fuzzy Portland Fox station and CBS from Salem. He had turned it off in disgust, and no one had tried it since.

The children played upstairs. An occasional thump accompanied by raucous laughter reminded Addy that they had not yet gone to bed. Dinner was late—Addy had refused to make it, and Loni had finally started when it became clear no one else would. Lisa had come in from the garden at twilight—Lord knew how long she had been out there—and helped. The smell of garlic, onions, and roast beef was making Addy's mouth water.

She took her glasses off and rubbed her eyes. After she had left Lisa, Addy had driven inland, away from the ocean until the air became crisp and light with a tang of pine—mountain air—and she could shake the salt from her feet. She had come back to Dory Cove feeling refreshed and strong enough to tackle her mother's papers.

Her mother had died a wealthy woman. Addy didn't know how she had managed that. When Addy's father had disappeared, her mother hadn't known how to make ends meet. They had worked side by side selling the garden produce so that they would have enough money to pay their meager bills. Her father had built the house from local materials, and apparently had paid cash for it, so there was no mortgage. Her mother's expenses had been low, and Addy had sent money when she could.

But that still didn't explain the balance Addy kept getting each time she punched the numbers into the calculator.

Her mother had died with $1.4 million in assets. The house was the largest. The rest were scattered in certificates of deposit, treasury bills, and money market accounts all over the state. At the end of her life her mother had not been a wise investor, and she had left Addy, as executor, with an inheritance-tax headache, but all of that paled when compared with the numbers.

One point four million dollars.

Where had it all come from?

"Bother you that you're not getting any of Gram's estate?" Marty stood a respectable distance behind her, his thumbs stuck through his belt loop. He had learned that habit as a young man in a vain attempt to imitate James Dean. The habit had stuck. The intent was probably long forgotten.

She shook her head. It surprised her, really. Aside from the anger at her mother's deliberate spite, Addy felt a certain relief that the money skipped a generation and went directly to her children. She would have given it to them anyway, except for the proceeds from the house. That money she considered tainted, and she would have tried to clean it by giving it to the church, an impulse she didn't completely understand.

"Then why do you keep going over the numbers?" Marty asked.

"Because," Addy said. "I don't believe them."

"Figure she's got more squirreled away?"

"I hope not. This is plenty."

He pulled up a chair, still careful not to look at the papers. She had taught her children respect for privacy, even when the knowledge would be in their own best interest.

"Then what's the problem, Mom?"

She picked up her glasses and twirled them by the ear guard. She used to yell at Marty for doing the same thing. He had clearly not forgotten. He grinned at her.

She had to smile back. Her son always had that effect on her. "I think there's something wrong with the documents I have. I must be adding the same things twice."

"Maybe you should check with Billy."

Billy. Somehow he had become like God to her children. He seemed to know everything about her mother, everything about this town. Like the rest of the locals, Lisa went to Billy with her problems, and her habits were rubbing off on her siblings.

"I probably will," Addy said, even though she had no intention of checking with Billy. Since she'd left Dory Cove, she had solved all of her problems on her own. She would continue to do so.

"You don't like Billy much, do you, Mom?"

She frowned at her son. He had turned the chair around and crossed his arms over the back the way a teenager would. The gesture seemed natural even though he was nearly fifty.

"Billy's not the man I remember," she said, and promptly wondered if *man* was the right word. Perhaps *boy* was better in reference to the Billy she had met all those years before. But Billy had had so many experiences when he arrived in Dory Cove that it felt, from her limited perspective, as if he had already lived a lifetime. His coffee-brown eyes had a world weariness she had never seen before.

The day she met him, she had thought she could see the old man hidden in the clean lines of his classic features. She hadn't been wrong. He had aged with grace and style, growing into his heavy features, gaining an elegance that his gangly, youthful self had lacked.

"I'm sure you're not the same either," Marty said.

Half of Addy's mouth moved into a smile, but she couldn't complete the expression. There was too much sadness behind it. "I think you're wrong," she said. "I think Billy finds me exactly the same."

A knock on the door made them jump. Addy glanced at Marty. He frowned as he got up and went to the door.

The voices in the kitchen stopped. Bruce peered over his newspaper. But the thumps continued upstairs, and as Addy concentrated, she realized the children were running. Loni's idea of discipline was much laxer than Addy's had been.

Marty was speaking to someone, using his formal tone. The voice that responded sounded familiar, but Addy didn't recognize its owner until he walked through the door.

The police officers who had been at the house the day before, when that boy had tried to pass himself off as Spence, had returned. Her mouth went dry. They probably had news, news she didn't want to hear.

The officers seemed bigger in the dark. The black man had the soft, squishy shape of an athlete going to fat, and his partner, the white boy with the Irish name, was whipcord thin, the kind of thinness that came from nerves and undereating.

She put her hands on the table and started to stand, when she noticed Marty behind them, shaking his head. She frowned. "You find anything more on that boy?"

"No, ma'am," the black officer said. She couldn't remember their names. She wondered if she had learned them. She doubted it, not in the turmoil of that awful afternoon. "He disappeared before we could find him, and no one else reports seeing him."

Addy bit off a defensive reply. Marty had seen him. All of her children had seen him. But they only had her word that he looked like Spence, and even she was doubting that. She hadn't seen Spence in fifty years.

"They're here to see Lisa," Marty said.

"Lisa?" Addy turned. Lisa was standing in the kitchen doorway, Loni beside her. They both wore aprons they had taken from the wall. Loni's matched her pale blue outfit. Lisa's looked comfortable. The difference between them.

"Forgive us for barging in on your evening," the white officer said. His tone carried regret, something it had lacked the day before. Authority still made Addy bristle, even at the age of sixty-nine. She wanted to ask if they were the only police officers in town or if they had just been assigned to humiliate her.

"You're not barging," Loni said in a silky tone she had inherited from her father. "But we are nearly done making dinner. Can we be quick about this?"

"I don't think so," the black officer said. He was looking at Lisa. "Is there a place we can talk alone?"

Addy finished standing. She took her hands off the table. She would speak for them all. "No," she said. "Whatever you have to say to Lisa can be said in front of all of us."

The black officer glanced at his partner, who shrugged. The white officer walked up to Lisa as if their nearness would give them privacy.

"Did you know Ian Kowen?" he asked.

She flushed, a deep reddish, painful flush that Addy hadn't seen since Lisa was in junior high and had questions about her menstrual cycle.

"Yes," Lisa said. Her voice was soft. "Why?"

"He's dead."

Slowly all the color drained from her face. Addy moved toward her, thinking she would faint, but Loni put a hand behind Lisa first. She swayed, but stayed upright.

"I'm afraid we're going to have to take you with us to the station," the officer said.

"You have a police station here?" Bruce asked. He had come in from the living room.

No one answered him. Addy stopped beside the black officer. "Why does she have to go with you?"

"Because," he said in a tone that implied he knew she was trying to intimidate him, "we need to question her in an official capacity, and this is not the proper place for it."

"Official?" Marty asked. "As in interrogation?"

"As in question," the officer said.

"Will she need an attorney?" Addy asked.

The black officer turned to her, stared at her, his gaze moving over her as if he were assessing her. She resisted the urge to clasp her hands together. Instead she met his look squarely. He nodded as if he saw the fear behind her strength.

"You might want to call Billy," he said.

"Billy?" Marty crossed his arms. "Billy handles civil cases."

"Billy's all we got unless you want to call to Portland," the officer snapped.

"Billy's fine," Lisa said. She took off the apron and handed it to Loni. "Cal Billy for me, will you, Mom?"

"No." Addy stacked the papers on the table and turned them over. Her children understood that meant they couldn't touch anything. "Loni will call. I'm coming with you."

"I'm coming too, Mother," Loni said.

"You're finishing dinner. You have two children to think of. I can wait." Addy didn't even look at her. Loni knew the drill. This was the pattern from her children's childhood all over again. Addy needed to take of something, so Loni took care of the house.

"Mother—"

Lisa put her hand on her sister's arm to silence her. "It's all right," Lisa said as if Loni believed Lisa didn't want Addy along. Loni shot a frustrated glance at her mother—this conflict was as old as Loni was and had nothing to do with Lisa—but said no more. She tucked Lisa's apron over her arm and went back into the kitchen.

Lisa picked up her purse and slung it over her shoulder. "Let's go," she said.

"You ride with them, Mother," Marty said. "I'll follow in your car."

Addy was about to protest when she realized what he was doing. He didn't want his sister alone with the police. Different generations. Addy had taught her children to respect the police. Marty had been clubbed at a sit-in in 1970 and still bore the scar.

The officers already held the door open. Lisa walked with them, Addy beside her. Lisa's eyes were wide, her expression still deadly pale. The death of this man terrified her. Addy could feel it. The terror echoed inside her. She took Lisa's arm and pulled her daughter close. Lisa shot her a startled glance. Addy was not normally possessive. But she wouldn't let this town take her daughter.

It had taken everything else.

15

THE DORY COVE police department shared a building with the local firefighters, the local government, and tiny Dory County's only courtroom. Billy hated the building, but walking through it always gave him a feeling of pride. The building was half a block long, made with the steel, glass, and cinderblock construction that seemed new and daring in 1951. The floors were the same gray tile he had swept when he was the building's first janitor, and the men's room still had the long rippling crack in the wall beside the only stall. Billy had put the crack there with the handle of a screw driver while he worked on the building crew; a carpenter from Portland was threatening him, saying a nigger shouldn't work with real people. Billy had gripped the driver like a knife. As he swung back to hit the man in the eye, the handle slammed into the wall and sent a crack rippling through the cinderblock. The force of the blow startled the other man. He hadn't bothered Billy since.

So each time Billy walked over these tiled floors, his briefcase in hand, or used the men's room where he could see himself in suit and tie, he knew how far he had come. The problem was, inside these doors, the janitor and carpenter's assistant were as close as the cinderblock walls.

Never, in all the years he had been coming to the city-county building, did he think he would do so at Addy's request.

The police department took up the back quarter of the building. It shared a driveway and the paramedics with the fire department. The glass doors that opened into the police area still had the original gold stenciling. Billy averted his eyes as he pushed the door open. He had been unable to do the stenciling himself, even though he had been assigned it. In 1951 he didn't know how to read.

Flat gunmetal desks with blond tops were scattered throughout the main floor.

Tourists were shocked when they came into this department. No one greeted them. The handful of police the city could afford doubled as duty officers and desk jockeys. Sometimes the dispatch was the only person in the office.

But not tonight. Addy sat in a green chair, its legs on castors, and she rolled back and forth like a child in her father's office. Her son was standing over the coffee machine, squinting at its stained sides, an empty coffee scoop in his right hand. Fitz and Jonah stood by the briefing room. Fitz was slapping a manila envelope against his right hand. The briefing room door was closed. Billy assumed Lisa was inside.

She had better be alone. If they had started without him, he would make more trouble for them than they had ever seen.

Addy saw him first. She stopped rolling the chair and got up. She came to him, hands outstretched, the strain of the last few days showing in her face.

"Billy," she said as she reached for him.

He didn't want to touch her in public. Old force of habit. He blocked her move by switching his briefcase to his left hand. She stopped in front of him. He scanned over her shoulder, still looking for Lisa.

"Where is she?" he asked.

"In that office," Addy said. "I've never been in a station so small."

"We don't need much." He started past her, but she grabbed his arm. Her warmth burned through his sleeve.

"You can help her?" she asked.

He glanced at her hand. The fingers were slender, the knuckles knobbed with a slight arthritis, the skin still a translucent white. "I don't even know what she's charged with, Addy."

"A man is dead."

"Have they accused her?"

"They want to question her. The—" she glanced at him "—black man, he said to call you."

Billy nodded. Jonah knew when things might get tight.

"But you don't handle these sorts of things, do you?" Addy asked.

"In Dory Cove," he said, "I handle everything."

She didn't take her hand off his arm. The warmth from her skin traveled along his side to his neck and face. Her son was watching them, the coffeepot wheezing beside him. No one else seemed to notice.

"She needs me, Addy," he said softly.

Addy's lips tightened. She let go as if touching him had been an accident in the first place. Perhaps it had.

He wound around the desks, nodding at Addy's son, and stopping by the officers. They had been talking softly. They stopped when Billy got close enough to overhear.

"What's this all about?" he asked.

"Don't know yet," Jonah said. He pushed open the door and waited for Billy to enter. Lisa was standing at the steel-meshed window, her hands clasped behind her back. She had Addy's stance, but Olivia's solidness. Her black hair shone in the fluorescent light.

The officers followed him in and closed the door. Jonah put a cassette recorder on the table. The plastic casing thudded against the blond wood. Fitz pulled back a folding chair and sat. Lisa did not turn around.

"Lisa," Billy said. "Your sister called me."

Her shoulders rose and fell in a sigh. For a moment she didn't move. Then she turned around. She didn't look at him. She didn't thank him for coming. Instead, she stood over Jonah.

"Do I get to find out what this is about now?" she asked him in a tone that Billy had never heard her use. It was imperious, Olivia on a bad day.

Fitz stuck a toothpick in his mouth, then ran a hand through his auburn hair.

"Found a dead man out by the Devil's Churn," he said. "His driver's license calls him Ian Kowen. He's got a PI's license too. Works for a firm in Portland. Maybe you've heard of them? DeFreeze & Garity."

"You know I've heard of them," Lisa snapped. "You wouldn't have me here otherwise."

Billy had started quivering at the mention of the Churn. He made himself take a deep breath. He had to help her before this got out of hand. "Lisa," he said, "don't volunteer anything. Let's hear what these gentlemen have to say first."

The contempt she shot him matched the contempt in her voice when she had spoken to Jonah. Billy felt like an old man, a janitor in his night blues, something he had never felt in her presence before. Olivia used to do that to him, too, sometimes. He swallowed the feeling back and motioned for her to sit down. She did, to his great relief.

"Is Lisa under arrest?"

"Not yet," Jonah said.

But she might be, depending on this conversation. Billy knew the drill. He also knew that the death of a Portland private investigator would require a better criminal lawyer than he was if this dragged on too long.

"Then tell me why she's here."

"Do you know this man?" Fitz asked Lisa.

"Fitz," Billy said. "I believe that was asked and answered at the house. I want to know why she's here."

"Because I—" Lisa started, but Billy held up his hand.

"I asked you not to volunteer anything," Billy said. "I mean it, or you can fight this without counsel. Did they read you your rights?"

"She's not under arrest, Billy," Jonah said.

"Yet," Billy reminded him.

"Ian Kowen was killed at the Churn," Fitz said. "You know the family history at the Churn, don't you, Lisa?"

She glanced at Billy. He shook his head slightly. His hands were under the table, shaking. He wondered if she did know the history at the Churn.

"That's not enough to bring her in," Billy said. "You can't bring anyone in based on fifty years of history."

"Kowen was working for you, wasn't he, Lisa?"

"What makes you think that?" Billy asked.

"This." Fitz slid the manila envelope forward. Billy didn't touch it. The envelope had Lisa's name written on the outside.

"That doesn't prove anything," Billy said.

"There's something marked preliminary report inside. It's addressed to you, Lisa."

She reached for the envelope, but Fitz snatched it back. Billy stood. "That's it," he said. "Either you charge my client, or we're leaving."

"Don't grandstand, Billy," Fitz said.

"I'm not grandstanding, but you're out of line. You're trying to interrogate my client before she has a chance to hear her rights. I won't allow it."

Lisa's hand was sprawled along the tabletop, her fingers wide. She slid it back as if her action had embarrassed her.

Fitz looked at Jonah. Jonah shrugged. Fitz took the toothpick from his mouth.

"Take her home, Billy. But don't let her out of town."

Billy stood. Lisa remained seated, staring longingly at the envelope. "Can I have that?" she asked.

Fitz shook his head. "Evidence," he said.

Billy held out his hand. "Lisa."

She sighed and stood, ignoring his hand. Together they left the briefing room.

Addy sat in her chair, clutching a cup of coffee like a lifeline. Her son was still standing near the coffeemaker, mixing and tasting the light brown liquid in his Styrofoam cup.

"You got her free!" Addy said.

"She was never under arrest." Billy had his hand tucked under Lisa's arm. He wasn't about to let her go in this station. Her behavior was odd, too odd for his tastes. When he got home, he'd make a few calls. His gut told him that Lisa would need a good criminal attorney. It was only a matter of time.

"Thank God," Addy said. "What was it about?"

Lisa's jaw was set. She didn't glance at her mother. "Nothing," Lisa said.

"It seemed like important nothing." Addy's son had joined them. Billy wanted to avoid a conference in the police station. He pushed the doors open and stepped into the hallway.

"Addy," he said. "Lisa is coming to my office for a while. I'll bring her home."

Addy's smile faded. "At least tell me what's going on."

Billy shook his head. He wasn't about to tell anyone anything. Except that criminal attorney. To that attorney he would explain the code Fitz and Jonah had given him. They had protected Lisa. She was a favorite. They had allowed Addy to send for him, and they had warned him that they had enough to begin a case against Lisa. He suspected her behavior in the room hadn't helped.

"Lisa?" Addy said.

"Nothing, Mother," Lisa said again. Billy hoped he wouldn't get the same response. "I'd like to go home, Billy."

He straightened. That tone again. He hated it. "Do you want me to represent you?"

"We're done, aren't we?" Lisa asked. "They let me go."

"They'll be back tomorrow with a homicide team from Portland. This thing is only just beginning."

"You're saying that so that you can get a fee," Addy's son said.

His words echoed in the empty corridor. Finally it was Lisa who shook her head. "No, Marty," she said softly. "Billy doesn't operate that way. He handles a lot of cases in town for nothing. Fees don't matter to him." She bowed her head and rubbed her eyes. He suddenly realized that her posturing hid terror. She was very, very frightened.

Addy realized the same thing. She put an arm around her daughter. "I'll go with you if you want," she said.

Lisa shook her head. "Billy's right. We need to talk alone." She was slumped against him slightly, the rigidity gone from her body. "We'll meet you at home."

Addy let go of Lisa and hesitated for a moment, as if she were waiting for them to change their minds. When they said nothing, she sighed. "All right, then," she said. "At the house."

Such interesting word choices. *Home* for Lisa. *House* for Addy. It described their relationship to Olivia perfectly. Billy said nothing as he watched Addy and her son walk away. He and Lisa turned down a different corridor. He had parked in the back lot.

When they reached his car, Lisa didn't act surprised by its opulence. She slipped in as if she had done so a hundred times. He got in and closed the door.

As he inserted the key in the ignition, she said, "I owe you an apology. I know you were trying to help me back there."

"You didn't make it easy," he said.

"I was stunned."

"Who is Ian Kowen?"

"A private detective I hired last year."

"Why?"

She was facing the windshield. A single yellow fog light illuminated a patch around the back door. Her face was in shadow. In the odd grayish-yellow light, she looked like Addy. He squeezed his hand around the key. The desire to touch her nearly overpowered him.

"I hired him to find out what happened to my grandfather."

Whatever Billy had expected her to say, it wasn't that. He pulled the key away from the ignition and set it on the seat. "Why?"

"I thought it would ease Grammy's mind if she knew."

"She did know. He was lost at sea."

Lisa shook her head. "They found his boat but not his body. And she kept trying to bring him back. He never came."

"People don't come back from the dead, Lisa," Billy said. Spence's face rose in his mind, curl plastered against his forehead, features battered by the rocks.

"Here they do," she said.

Her calmness sent a shiver through him. Now she sounded like Olivia. But Olivia had never faced police who hinted that they might charge her with murder.

"What's in the report?"

Lisa shook her head. "He called me two weeks ago and said he'd found something. I asked him to meet me at Mo's, but he never showed up. I thought maybe I missed him. Then I came home, and Grammy was missing. They found her on the trail, and we took her to the hospital." Extenuating circumstances. But not enough. Yet. "Did you call him?"

"No," she said.

"Why not?"

"I forgot about it. Gram was dying. It didn't seem important any more."

The words were clear, the sentiment made sense, but a prickly feeling along the back of his neck told him she was lying. "They're going to charge you with murder, Lisa."

"They let me go," she said.

"They're small-town cops. They know enough to know that they could mess this up if they act incorrectly. Just allowing you to bring me in might get them in trouble."

"So why did they let you in?" Her voice was soft, curious, no rancor in it. This was the Lisa he knew, not the shrill, condescending woman from the briefing room.

He didn't know how to explain his relationship with Jonah. In some ways Billy was Jonah's mentor. In others Billy envied Jonah his lifelong opportunities. The relationship was balanced. Jonah knew Billy would never forgive him if a Hawthorne got in trouble and he hadn't had a chance to help.

"Because of Olivia," Billy said. "Because they know and like you."

"That's all?" she asked.

"No," he said. "This little interaction was a signal to me. You'll need a high-powered attorney, Lisa. They have enough evidence on you already to make you a prime suspect."

"Then why didn't they arrest me?"

He had already answered that question. He wasn't going to explain this over and over again. That wasn't why he wanted to see her. He needed honesty from her, as much as he could get.

"What's in that report, Lisa?"

"I told you," she said. "I don't know. That's why I grabbed for it."

"He had to have told you something when he called to arrange the meeting. What was it, Lisa?"

She licked her lips. The movement was nervous, not seductive. Even though his eyes were getting used to the odd light, she still appeared to be in shadow.

"He said the report would surprise me," she said.

Surprise her. That curious light feeling that he had had for the last few days rose again. He swallowed. "What do you think he meant?"

"I don't know," she said.

"You don't know, or don't want to say?"

"I don't know."

Billy picked up his keys. He was about to start the car when he paused. The keys swung back and forth, jingling in the silence. "What were you expecting him to find?"

"Something overlooked," she said. "Something that would point toward my grandfather's body. Something that would give Grammy peace."

"Now? Olivia's health had been fading for the past two years. Why now?"

Lisa sighed. "Because she was talking about dying. About joining him. And how could she join him if he wasn't where she thought he was? I thought maybe I could help. I thought maybe I could get him to join her. If he was going to come for her, he had to do it soon."

"Come for her?" Billy had never realized that Lisa shared Olivia's beliefs. It made him nervous. Lisa was too young, too vibrant to obsess the way Olivia had. He wondered if Addy knew, then hoped she didn't.

She had been afraid of becoming like Olivia herself. She had said so the night Spence died. "You actually believed your grandfather was going to walk out of the sea one day?"

"I've seen stranger things," Lisa said.

Suddenly he wanted this conversation to end. He was her attorney for the night, but by tomorrow she would have a high-priced criminal lawyer out of Portland. He knew several candidates who could work with Lisa. Several who could either hide or use her delusions depending on what she needed.

His gut told him she would need a lot.

His gut told him she had more to do with this death than he wanted to know.

"I promised your mother I would drive you to the house."

"I thought we were going to the office," Lisa said.

He shoved the key into the ignition, hearing the scrape of metal on metal. "We had our conversation here."

He turned the key. The car purred to a start, forgiving him for the force he had used a second earlier. He flicked on the lights, put the car in reverse, and backed up. The parking lot had an odd wet look caused by the yellow light on the blacktop. Then he shifted to first and drove out of the lot, turning down the winding streets until he found 101.

The ocean looked as if it had its own special lighting. The water had a brightness as it pushed against the shore. He always found that odd, that no night was completely black near the ocean.

"You think I'm crazy, don't you?" Lisa asked. "You think Grammy was crazy and you think I'm crazy."

He kept his hands loose on the wheel, his gaze on the road. The highway was empty. It was after ten. "I think you were taking care of your grandmother," he said.

"Perhaps," Lisa said. "But I wasn't humoring her. I knew she was right."

The highway curved sharply left. Two abandoned shops sat on the corner. The stoplight was green. He said nothing. If he said anything at all, he would argue with her.

"Grandfather didn't come back for some other reason, some reason that defied the magic."

Billy turned onto Jetty Drive and followed the road to Olivia's house. It looked lonely, perched at the top of the cliff. Lights blazed.

"You understand, don't you, Billy? She said she talked to you about him."

Billy drove up the slanted driveway, stopping on the incline and pulling on his emergency brake. He let the car idle. "I'll call you in the morning. You call me if the police come back."

She opened the door. "You really think they're going to charge me with that man's murder?"

Until then no one had used the word. He was glad she had said it to him, alone, without the police present. "A lawyer has to plan for all eventualities," he said.

"I wish you could be my lawyer, Billy." Her voice was wistful.

"I can't, Lisa. If they come back for you, you'll need someone better than me." Besides, after this conversation he wouldn't take the case.

Not even if he had the experience.

Especially not then.

16

A MAN could not describe fifty years in the space of a day. Just explaining the changes in kitchen technology took Charlie half the morning. Television took much of the afternoon. It wasn't that Spence didn't understand. He did, often after only a second or two ("television is like visual radio") but he wanted to know how it came about, what its influence was, and how it was used.

He also wanted to know what had happened to Charlie.

Charlie preferred discussing television. That way he didn't have to face the fact that he was now forty-eight years older than the boy who once had a long two-year lead on him. Spence had been his hero—Spence who was now little more than a naive boy, stuck in a situation he did not completely understand.

Charlie, at least, knew that the world owed him no explanations. He had stopped searching for them when he came back from the Pacific. The parades had been nice, the deference to an injured veteran even nicer, but no one wanted to talk about the war. It was over, it was past, the world was great, and America was on top thanks to the boys in uniform. Thank you very much for your service, and please, stop reminding us how we got here.

He couldn't explain that even if he were willing to try.

Spence sat in the middle of the living room floor. He had taken apart Charlie's television remote and was staring at it in bafflement. Charlie understood, although he said nothing. The days when a man could take a machine apart to see how it worked were long gone. A few wires, a battery, and tiny chips shouldn't make anything function. But they did.

Magically.

Like Spence's return.

Charlie sat on the couch. He had napped while Spence played with the television and took the remote apart. His stomach had awakened him. He needed to eat.

But he needed to think even more.

As the day progressed, he had become more and more convinced Spence was with him. The little things convinced him—tiny movements he thought he had forgotten—the crook of Spence's smile, the wink when Spence was kidding, the way he stroked his chin when he was thinking. His beard grew in patches that suggested Indian blood in his background, as did his high, flat cheekbones and dark coloring, a thought Charlie hadn't had since the war. The small hitch at the end of Spence's laugh, the way he focused on a problem, and his studied nonchalance. Charlie, the adult, saw through the nonchalance to the terrors it hid, but Charlie, the boy, never had.

Spence had given him a lot in those days, a way of being, a way of believing.

Charlie now had a chance to give back.

But he didn't know how. Nothing he had ever done, nothing he had ever heard of, prepared him for this moment. Over lunch Spence had mentioned how he had frightened Addy, and casually he had asked after his parents. He excused himself and spent fifteen minutes in the bathroom after he learned of their deaths. When he returned, his eyes were bloodshot, but his coloring was normal, as if nothing had changed.

Everything had changed for him, though. He remembered being in the Churn.

He remembered his struggle to survive, and he remembered losing consciousness under the waves. The next thing he remembered, he said, was pulling himself out of the ocean, walking to the Churn, and collapsing on the lava rock, soaking wet and cold. It wasn't until he reached Addy's by the back path that he realized something was wrong.

Charlie, who had experienced dislocation when he returned from the war, could not imagine what Spence was going through. Rip Van Winkle, waking up years later, saw that the people around him had changed, but not the world. And not so dramatically.

"I don't get this thing," Spence said, tossing a piece of plastic on the lint-covered carpet. "Lasers, computer thingies, wires. It makes no sense."

"It makes no sense to me either," Charlie said, "and I was around as these things developed."

Spence leaned his head back against the couch and closed his eyes. He seemed calm except for his left leg. It jiggled, as if the energy inside him had to come out somewhere.

Charlie sighed. He had known this moment would come. He had hoped to put it off for a while, but he also knew that was unrealistic. Spence needed help dealing with the changes. Charlie would have to do what he could, and then he would need some kind of professional assistance.

Not a shrink, though. A shrink would think Spence was having an elaborate delusion. No. Charlie had to turn to someone he trusted. Someone who would believe both of them. Someone wouldn't assume that Spence was crazy.

Maybe one of the guys who used to work at the Vets' Center in Eugene. A couple continued the Center with private funding after Reagan cut CETA, but most had disappeared into "the real world." He would have to check. He had known a few men with minds open enough to accept Spence. Charlie would try to track them down.

"Spence," he said. "It's nearly time for dinner."

"Yeah." Spence spoke without opening his eyes. "I'm hungry."

He had a teenage boy's appetite, a teenage boy's build, and teenage boy's attitudes. But he had been born in 1919.

"I don't have enough here for a good meal," Charlie said. He took a deep breath. "I was thinking of taking you out."

Spence didn't answer. He kept his eyes closed.

Charlie swallowed. "I can keep you here indefinitely if you want. There's easy access to the beach if you need to get out of the house, and I can have my food delivered if that's what you want. Or I can go out and leave you at times if you want privacy. But you need to decide. You need to figure out if you want to explore this Dory Cove and risk seeing Addy, risk having the changes reinforced. You have to tell me."

Spence brought his head forward. He rubbed his eyes, his shoulders hunched, his back curved. He looked like a little boy expecting to be hit. Charlie reached out. His hand hovered over Spence's back, then pulled away. Not yet. Men of his generation didn't believe in touch, even for comfort. Charlie would startle him at best, terrify him at worst.

"You don't have to decide now," Charlie said.

Spence shook his head. The edges of his black hair brushed his collar. He took a deep, shuddery breath. "The beach is the only thing that hasn't changed," he said. "When no one's on it, it looks the same."

Charlie rested his hand against the couch. The upholstery had thinned. It had probably scratched Spence in his sleep.

"But there's nowhere for me to go." Spence sat up. He picked up the plastic remote frame. "Even in a house, the little things are different. The shape of the toilet handle is different. My family never had a shower bath, and the stove took me half an hour to figure out. Even the air smells different."

Charlie remembered that. Landing in San Francisco after the war. The air smelled of coal, of promise, of progress. It didn't have the thick, humid, languid feel that he had gotten used to. A feeling that he still associated with death.

"So it doesn't matter if I go or if I stay. I still don't fit."

This time Charlie did touch Spence. He put a hand on the boy's shoulder.

Spence was thin. His bones dug into Charlie's palm. "None of us fit, Spence," Charlie said. "It's all pretense."

Spence bolted out of his grasp and walked to the television. He held its corner and still had his back to Charlie. "You don't understand."

"Not completely, you're right. But I probably understand better than most."

Spence turned. He was probably thinking of Charlie's leg, of the way Charlie lived, alone and outside of the community. Charlie was thinking of the war. Not a day went by when he didn't think of the war.

"So what do you think I should do?" Spence asked.

"Take it slow," Charlie said. "The more you expect of yourself, the harder it will be. Take it slow."

Spence nodded. He ran a hand through his hair. The curl fell against his forehead, like it always did. His casual look—the one Charlie had always admired—came from his nervousness.

"I can't stay cooped up here," Spence said. "I never stay in one place this long."

That was true to Charlie's memory. Spence was never still. He was always jiggling a foot or urging his friends to move on from the place they were at.

Charlie had learned the habit, and it had kept him alive.

It had also almost killed him.

"I'll take you to Ruthie's," Charlie said. "She serves diner food. That's a good place to start."

"Will people recognize me?"

"Maybe," Charlie said. "But most folks my age will assume you're somebody's son. Or somebody's grandson. They won't put it all together."

"Will Addy be there?" Spence's voice held pain. The meeting the day before must have shaken him more than he had admitted. In his mind it had only been a week or so before that they were engaged. Now she was an old woman who believed Spence to be dead.

"I've never seen her at Ruthie's," Charlie said. He levered himself off the couch, then grabbed his cane for balance. "Cars are different. Mine is about twenty years old. And no, I don't know how it works. You'll see the Cove too. It's grown. We'll discuss each business when we get the chance."

"You're as tired of explaining as I am of listening," Spence said.

Charlie nodded.

"You know," Spence said, "*Thrilling Wonder Stories* had this story about a guy who could travel to the future. I always thought that would be so swell. But he could get back. I might like this if I knew I could get back."

Charlie's heart ached. In one sense Spence was right. But Charlie had always thought he could go back, that home would be the same when he arrived. But he had come to Dory Cove in '46, his parents dead, the store his, and half his friends gone. He'd missed the bunkers and the black-outs, the fear of Japanese subs along the coast. He also missed the booms and the growth. In the five years he lived outside the state, Oregon had gone from a tiny backwoods place to a state filled with people. Washington was worse, with Boeing and all the munitions plants.

People came here to work, and work they did. But the war marked the end of the frontier for the coast and the beginning of the modern period. An historian had once told him that the Depression had done that. But Charlie had lived through the Depression and the war. The historian was wrong.

Spence was watching his face. "What were you thinking just then?"

Charlie leaned on his cane. His arm ached. "Sometimes I wish I could go back too," he said.

They smiled at each other. For the first time, Charlie felt as if he had reached across the gap of strangeness to Spence himself.

Slowly Spence's smile faded. "Charlie," he said in a small, lost voice. "What am I going to do?"

Charlie put a hand on Spence's back. "Walk forward, kid. It's all we can do."

17

EVELYN PARKED on the road below Olivia's house. She had been driving ever since she left the police station. She had had to describe again and again how she found that man, how she hadn't noticed him when she first arrived at the Churn.

She also had to describe what she was doing there. That had been the hardest of all. She still didn't think Detective Huffman believed her. He didn't understand why an old woman would risk hurting herself for a few moments of peace and quiet beside the Churn. She wasn't certain she understood it either. No one else meditated near the Churn. But she couldn't think of any other explanation. Describing the herbs would have taken too long.

And would have made her seem crazy.

So she had said nothing about that. Nor had she explained how she had gotten so wet except to say that she'd gotten splashed. Everyone had been to the Churn at least once. The officers should have understood the way the water leapt at the unwary, the possessiveness it felt toward everything on its banks.

She didn't explain that either.

The remains of a Big Mac sat on the seat beside her. Despite the ordeal—or maybe because of it—she had been ravenous. The coffee she bought cooled in the cup holder built into the dash. She had thought she wouldn't drink it, needing the sleep tonight, but it tempted her.

She doubted she would sleep until August ended.

Until the Storm had passed them by.

Lights still blazed in Olivia's house. Set against the dark sky, the house looked like part of a painting on a gothic-romance cover. The shadows were brushed, the edges blurred. Only the light, the sea, and the sky were visible. She half expected a woman in a white nightdress to run out of the front door, screaming.

But no one did.

She wished Olivia were still alive. Olivia would tell her what to do.

That left Lisa. Lisa had been the repository for Olivia's knowledge. Maybe Lisa knew something that Evelyn didn't.

The man shouldn't have died. Not that way. The magic had caused a death like that before, when Olivia had tried to bring Spence back. But she had failed, she said, because in reality she was trying to keep Addy in the Cove. If Olivia's motives had been pure, Spence would have come back the day after he drowned.

Spence might be back now.

Evelyn shuddered. Her clothes had dried, but they still stuck to her skin. She would make no assumptions until she spoke to Lisa. Together they would know what to do.

How to talk to her about it in front of Addy was another matter. But Evelyn had been worrying about others all of her life. She couldn't afford to now.

She got out of the car and slammed the door. The thud echoed through the silent neighborhood. The sea smell was strong here, and the roar of the waves against the beach sounded like the warning of a giant cat. Just over the ridge, two miles away, the Churn boomed in the darkness, waiting. Always waiting.

As she walked up to the house, the muscles in her calves pulled. She hadn't had this much exercise in a long time. It had been silly to think she wouldn't sleep. She would pass out from exhaustion if she wasn't careful.

The wind came up as she topped the crest of the walk. It teased her hair and touched her face like a long-lost lover. She shivered. Sometimes she felt the presence of the gods as one god. Its being filled the sea, the beach, and the Churn.

The wind provided its hands, the rain its tears, and the sea its wildness. But like any other god, this one was unfathomable. It always seemed to want something no one could provide.

At the door she paused to catch her breath. Even after all these years the house had the odor of Douglas fir. Zeke had built the house carefully, making certain he only used the trees Olivia had chosen, and she had chosen those from the Churn itself. Then he had laid the boards with the grain always running in the same direction, again to Olivia's order. He had made the furniture the same way.

Sometimes Evelyn felt as if the house could catch the wind and hold it. She felt that way tonight. The wind had died down here, as if it had never been. Only the swaying branches of the trees away from the house convinced her otherwise.

She rang the doorbell, a small, delicate chime, Olivia's concession to the changes of coastal life. Lisa had convinced Olivia to update the kitchen and the bathrooms, but Olivia had supervised those changes just as she had supervised Zeke. Evelyn remembered the contractors griping about the crazy old woman on Jetty Drive who wanted everything perfect, down to the direction of the grain of the wood.

The door swung open slowly. Marty stood in front of her. He hadn't aged well.

He still had a youthful leanness, but he was balding, and his skin was criss-crossed with wrinkles. The look he gave her was at once wary and weary. She half expected him to turn her away.

Instead he moved aside. "Mother's in the kitchen."

A chill ran down Evelyn's back. Addy hated that kitchen. Still, she had to be in it sometimes. Evelyn stepped in, grateful for the warmth. Even though the wind didn't seem to blow near the house, the house's exterior had its own cold, one that seemed to exude from the wood.

Papers were scattered on the dining room table, and someone had left parts of a newspaper all over the living room floor. Olivia would never have stood for such mess. Children's toys littered the hallway leading to the kitchen. Evelyn picked her way around them as she walked.

The house smelled of roast beef, but the smell wasn't fresh. She had missed dinner by a few hours, she would guess, and she was grateful for her Big Mac.

Two exhausted children sat at the table, picking at pieces of cake leftover from the memorial service. Loni wore an apron and leaned against the counter, her arms crossed. Her husband was running water in the sink. Lisa and Addy were eating a dinner of roast beef, mashed potatoes, and brown gravy that had the dried look of something improperly heated in the microwave. Another half-full plate sat in front of the fifth chair.

Through the windows behind Lisa, the sea frothed. The waves rolled in white, reflecting the ambient light in the sky. Evelyn had never been in this room at night. The windows created an optical illusion, as if the kitchen were part of the outdoors.

Addy set her fork down. "Evelyn," she said. "I have no emotions left tonight."

"I actually came to see Lisa," Evelyn said.

Lisa flushed. Addy looked at her daughter as if she had never seen her before.

"I never realized you were such a part of this town, Lisa," Addy said.

Evelyn wanted to say that she had known Lisa a long time. Everyone did. Lisa had been there for Olivia. But something held the comments back. Addy had a vulnerability that Evelyn both disliked and wanted to protect. Besides, Lisa could take care of herself.

"It's been a long day for me, too, Mom," Lisa said.

"It'll only take a minute," Evelyn said.

Marty walked around her and grabbed his plate. "It's almost time for the news anyway," he said. "Think we can get a good picture with this wind?"

Addy shuddered. She pushed her plate away, then crouched beside her grandchildren. "You guys want to hear a story?"

They nodded. The boy put his finger in his mouth. He probably wouldn't last through the first page.

"Thanks, Mom," Loni said.

"I'll help with dishes later," Marty said to his sister and her husband. "Come watch the news with me."

Loni shot a glance at Lisa, who was pushing the potatoes around on her plate.

When she didn't respond, Loni took off her apron. "Why not? Better to do the dishes all at once."

Her husband shut off the water and dried his hands. Addy led the children to the door that blocked off the second-story stairs. Marty took a napkin and, balancing his plate on his right hand, walked out of the kitchen. Loni and her husband followed. The door closed behind Addy.

Evelyn was alone with Lisa.

"I suppose you can sit," Lisa said.

She looked miserable, her hair dull and lifeless, her eyes red-rimmed. She had rearranged the food on her plate, but had obviously eaten little of it. A half-full bottle of Alaskan pale ale rested near her right hand.

Evelyn was already regretting her decision to come. Olivia had always made her feel welcome, even when she wasn't. Lisa, while known for her kindness, obviously didn't know how to be gracious.

"I was at the Churn today—" Evelyn started.

"Well, I wasn't," Lisa snapped. "I haven't been to the Churn since Grammy died. I told the police that. If they want more information, they'll have to ask themselves."

Evelyn sat because if she didn't, her legs would give out. She leaned her bare arms on the plastic tablecloth. Something sticky pulled at the fine hairs on her skin. "You know," she said.

"Know?" Lisa shoved her plate away. "Billy thinks they'll charge me with murder."

"Billy?" Everything was moving too fast for Evelyn. "How did Billy get involved with this?"

"I called him," Lisa said. "Or rather, Mother had Loni call. Billy says it's good that we did. He's going to get me some fancy criminal lawyer from Portland."

"You knew that man?"

"He's a detective," Lisa said. She took the ale by the neck and cradled it against her chest. "I hired him."

"Why?" Evelyn asked.

"To find out what happened to my grandfather."

The waves had grown. That meant the wind was up. Evelyn couldn't remember the sunset. For the first time in fifty years she had forgotten to look for the green glow.

"What good would that have done?" she asked softly.

Lisa took a swig like a practiced pro. Evelyn had never seen this side of Lisa.

She wondered if Olivia had. "It would have answered some questions. It would have given Grammy peace."

Evelyn shook her head. The ache in her legs had risen to her lower back. She had strained herself today.

"It was too late to give Olivia peace. She had finally come to terms with it. In the last few years, she talked about Zeke. She said she knew he would never return."

Lisa set the beer down. She tilted her chair back and rested her head against the window glass. The ocean looked as if it were painted behind her. "Are you saying he didn't want to come back?"

"Or maybe the sea didn't kill him. The gods can't resurrect what they don't kill themselves."

A half smile crossed Lisa's face. "Did Grammy tell you that? Or did you learn it on your own?"

Her voice had an edge of bitterness to it. "What happened to you tonight?" Evelyn asked.

Lisa set her chair down, slid it back, and walked to the door. The windowpanes shivered in the wind. The light on the ocean seemed dimmer. "I'm scared, Evelyn," Lisa said. "Everything made sense when Grammy was alive. None of it makes sense now."

Evelyn understood that. She had been thinking the same thing all day. How much of her life had she spent living the way Olivia had wanted her to live? How much of her life had really been her own?

"What doesn't make sense?" Evelyn asked, hoping Lisa would talk about keeping the house, hoping that she would ask for advice.

"That man," Lisa said. "He died at the Churn, but what was he doing there? He was supposed to meet me at Mo's."

"It's a scenic site. People stop."

"But how many die there and don't fall into the Churn?"

"Only two that I know of," Evelyn said.

Lisa turned. "Mom's first boyfriend? Spence?"

Evelyn shook her head. "A hobo died the day after Spence. I found him too."

Lisa inhaled sharply. "And the Storm is coming. Oh, God, Evelyn, do you think I killed that man?"

The kitchen no longer seemed warm. The homey scents had fled like Lisa's family. "What did you do, Lisa?"

Lisa's eyes were wide, her face as pale as the froth on the ocean. "I did the spell," she said. "I found Gram's notes and I did the spell."

"But the spell calls for the beloved to perform it." Evelyn didn't want to hear this. She didn't want to think about it. Olivia had performed the spell after Spence died, and had failed. Addy had left, and Olivia never performed the spell again, although she continued to watch the sunset.

Olivia had believed the spell dangerous. It took a life even when it failed.

"The spell calls for the beloved or the beloved's family to perform it. I qualify."

And Lisa, unlike Olivia, had the right motivations. No secret agenda, only a very real desire to bring the dead up from a watery grave.

"Oh, God," Evelyn said. She got up. The soft skin under her forearms was sticky. She went to the sink, grabbed a rag, dipped it in the soapy water, and washed. Her hands were shaking. "I thought Olivia wouldn't let anyone touch that Book."

"She put it in the basement, in a box. I found it one afternoon."

Evelyn took the towel off the rack and dried her arms. They felt no better. It was almost as if she had gotten into some pitch. Turpentine would take it off, but she didn't want to ask for any. Not in this house. Take no hospitality in a cursed place. Olivia had drummed that into her as well.

"Did you ask her about it?" Evelyn said.

"She said she was afraid to burn it, afraid of what it would release. She couldn't bury it because she was afraid someone would find it. She asked me to find a good combination lock, put the notes back in the box, afix the lock to the handle, and lose the combination."

"Why didn't you?"

Lisa's brow furrowed. Evelyn realized the girl was holding back tears. "Because she deserved one more chance to see him. I couldn't imagine living my whole life waiting for the only person I loved to come back to me."

A gift, then. She had meant it as a gift. The gods always liked that sort of thing.

"Then why the detective?" Evelyn asked, half afraid of the answer. She hadn't liked what she had heard so far.

Lisa ran the back of her hand over her nose. All the bluster and rudeness was gone now. In its place was a young, frightened woman. "Because," she said, "I thought if he could find evidence that someone had shot my grandfather or killed him before he fell into the sea, then I would know why Grammy had failed. She had strong powers, Evelyn. She should have been able to bring him back."

"Maybe he didn't want to come back," Evelyn said. "Have you ever thought of that?"

"The spell says the dead has no choice. The spell says that the dead must come back if called and resolve all that was left unfinished."

"And what if nothing was left unfinished?"

"Grammy said they never got a chance to say good-bye to each other. Grammy said that they had always promised to do that."

Evelyn leaned against the sink. The cold porcelain lip felt good against her aching back. She braced her hands against the cabinets below so that Lisa couldn't see her trembling. "Olivia had strong powers, Lisa, and that Book terrified her. Its spells had mislead her more than once. What made you think you could control it?"

A single tear rested on the lower lashes of Lisa's right eye. The tear was as shiny as the sea. Then she blinked and the tear fell, catching on the lower part of her cheek, the trail glinting in the kitchen light. "I thought maybe she was too involved. I thought maybe she didn't have the powers then that I do now. I thought—oh, God, Evelyn." Lisa's voice broke. "Did I kill that man?"

Evelyn's heart raced. She flattened her hands against the wood cabinets, relishing the pain in her arthritic knuckles. "I don't know," she said.

"I keep thinking that I must have. He was at the Churn and I did the spell and something got him, right?"

"I don't know," Evelyn said again. "I wish we could ask Olivia."

"But we can't. She died in the hospital, away from the sea."

Evelyn crossed her arms in front of her chest. The chill in the air had grown.

Outside, she heard a faint whistle, and knew it to be the wind. "Even if she had died in the sea, Lisa, we wouldn't have tried. We have to get rid of the Book."

"How?" Lisa asked.

"Olivia wanted it locked away. We'll do that, at least."

"And throw it in the sea."

Both women turned at the new voice. Addy stood behind them, looking like an avenging angel. Evelyn had never seen such a frown on Addy's face.

"You didn't think I knew, did you?" Addy asked. She pushed the upstairs door closed. "You thought I never knew about Mother's magics and tricks. She raised me in her religion. I used to reach into the Churn for her when I was little more than a baby. The water would calm for me. Remember that, Ev? And when she was trying to get me to come back, she said she had given all that up. Stupid me, I believed her until tonight."

"Tonight?" Lisa asked, her voice trembling.

"When I was going over the books. The math doesn't work, Lisa. Your grandmother would have had to have been a financial wizard to make the sale of Father's business into a one-point-four-million-dollar estate."

"It happens," Evelyn said.

"Not to a woman with a second-grade education, it doesn't," Addy said.

"Maybe she had some good advice," Lisa said.

"Or maybe she cast sea sand each time she filled out a form," Addy said. "See? I remember. Sea sand for money, desert sand for numbers. Shells to cut and wood to bind. I remember it all. And I walked away from it. Why didn't you?"

"I didn't know you'd left it behind," Lisa said.

"For God's sake," Addy said. "I raised you in the church. Didn't you listen to all that talk of demons and false gods? Didn't you listen?"

"It didn't mean much to me, Mother," Lisa said. "I didn't know those texts were written about Grammy."

"I don't need the sarcasm," Addy said.

"Maybe if you had wanted me to stay away, you should have told me why."

"I did," Addy said. "I told you that your grandmother was a dangerous woman who would fill your head with dangerous things. I told you not to listen to her. I told you to take everything she said with a grain of salt."

"I loved her, Mother, and she loved me back. Was there any harm in that?"

"I don't know," Addy said. "Maybe you should ask the dead man at the Devil's Churn."

Evelyn's arms wrapped more tightly around herself. She had been wrong to come here, wrong to start this discussion. Through the window, she could see the shrubs in the back garden dancing in the wind.

"That's not fair, Mother," Lisa said.

"Isn't it?" Addy asked. "Mother cast the same spell you did, and a man died at the Churn."

"Two men," Evelyn whispered.

Addy turned her gaze to Evelyn. "Because she failed. Because she never had control of the magic, although she thought she did. You knew that and you still did as my mother bid. Didn't Spence's failure to return convince you that Mother was wrong?"

"She said she miscast the spell. She said she wasn't using it to bring Spence back, but to find a way to keep you from leaving the Cove."

"You know what she said to me that night?" Addy asked. "Do you?"

Evelyn shook her head once, a small, involuntary movement. She felt like a mouse cornered by the biggest cat she had ever seen.

"She said that you should have been the one who died. You were the one marked. You should have died, not Spence. And then she took out the book, showed me the notes, and asked me to help her bring him back. 'If we do it quickly, Addy,' she said, 'we can get him. I know we can.'"

"And you ran."

"I ran. Enough people had died, Evelyn."

"It was a storm," Evelyn said.

"It was my mother." Addy's voice rose above the wail of the wind. "And you both know it."

"Gram never harmed anyone," Lisa said.

"That's not what Evelyn just said." Addy stepped deeper into the kitchen. "She said Mother killed a hobo trying to bring Spence back. You know the rules, Lisa. You have to. They're in the Book. A life for a life. The gods don't create the life force. They just move it from being to being. Or keep it for themselves. They kept that hobo's life. Spence didn't come back. Not then anyway."

Outside, the darkness had grown. The crest of the waves were the only visible parts of the ocean. A storm was blowing in. Evelyn inched to the edge of the counter. She didn't want to be in this house during a storm.

"If you really believed that your grandmother never harmed anyone," Addy said, "then why did you grab for that report at the police station tonight? Didn't you ever wonder what Mother and Father's unfinished business was? Or why Mother gave up the dark powers? Did you ever think that maybe Father's death wasn't an accident? He fought with Mother that morning. I heard them. Their voices carried upstairs from this very kitchen. And then he slammed the door and he never came back."

"That doesn't mean she killed him," Lisa said.

"No, it doesn't. But when I came downstairs, she was gone too. She came back drenched, sand-covered, and she threw her dress away. Clothing was precious in those days, Lisa. Women didn't throw garments away. They took stains out.

Unless the garment was ruined. She went to the Churn that day. And he never came back."

A tree limb tapped against the window. The house no longer protected them from the storm. Evelyn squinted. The clouds were low, thick, and heavy. Far out to sea, a silver swirl was all she could see of a sea squall.

"If Olivia had killed Zeke," Evelyn said slowly, wanting to be calm, wanting to be rational, so that his conversation could end and she could be on her way, "then she wouldn't have tried so hard to bring him back."

"Did she try?" Addy asked. "I never saw her try. And if she used that spell, the one she tried for Spence, more people would have been found dead near the Churn. We only have her word for what she did. There are a lot of spells in that Book. What if she watched the sea out of fear, fear that he would return? What if she did a binding spell, tying him forever to the bottom of the sea?"

"Then I would have reversed it," Lisa said, "when I did my spell. He should have come here by now."

Evelyn shuddered. A long-dead vengeful ghost, seeking the wife who had murdered him in cold blood. That would have been what Lisa called up in the name of love. But why would such a man kill a private detective and then disappear?

"There's no timetable on that spell," Addy said. "The magic happens when it happens. You know that."

"I don't know any of this," Lisa said. "You have spent your whole life trying to prove everything Gram did was wrong. You could be making all of this up."

Addy shook her head. "I can't believe you still defend her. She caused one death that we know of, and you defend her."

"We don't know anything," Evelyn said. "We only have our suspicions."

"And you're more suspicious than most, Mother," Lisa said.

"I grew up with her. I know what she could do."

"And you doubt that a woman could learn in her lifetime, that she could understand stocks and the market and parlay a small amount of money into a large one." Evelyn walked over to Addy. "I only have a high school education, Adelaide. I tripled the money my husband left me in less than a year. You base your suspicions on nothing."

"You were my mother's acolyte. You learned from her."

"I learned from the *Wall Street Journal*." Evelyn hoped her fear showed as disgust. She had to get out of the house. "Now, if you'll excuse me, I'm going to leave before it starts to rain."

Addy grabbed her arm. Addy's grip was tight, her lips thin. "Why did you come here, Evelyn? To upset my daughter?"

Evelyn shook her head. "It doesn't matter now."

"It does to me," Addy said.

Evelyn glanced at Lisa. "I came for advice."

"Advice, from a girl half your age?"

"Advice from the only other person Olivia confided in."

The remark stung as she hoped it would. Addy let go of her arm.

"What kind of advice?" Lisa asked.

Evelyn closed her eyes. She didn't turn around. She had to get out. Couldn't they see that? "It doesn't matter anymore," she said.

"Yes, it does," Lisa said. "It always matters if it's about Grammy."

"Your grandmother is dead," Evelyn said. "I think that's what I learned tonight. Olivia is dead, and no matter how much we talk about her, no matter how much we need her, we'll never have her again. Nothing in that Book, nothing we know will bring her back. I thought maybe she confided in you, but I can tell now that she didn't. No more than she confided in me."

"She told me everything," Lisa said.

Addy snorted, but said nothing.

"If she had told you everything," Evelyn said, "you would never have used her Book." She waited, half out of politeness, half out of fear, to see if Lisa would respond. But Lisa said nothing. Addy watched Evelyn, her look challenging.

Evelyn wasn't up to meeting the challenge. Olivia would have comforted her, given her advice that she could have used.

But Olivia was dead. Lisa was not her grandmother, and Addy—Addy hated all that they stood for.

"I'm sorry to have taken your time tonight," Evelyn said. "I can let myself out."

She had to force herself to walk to the door. Outside, the wind whipped. If she wanted to arrive home before the storm, she would have to hurry. Without Olivia, the house provided a haven for no one. The sooner Olivia's family discovered that, the better.

18

ADDY HADN'T MOVED from the doorway. Evelyn was gone—the front door had closed quietly behind her—and Addy and Lisa were alone in the kitchen.

Addy was shaking. She hadn't realized that Olivia's influence on Lisa had gone so deep. Addy's mind couldn't quite wrap around what she had learned: that Lisa had used Olivia's Book to bring back Addy's father. And a man had died.

"What did your grandmother teach you?" Addy asked.

"She taught me how to live a real life," Lisa said.

"Like hers? Trapped in this house? Waiting for my father to return?"

"She loved it here. She loved the sea and the land around it. She even loved the Churn. She didn't do anything she was forced to do. She did everything because she enjoyed it."

"Really?" Addy said. Addy couldn't control her voice. Her fear had crept into it. She had failed with Lisa. She had failed completely. "You know that for certain."

"I watched her. I spent time with her, unlike you."

"You spent time with an old woman. I knew her when she was young," Addy said. "You wouldn't have liked her then."

"You don't know what I like and dislike," Lisa said. "You haven't been around enough."

Tree branches tapped on the house in the growing wind. Below, the ocean crashed and boomed. Addy had hoped she would be gone before a storm hit this house. She hated the coast in storms.

"I was around every day of your life," Addy said.

"You were never there when I needed you."

Addy sighed and closed her eyes. Lisa would never forgive her for failing to be an ideal mother. But Addy had had no choice. Donald Rustin had been a handsome man with a good job when Addy met him. But he had been embezzling from the company, and he got fired. He also borrowed money from everyone he knew. He had a silver tongue and got car loans he couldn't afford, consolidation loans in the days before banks routinely gave them, and credit at every store he ever frequented. Addy never had that kind of charm. When he died without savings, without life insurance, without assets, the companies wouldn't work with Addy. All they wanted was their money. All they wanted was to prove they hadn't been screwed.

Try as she might, Addy wouldn't be able to explain those days to Lisa. Not the gut-wrenching fear that she carried from moment to moment, the nights with no sleep as she juggled one bill to pay the other. Marty, bless him, had finally gotten a paper route, and some weeks his tiny salary had paid for their food.

"Sometimes," Addy said, "being there for a child means providing for that child. Sometimes a person can do no more than that."

"Then thank your Christian God for Gram," Lisa said. "At least she taught me what love meant."

Addy shook her head. She opened her eyes. "My mother taught you how to hate people. She started by training you to hate me."

"She taught me how to coexist with the natural order. She taught—"

"If she had taught you that, then you would learn to accept death. It is the natural way." Addy clenched her fists. She didn't know how to stop this argument. It was as if she and Lisa could only talk about this, not anything else.

And they needed to, especially if the police really thought that she killed that man.

Especially if Lisa thought she had.

The wind howled. Raindrops splattered the window with the ferocity of gunfire. Marty had come into the kitchen. He was carrying his plate. He put his arm around Addy and pulled her close. He knew her terror of storms. He had spent many a night with her in the living room of their tiny apartment, watching old movies on the tiny black and white television they hadn't been able to afford, but which Addy had refused to give up.

"You all right?" he asked.

"Let her alone. She's old enough to live with storms," Lisa said.

His grip on Addy tightened. She felt like burying her face in his shoulder. "You need to learn compassion, Lisa," he said. "Mom survived one of the worst storms on record in this town. Her boyfriend died."

"He wouldn't have had to if Mom had listened to Grammy," Lisa said.

Addy straightened. She patted Marty's hand as she moved out of his embrace.

She approached her youngest daughter, the only child she had never completely understood, and stopped a few inches away from her face.

"Your grandmother's art was the art of selfishness," Addy said. "She wanted people to cater to her. She didn't care that my father had left, at least not for me, but she cared about her pride. He had left her, and she was going to do everything she could to bring him back, even cheat death. Well, it failed, Lisa. Everything my mother did failed. Even raising me."

"Mom." Marty's tone was chiding. Addy recognized it. It was his I-don't-want-to-hear-this, let's-humor-Mother-and-make-her-stop voice.

Addy would have none of it. Her children would at least hear her side, even if they didn't want to accept it. "Think about it, Marty. I didn't stay here. I didn't try to become the Good Witch of the North. I didn't try to raise Spence from the dead. Instead I went inland, away from Mother's precious sea. I married two losers, and I never built a proper home. I even became a Christian."

"And you raised three children—" Marty said

"One of whom hates me."

"—and pulled yourself out of horrible debt in an era when a woman shouldn't have been able to survive on her own, and you became your own person. Those are things to be proud of, Mom."

"You always defend her, don't you?" Lisa asked. The rain was running down the windows behind her. The kitchen was dark. The electric lights couldn't cut through the gloom. "She stole your childhood, too, and you still defend her."

"You had a childhood," he said. "Loni and I made sure of that. You had the toys you wanted, and the time you needed, and you didn't have to work until you were sixteen years old. Mom even wanted to spare you that, but Loni thought you needed to learn fiscal responsibility like the two of us did."

"So why do you defend Mom? You had no childhood."

"I'm at least adult enough to look at Mom's life. She did the best with what she was given."

His words made tears rise in Addy's eyes. She turned away from Lisa so that Lisa couldn't see. No one had noticed before. No one had said anything about all of those years except to criticize her and accuse her of abandoning her family, from her children to her ever-precious mother.

"Have you ever thought," Marty said, lowering his voice, "that your embrace of Gram's lifestyle is a betrayal to Mom?"

Addy shook her head. "Don't, Marty. Lisa's grown too. She makes her own choices." Addy walked to the sink, took a paper towel off the roll, and wiped her face.

"Did I hurt you, Mom?" Lisa asked, voice small.

"It seems more like you hurt yourself," Addy said. She tried to sound calm, but she was terrified. If Lisa had done as she claimed, then she might have had something to do with that man's death. She might have had her hands in too many different things. Things she didn't understand.

"Did you want to hurt her?" Marty asked.

Lisa didn't answer. Addy threw the paper towel in the garbage under the sink.

The rain kept thudding against the window, the wind howling around them.

"Did you?"

"Let her alone," Addy said. "She loved her grandmother. That's enough reason for what she did."

"You make it sound like I did something wrong," Lisa said.

"Mother was afraid of that Book," Addy said. "And Mother wasn't afraid of much. Going against her wishes, even with her best interest at heart, was probably wrong, Lisa."

Lisa shook her head. "I only have your word that Grammy didn't like that Book."

"My word and the fact that she kept it locked away," Addy said.

"She probably didn't want people who lacked experience to use it."

People like you. Addy heard the context. She wasn't sure if she liked it. "Did you tell your grandmother that you had done this?"

"No," Lisa said.

"Why not?"

"Because I wanted to surprise her."

"Or you wanted Father to surprise her," Addy said. "Did you ever think what seeing him might do to her? It might have killed her quickly."

"It's what she always wanted," Lisa said.

"That doesn't mean she would have liked getting it. Sometimes the quest is more important," Addy said.

"You know where Grandfather is?" Marty asked.

Lisa shook her head. "Apparently I don't know anything," she said, and ran from the room.

Marty sighed. He put his plate beside the full sink, then bowed his head and rubbed his eyes. His hair was thinning in the back, and he had frown lines around his mouth. Even her children were getting old. "She had it the best of all of us," he said.

"No." Addy was still standing by the counter. In the rain-covered windows, she could see herself and her son. They looked like ghosts in her mother's kitchen. "She didn't. You had me at home for part of your childhood, and you had Donald in the good days. She only had me. And I was gone. She was so young when he died."

"She had us too. She just made this up about needing love."

Addy shook her head. "We don't know. We really don't know how she felt. We can't belittle it, Marty. Maybe I didn't treat her right. Maybe I sent her here."

"The police think she killed that man."

"I know."

"Do you?"

Addy didn't want to answer that question. But she knew it would come up over and over again. "I don't think she bashed him on the head like they said."

"They have to have a pretty solid case against her."

"She hasn't been arrested yet," Addy said.

"But Billy thinks she will be."

"Billy can be wrong." Addy glanced at the window. The darkness wasn't so absolute. The wind had died down, and the raindrops had beaded on the window. "The storm's passing."

"Thank God," Marty said. "This house is too close to the sea for my taste."

"Mother always said it provided excitement."

"I don't need that kind of excitement." He went over to the door. "Clear sky over the ocean."

"When I was a little girl," Addy said, "I used to love the way the storms blew over. For the first year after I moved to Chicago, I used to think that rain would stop after a half hour or so. It took me two summers to realize that gray and drizzle could last for days."

"That wind was really gusting," Marty said. He flicked on the outdoor light.

Instantly the view of the ocean was gone, replaced by a spotlit view of the remains of the garden.

"Mother," he said in a strangled voice. "I think you should come over here."

"I don't want to go out now," Addy said. "Even though the rain has stopped." She hated the smell of sea salt and fresh rain. It haunted her for years. Once, on a business trip to Boston, the smell had wafted over her, and she disappeared from the meeting she was supposed to attend. She had reached the harbor before she realized what she was doing and stopped herself.

Marty pulled the door open. The smell filtered in, turning Addy's stomach. She put a hand to her mouth.

The air was cold and damp, but the wind had gone. Marty walked out to the stoop. "Mother, can you get me a flashlight?"

She opened the drawer beside her, the drawer in which her mother used to keep candles. Boxes of white votive candles lay inside, and two flashlights, just as Addy had expected. Only one worked. She handed it to Marty.

He walked off the stoop and tapped the ground with the toe of his shoe like a blind man. He did the same with the next step, and the next until she realized what he was doing.

"Stop!" she screamed.

She ran to the door, finally seeing what had shocked him.

The shrubs were gone. The back yard, from the tiny trees to the shrub barrier had fallen away. It hadn't looked as if the waves had been that high from inside the house, but maybe they had, or maybe they had eaten away the sand at the bottom.

"Come back in!" she cried.

"I want to see how far it goes," he said.

"No!"

"Mom—"

"No!" She screamed so loud her throat was raw. "It eroded from underneath. Your weight could make it all fall."

He clearly hadn't thought of that. He glanced behind him, at the path he had walked, then ran to the door. He put his hand on the doorframe and leaned his forehead against his knuckles, breathing hard. Below, the sea whispered as if nothing had happened.

"My God, Mother," he said. "Twenty feet of property is gone."

She nodded. "See why I want to sell it?"

"That wasn't a very big storm. It's amazing that this didn't happen more often."

"The bottom of the cliff face gets worn away. Then it topples. It doesn't take much after years of erosion, Marty." Addy put her arm around her son, and pulled him inside. For the first time in Addy's memory, her mother's kitchen seemed welcoming. "When I was a little girl, there was an entire town between Lincoln City and Tillamook that got washed away. They built it on a sandbar, and the town lasted for thirty years. Then one stormy night half the buildings washed away."

"My God," Marty said. "Why do people live here?"

"You're asking me?" Addy said. "I belong in Chicago." She would rather face the crime, violence, pollution, and poverty than this coastline. She could at least understand the human monsters. The sea had a life of its own.

"You don't think we'll get another storm tonight, do you?" Marty asked.

"No," Addy said. "But we'll get one soon." She hoped it wouldn't be too soon.

She wanted to be back in prairie country when the storm hit, as far away from the sea—and the Churn—as she could get.

19

THE WIND howled outside Billy's office. Twice today the storms had come up, and twice he found himself hunching against the weather, struggling to keep his mind—and his memory—away from the Churn. Billy's office had been built in the 1950s. He had bought it for a song during the late sixties and had fixed it up as best he could. He still meant to replace the electric heat that blasted through a square wall blower, but hadn't gotten around to it. The office was hot near the heater, and frigid everywhere else.

He clutched a cup of coffee in his aching fingers. His arthritis had flared up again, probably brought on by the weather. He stood next to his boxy fax machine, watching the paper curl as it rolled out. The machine growled as it reproduced the tiny type, and he saw names he recognized scattered throughout.

He set the coffee cup down and ripped the sheet between two pages, wishing that he had bought the machine one grade up, the one with the automatic paper cutter.

He had never thought he would rely on a fax so much. Technology he didn't even know existed a year ago had become a lifeline in his business.

When he had dropped Lisa off, he returned to the office and called Jason DeFreeze, one of the partners in DeFreeze and Garity, the private detective firm Lisa had hired. DeFreeze and Garity were the largest PI firm in the state, handling everything from the seedy divorce case to murder investigations to gathering information on U.S. Senators. Billy had worked with them on a case several years back involving a five-star resort and a world-famous golfer, and somehow he and DeFreeze had hit it off.

The two men couldn't have been more different. DeFreeze had been born into privilege. He was from one of Portland's oldest families, and his skin was the pure translucent white that came from Nordic blood. His dark hair was going silver, giving him a patrician look, and he had power that Billy could never achieve. But DeFreeze believed in men like Billy and had helped more than his share. His contribution had been the bulk of the money behind the second-year scholarship Billy had won to law school. DeFreeze never viewed him as a project, always as an equal, and made a point of seeing Billy each time he came to the coast.

Billy, in turn, hired the company whenever he needed an assist in Portland. He had never asked for a favor before. Calling DeFreeze had almost felt like a betrayal, but if asked to choose between his loyalty to DeFreeze and his loyalty to Addy, he chose Addy. He had been keeping her secrets longer.

DeFreeze had left three messages on Billy's machine about Kowen's death. But by the time Billy called, DeFreeze had given up on hearing from him and sent a man blind. Billy promised to help DeFreeze's operative as best he could if only DeFreeze would fax a copy of the report.

DeFreeze had made the perfunctory objections. He had also sent the report.

Billy used the edge of his desk to rip the sheets into the proper size. The report was twenty-five pages long, double-spaced, and printed on a dot-matrix. The fax was difficult to read. Billy grabbed his coffee, sat in the overstuffed chair behind his desk, and took his glasses out of his pocket.

The howling wind disturbed him. He thought about turning on the radio, but knew he needed to concentrate. Wind found its way through the poorly built boards, leaving half of him chilled and the other half too hot. He took off his suit coat, and rolled up his shirtsleeves.

Then he read.

Kowen had been on this case a long time, longer than Lisa had let on. She first contacted him in 1985, shortly after she had moved to Salem. She hadn't had much money, so she asked Kowen to investigate when he had a chance. In the covering letter that Kowen submitted to DeFreeze, he had explained that the wealth of detail in the report came not because he expected a fat commission but because the case intrigued him.

When Lisa contacted Kowen, all she had known about her grandfather was his name, the fact that he had married her grandmother, and that he had built their house in Dory Cove. She wasn't even certain what year he had died, but knew it to be in the early 1930s. She also mentioned that her grandmother had never gotten over the death, and anything Kowen could tell them would be appreciated.

Billy sipped his coffee, marveling at Lisa's understatement. The girl had been digging into this for a reason. He was no longer certain if she had done so, as she claimed, because she wanted to help her grandmother. If that were true, she had no reason to lie, especially to the police. Instead it seemed as if she were trying to resolve her confusion about Zeke, for if she did, then she might be able to resolve her confusion about her mother and her grandmother. Maybe if she found out who her grandfather was, she would learn more about Addy and Olivia.

But Billy had learned long ago he was no psychologist. People often did things he didn't understand for reasons more illogical than Lisa's.

Between cases, Kowen investigated. He discovered Addy's birth certificate, but he couldn't locate Olivia's marriage certificate nor any newspaper accounts of the nuptials. He also couldn't find any death certificate for Zeke Hawthorne. Kowen included a photocopy of Addy's birth certificate. He noted that she had two on file. One done the day of her birth and one recopied the day after. Apparently the one the courthouse always sent out was the second one. The first one had the father's name crossed out.

Billy set the birth certificates aside. He would go to the courthouse the next day and examine the originals himself. Rain tapped against his window, and lights from a passing car illuminated his empty porch. He hated being here alone at night. It made him feel vulnerable.

He got up, closed the blinds, took the remaining paper off the fax machine, and went back to the report.

Olivia's maiden name was not listed. From everything Kowen could find, she had been born in Dory Cove, but again, he found no legal registration of the birth. This he attributed to Olivia's odd religion and the fact that her family had never attended a regular church. He couldn't even cross-check baptismal records, and he had found that both odd and frustrating.

Zeke Hawthorne, on the other hand, had been born in Portland to a logger and his family. Zeke had loved the sea from an early age and, after a family vacation in Astoria, had decided to travel down the coast. On that trip he had met Olivia and decided to remain in Dory Cove.

Much of Zeke's information did have a paper trail. Kowen had found the rental papers for the office that housed Zeke's fishing business. He also found the papers tracing the ownership of the boat Zeke had died in.

Zeke had owned neither. Olivia had lied about that. On the day Zeke disappeared, he had been so deeply in debt, a decade's worth of good fishing wouldn't get him out of it.

Kowen couldn't trace where Olivia had gotten her money. He suspected she always had it, and that she, not Zeke, had been the family's sole support. During the thirties Olivia had no obvious source of funds, but her name started appearing on stock certificates and treasury bills in the forties, when it became safe to invest again. She had quadrupled her income in the space of four years.

Billy's coffee was cold. He took off his glasses, rubbed the bridge of his nose, and stretched. When he had gone back to school, he had learned to read and write with the intent of becoming a judge. Judges, in his estimation, were the wisest men on earth. Judges had opened the doors for people like him. Judges had ordered changes in systems hundreds of years old. They had given him a feeling of real power for the first time in his life.

But to become a judge, one had to be a lawyer. The more he learned about law, the more he loved it. He loved the way it twisted and turned, the way one point rested on another point. The young kids in school with him all complained of the disillusionment, the way that the professors forced them to become cynics, to take the harsh view, the see the seedy side of life. But Billy had always been a cynic, had always taken the harsh view, had lived on the seedy side.

He was prime lawyer material.

Until he had to practice.

Then his disillusionment began. His mistake had been choosing to practice in his hometown, with the people he knew. Dory Cove's only lawyer had died two years before Billy hung out his shingle, and Billy had thought it a natural market.

It was.

But he learned things about his friends, his neighbors, even his enemies that he never wanted to know.

And Olivia, for all her strangeness, had been a friend and a constant in his life for more than fifty years.

Olivia, who had lied about her marriage, her money, and herself all that time.

He should never have answered the phone.

He should have said no when Loni asked him to take this case.

He had said no when he learned how difficult it would be, but by then it was already too late.

Fitz's handling of the report had made him curious. The Portland lawyer wouldn't arrive until tomorrow afternoon, and Billy knew Jason DeFreeze.

Billy had made the wrong choices all along, but his curiosity got the better of him, as it always did.

Always.

He picked up the rest of the fax. He had started. He might as well finish.

Kowen followed the obvious trail. He checked medical records, interviewed people, listened to the stories of Zeke's death. He contacted communities up and down to the coast to see if a body had washed ashore.

He learned the following:

Zeke's office was closed a week before he died. He owed six months back rent.

And, more important, Zeke's boat had not been out the day of Zeke's death.

The owner had repossessed it, citing Zeke's inability to pay as the reason. Kowen had attached that document as well, a hand-written scrap of paper a Portland shipping company kept as a way of covering themselves in case Zeke decided to pursue the matter.

He didn't.

Instead he disappeared.

Kowen had told Lisa of these developments, and she had told him to keep looking. Perhaps, she had said, her grandfather was shipping in someone else's boat. Perhaps someone had killed him and made up this information as cover.

Perhaps bits and pieces of the story she had heard were confused with other bits and pieces in her memory.

He checked.

In his report he covered each of Lisa's concerns. He tracked down the case as she instructed him to do, and it led nowhere.

Then he found a man who claimed to have known Zeke.

In 1952.

Billy stopped reading again. He got up, made more coffee, and sat back down.

He would never be able to sleep, and part of him didn't care. The rain battered the roof. The storm left him as unsettled as this fax had.

A part of him had always wondered if Zeke were alive, and the thought had felt like a betrayal of Olivia. She had said he was dead, the whole town had acted as if he were dead, and her grief was all she held onto.

It was false.

It had always been false.

Billy paged through the fax. He couldn't tell if Lisa had learned of this before Kowen died. The only way he would get answers was to keep reading.

So he did.

Kowen tracked Zeke Hawthorne. It soon became clear why he was fascinated with the case. It presented a challenge to any detective's skills. Zeke was one of an estimated twelve million unemployed men in the 1930s, always on the move, a dusty face hidden by a battered cap, walking with a pack on his back toward a future he didn't completely understand. Kowen found traces of Zeke using false names in San Francisco in 1935, in Seattle in 1937, and in Boise in 1940. In December 1941 Zeke tried to enlist under his own name in Missoula but was turned down because of his health and age.

He didn't resurface again until 1950, when he got a job running a pilot ship on Lake Superior. Gradually his work piloting ships brought him to Lake Michigan, which brought him to Chicago. He retired in 1965—documents made the retirement look forced—and collected excellent benefits and Social Security. He lived in a house not far from Addy's until he died in 1987.

Kowen even had proof that Zeke kept track of his daughter. Two photographs, which faxed as big black sheets, were enclosed: one from Zeke's effects (which Kowen said he got from a friend) of Addy and her children; another of Addy eating alone in a restaurant, reading a newspaper, Zeke watching her wistfully from a table a few feet away.

Billy turned the photos over quickly. He almost shredded them, then realized that if charges were brought against Lisa, Addy would see them anyway. Addy had thought her father dead since she was twelve years old. To learn that he had run out on her and her mother would devastate her. To learn that he knew where she was and never spoke to her would tear her up even more.

Even now, fifty years later, Billy wanted to protect her.

But he couldn't. He had never been able to.

That was his curse.

Billy sighed and read the last few pages of the report. Kowen's conclusions were curious. He wrote that if he had done a cursory investigative job, he would have assumed that Zeke left because of his family's economic circumstances, to find a new job, and to send money home, as so many men did in those days.

But all the evidence indicated that Olivia had money of her own and that the family was doing fine. She clearly didn't share her money with Zeke's business—or else he had never told her of his financial problems—but the family never hurt for food, cash, or shelter. Zeke's disappearance coincided with an argument he had had with his wife, and he worked hard in the first nine years of his flight to make certain his picture was never taken and his true name rarely used. Only after his attempt at enlistment in 1941 did he revert to Zeke Hawthorne, the name he used until the day he died.

He never tried to contact Addy, a fact the friend who had survived him found curious. He seemed, the friend said, both fascinated by her and afraid of her. He watched her from afar, but he never told her who he was. Zeke Hawthorne remained, for his daughter, dead.

Kowen concluded that all the facts pointed to Zeke as a man on the run. He had escaped his family at a time when such escape was easy. Men on the road weren't questioned. Their circumstances were thought to be known. Zeke never returned to Oregon, never made contact with his family, and except for that one friend, never spoke of his past to anyone. Something had happened there, something he didn't want to face, something that had forced him to leave his family behind.

Kowen believed that it had something to do with Olivia, but he didn't know what. At the end of his report he said he would speak to Lisa about continuing.

By now he was perhaps as curious as she was to learn what had happened and why.

Billy turned the page and looked at Kowen's signature. It was a firm, legible signature, slanted slightly forward. It had authority, just like Kowen's writing style.

His interest in a case that should have been perfunctory made Billy admire him.

They would have been friends if Kowen had lived.

But he hadn't.

He had died in Dory Cove, after he had contacted Lisa.

No wonder the police had picked her up.

Billy didn't know the particulars of the rest of the case. He gathered that Kowen had been killed by a blow to the head while he was in his car, the kind of wound anyone could make. Kowen had turned his investigation of Zeke into an investigation of Olivia, and the results made Olivia into a liar or worse. Instead of the great romance that Lisa had hoped for, she discovered that her grandfather had run away from his family and had refused to reestablish contact. All her familial beliefs would have been shattered. Addy's version of reality would have won, and Lisa would have hated that. She would have responded in anger to something Kowen said, struck him, and been startled to find him dead.

That was only one scenario. There were others, equally damning, some more ugly.

Billy turned over the last page and bowed his head. The rain slapping on the building reminded him of the aftermath of the storm, when Addy had come to him, her battered suitcase in one hand. She had only been in his shack once before and never when it rained. The water dripped through the ceiling into rusted pots and old soup cans he had scattered around the room. And it was cold in there, always cold. He could never keep it warm, not in all the years he lived there. It had seemed even colder that day.

She wants me to be just like her, Addy had said. *She's evil, Billy.*

She's your mother, he had said.

I know, Addy had said. *But that doesn't mean I have to be her. I'm nineteen years old. I don't want to spend the rest of my life staring out to sea, waiting for the return of a man I never loved.*

Billy sighed. Time passed too quickly, and a man who understood life was too old to appreciate it, or so the adage went. He was still agile, his mind was quick, and he had made a way for himself. But he didn't understand life. The older he got, the more mysterious it got. Sometimes he longed for his youth because the choices he had then seemed simpler than the choices he had now.

The coffee churned in his stomach. The caffeine, the tension, and the memories would never let him sleep. He glanced at his watch. It was only ten-thirty.

It seemed so much later.

He gathered his papers and put them in the top desk drawer. He had to search for the drawer key, found it, and then locked the drawer.

Even though his part-time secretary wasn't due for three days, he didn't want her to see the report. The fewer in Dory Cove who knew Olivia's real history, the better.

Ruthie kept the diner open until midnight, although she had someone else close up. He would go, eat something full of grease and lard, and see how much he could forget.

Tomorrow would be another hellish day. He needed to be ready for it.

20

AFTER THE DINNER RUSH, the crowd at Ruthie's was small. A few teenagers sat in the booth nearest the door, drinking milkshakes and smoking cigarettes. A girl was perched on the booth seat, her feet tucked beneath her as if she were too restless to put them on the floor. Her stretch pants revealed legs too thin, and she wore white pancake makeup that made her look dead. Charlie had seen the look before. He particularly hated the black lipstick. The girl would look like that soon enough. No sense hurrying the inevitable.

He ushered Spence in. They passed the truck drivers sitting at the counter and sat in a booth near the kitchen door.

Cigarette smoke bumped the ceiling like a thick mist. Ruthie didn't enforce the state's no-smoking regulations, claiming it would drive most of her customers away. Charlie never minded back in the days when he smoked—he always appreciated her no-nonsense policy—but after he quit five years ago, he found the smoke a cloying reminder of all the things he had used to kill himself and failed.

Spence had not said a word on the entire drive over here. His eyes were sunken, lined with dark circles, speaking more eloquently than he could of his exhaustion. Charlie pulled the folded and stained menus from their spot between the large sugar container and the wall. He ordered two well-done cheeseburgers with fries and two Classic Cokes from the pimply-faced boy wrapped in chef's whites. When the boy left, Spence sighed.

"The details are wrong," he said.

Charlie frowned at him, not completely understanding.

"The details. They're wrong," Spence said again. His voice had that agitation Charlie was coming to dread. "The clock in the window has only numbers, no face. The newspaper has funny type. There's pink packets near the sugar container."

He picked up the Sweet 'n Low and scattered it across the table. "Is this going to be my whole life, Charlie? Details I don't get?"

Charlie picked up one pink packet. The fake sugar was packed into one thin paper corner. "On December seventh, 1941," he said, "the Japanese bombed Pearl Harbor, Hawaii, damaging or destroying nineteen U.S. naval vessels and killing three thousand Americans. On December eighth we declared war against Japan, and on December ninth I enlisted, just like I thought you would do."

"Me?" Spence swallowed. "You didn't even know me, Charlie."

Charlie smiled. The smile was small. "I followed you everywhere, Spence. You were everything I wasn't. You were handsome and smart and fearless, and I wanted to be just like you."

"Fearless." Spence made a small snorting sound through his nose. "I was stupid, Charlie. I still am."

Charlie shook his head. "Not to me." He set the sugar packet down. "I held you up like a light through everything. What would Spence have done? Would Spence have been scared here? Would Spence have run away? Sometimes I think I served for both of us."

"Charlie—"

Charlie held up his hand. "Let me finish."

The cook set down the Cokes so hard the liquid sloshed from the glasses, spilling on the fake sugar. Spence grabbed napkins out of the dispenser and mopped up, creating a pile at the edge of the table.

"You got me through, Spence," Charlie said. "The bugs and the heat and the long days of boredom followed by the deepest fear I've ever felt. You got me through. You saved my life."

"I wasn't there," Spence said.

"You were to me." Charlie picked up his straw, peeling the wet paper from it, and stuck it into the Coke. He slurped half. Coke always tasted like his teenage years to him, syrupy, bitter, and sweet at the same time.

"Charlie—"

"I'm not done," Charlie said. He wiped a hand over his face. "This is hard to talk about. I've never talked about it to someone who hasn't done it." He frowned. He wasn't sure how to convey what he wanted to say. "It wasn't the going. The going and the war and the fighting and the horrors, they were awful and they were alien, but they weren't *home*. They happened in places I'd never seen and would never see again. In some weird way it was normal because it was new. But then I came back to the States, first to Hawaii, then to the Cove."

Spence's hands were wrapped around his own Coke. He was leaning forward.

"It was 1946 before they fixed me up good enough to come home. My parents were dead. The store was closed. But that wasn't the worst of it. The town had people I didn't know. No one cared about the war. It had been over for two years. We won. No one needed a guy like me around, missing one leg and barely able to use the one that was left. I was in such pain some days, I couldn't get out of bed. The government sent me money, but folks here, they thought I was some kind of deadbeat."

"But you got hurt in the war, defending the country, right?" Spence asked.

Charlie nodded. "When I enlisted, all people talked about was the Japs this and the Japs that and the Krauts this and the Krauts that and when we get over there, we'll kick their ass or maybe we shouldn't fight, and when I got back, no one talked about it at all. We won. There was money everywhere. Guys had jobs and women—they wanted to keep working like they did in the war. They swore and earned their own money and people were buying homes and going to movies and driving fancy cars and—" his own voice broke. It could barely take the strain of the memories—"and the details were wrong. It was like I came home to a different country, one that didn't want me."

"It isn't the same," Spence said.

"It's just the same," Charlie said. "You and me, we're reminders of things people don't like to think about."

"No one but you even knows I'm here."

"Addy does," Charlie said. "And she chased you away."

"You gotta admit, me coming back is hard to believe," Spence said.

Charlie nodded. "But I made the leap."

"You made the leap," Spence said slowly, "because you been there?"

"In a way," Charlie said. "I can help you, Spence, if you let me. It'll take time, but I can."

"Why would you want to?" Spence asked.

The boy set two steaming burgers down. The soft buns were separated, lettuce, tomato, and onion on the top, the cheeseburger on the bottom. Some of the cheese had melted onto the fries. The smell of the grilled meat made Charlie's mouth water.

Charlie put his burger together, unsure how to answer Spence's question. There were so many reasons, but explaining them was another matter.

"I was over fifty years old when I realized other guys had the same experiences I did," Charlie said. "Almost thirty years since I'd come home and one war later. Thirty years feeling like you do now."

"You're helping me because you think you been here?"

"In a small way," Charlie said. "But I'm helping you for a bunch of reasons. Mostly because you helped me."

"Me?" Spence started, nearly spilling his Coke.

"You got me through," Charlie said.

"I'm not the person you think I am," Spence said.

"I know that," Charlie said. "But it doesn't matter. Knowing you made me make choices I wouldn't have made otherwise. Knowing you helped me. I owe you for that."

"'Owe' me?" Spence said. There was sadness in his voice. "I don't want you to do this just because you owe me."

"I'm not," Charlie said. He picked up his burger and squished it to bite-size with his fingers. "I never do anything I don't want to do."

Spence smiled. He put the pieces of his burger together, added pickles from the side, and took a bite. As he ate, his gaze roamed around the diner.

Charlie relaxed. Spence had his moments of withdrawal, but they didn't last.

He would be fine, at least so far as Charlie could tell.

If he didn't think about the fact of Spence's existence. Charlie wasn't a religious man. He hadn't been in a church since he'd left Dory Cove in '41, but he worried that Spence's return had some significance beyond Charlie's ken.

Miracles didn't happen every day, and Charlie couldn't believe they happened at random. They had to have a purpose. Perhaps the purpose was one he couldn't decipher, but it had to be there.

A blast of cold air hit his back as someone new came into the diner. Spence stopped eating mid-bite. He dropped his burger, and before Charlie could move, had launched himself out of the booth.

"You goddamn bastard!" he shouted as he ran.

Charlie tried to turn and get up at the same time, but his leg caught him.

Something crashed behind him. People were yelling. Charlie got to the edge of the booth to see Spence on top of a man on the floor, holding him down and punching him repeatedly in the face. The teenage boys who had been at the table by the door were trying to pull Spence away, but he shook them off with the agility of a prize fighter.

"You uppity goddamn nigger!" he shouted, his fists making a sickening sound as they hit flesh. "You apologize for what you did to Addy. You apologize."

The other boys were yelling now too. They levered Spence away, but he pushed free and fell on the man on the floor again, screaming obscenities. Charlie grabbed his cane and forced himself to his feet. The door swung open and other patrons stood there, waiting for the fighting to end. The cook was on the phone to the police.

Charlie didn't want them to come.

His heart was pounding so hard he thought it was going to beat a hole through his chest. He limped across the floor, careful to stay back from the shouting boys, the flailing arms.

Finally he used his cane as a weapon, shoving the boys aside. He shoved the cane into Spence's side as hard as he could. Spence whirled, grabbed at it, and Charlie said, "Let him go, Spence."

"Goddamn nigger raped my girl," he said.

Charlie sucked in a mouthful of air. The teenagers let out a cry of denial. The man on the floor had his arms over his face, protecting his head.

"Get off him, Spence," Charlie said.

"He's mine, Charlie. He should die for what he did."

"Get off him," Charlie said. He was shaking. If Spence grabbed for the cane again, he would knock it free.

"He raped Addy," Spence said.

"No." The voice spoke from behind the teenagers.

Charlie looked up as Spence did. Billy was standing there, his mouth a thin line.

"I don't know who you have beaten up," Billy said, "but I can guarantee you have the wrong man."

The man on the floor moaned. The teenage girl made her away around Spence and pulled the man's arm away from his face. It was swollen and covered with blood, but even from Charlie's distance he could tell that Spence had beaten up a man young enough to be Addy's grandson.

"You're Billy Malone?" Spence asked in wonder.

"Have been for seventy-four years," Billy said.

Spence started for him, but Charlie was ready. He pulled back his cane and whacked Spence across the spine so hard that Spence doubled over coughing.

The teenagers were gathered around their friend.

"Tell the police they're not needed," Charlie said to the cook, who was still holding the phone.

The cook shook his head.

"Tel them," Charlie said. "Ruthie doesn't need this kind of publicity during the tourist season."

"He needs a doctor," the girl said.

The boy was sitting up. Since he had already been moved, moving him more wouldn't hurt. "The hospital's at the bottom of the hill," Charlie said. "It'd be quicker to take him there than to wait."

"Who're you, Mister?" One of the other boys asked.

"It doesn't matter who he is," Billy said. He pulled a business card out of his suit pocket. "I'm Billy Malone. I'm an attorney. If there's a problem, you call me. I'll take responsibility for this."

"Billy—" Charlie started.

"It's mine," Billy said. "It has been for fifty years. Just took a while to catch up with me, is all."

The teenagers looked confused, but they were more concerned about their friend. They helped him to his feet and led him out of the diner.

Blood spatters covered the floor and the sides of their booth. Spence was still beside it, gasping for air from Charlie's blow.

"They didn't pay their bill," the cook said.

"Add it to mine," Charlie said. He went over to Spence, put his arm around him, and eased him up. Charlie had caned enough people to know that he hadn't done a lot of damage, just enough to protect Billy.

Billy was watching, a sadness on his face that Charlie had never seen before.

"It really is Spence, isn't it?" Billy asked.

Charlie nodded. His mouth was dry. How had Spence convinced Billy so easily? That line about rape? Charlie leaned against the bloody booth. Beneath his hands Spence was taking deep, shuddery breaths.

"What did you do to Addy?" Charlie asked, not sure he wanted the answer.

"It wasn't rape," Billy said.

"You lie…you filthy…coon," Spence wheezed. He tried to stand, but Charlie kept his hand on Spence's back, holding him down. "You lie."

Billy's mouth thinned, but he said no more, standing impassively as he had always done, the man in the shadows, the man Charlie had only noticed a handful of times in his life, until one day Billy became the subject of newspaper articles, a lauded man, a man with a future, a man with a dream.

A man who had faced the system and beat it.

One of Dory Cove's most upstanding citizens.

One of Oregon's.

A man decorated by the Oregon NAACP, a man written up in the *Oregonian,* a man known nationwide for succeeding against frightening odds.

A man who had raped Addy Hawthorne?

"Let's sit," Billy said.

"I'm…not sitting…with you," Spence said.

Charlie hadn't relaxed his protective touch on Spence's back. "Times are different now, Spencer. You'll sit with him."

"It's all right," Billy said. "No reason he should." Billy's voice sounded calm, but his eyes had a panic in them that Charlie had only seen on the battlefield. He attempted to smile at Charlie, but the smile came out as a grimace. "I'll leave you two."

Then, without waiting for a response, he turned and pushed open the glass door. The wind had died down, but the chill remained, a damp chill, promising more rain.

Spence stood up, his body shaking. He gripped the booth as he watched Billy leave.

"Spence," Charlie said, trying to placate something he wasn't sure he wanted to understand, "he's an old man now."

"I don't care," Spence said.

"It's been fifty years," Charlie said.

"For him. And you. But not for me."

"Spence—"

"You think I should forgive him, Charlie?" Spence turned to Charlie, dark eyes flashing. "He stuck his dick into my girl."

"Spence, times are different."

"Are they?" Spence's breath was coming hard. "So maybe it's okay to let some nigger fuck a white girl, but I'll bet attempted murder's still illegal."

Charlie leaned on his cane, unable to stand without it. "What?"

"You said you followed me everywhere, Charlie. Don't you remember what happened? Or maybe you didn't see it."

"See what?"

"See your good little nigger friend there," Spence said. "The day he shoved me into the Devil's Churn."

21

THE POUNDING on the door awoke her. Evelyn pushed up her sleep mask and squinted at the clock: 11:45. She had been asleep for fifteen minutes.

She grabbed her robe off the side of the bed, stuck her feet into her mules, and tossed her mask onto the pillow. She gathered the robe around her as she made her way out of the bedroom.

The pounding sounded so hard, she thought the door would cave in. She was tempted to call the police. But that made no sense. A robber wouldn't knock. She stopped in the entryway a few feet from the door and yelled, "Who is it?"

"Billy."

He didn't sound like himself. His voice had a wild edge that she had never heard before. A chill ran down her back.

"You woke me up," she said.

"I don't care," he said.

Who did he think he was, waking her out of a sound sleep? She pulled the robe tighter. "Call me in the morning."

"No," he said. His voice boomed as loud as the pounding had. "You open this door now."

"I don't take orders from men like you, Billy," Evelyn said.

"Open it, Evelyn, or I'll kick the damn thing down."

She stood for a moment, her hands shaking. He had never talked to her like this. Never. Who the hell did he think he was?

"Evelyn, you've awakened me plenty over the years."

"Go away, Billy."

She started down the hall. He pounded again. The doorframe rattled.

"I'll break it," he said.

He was scaring her. If she continued to walk away, he just might break the door down, and where would that leave her?

She walked to it, put her hand on the knob, and felt the door vibrate from the force of his blows. "Billy," she said. "Come back when you're calm."

"Evelyn." He stopped hitting the door. "Evelyn, please." His voice broke.

Something awful had happened. Something awful had happened, and he was coming to her.

She turned the dead bolt and pulled the door open. He staggered inside. His suit was covered with tiny rain drops, but other than that he looked no different.

The storm had died down. Only a fine mist was falling. She shut the door behind him and flicked on the hall light.

"What's happening?" she asked.

In the few hours since she had seen him, he had aged. New lines ran from his eyes to his mouth. His dark hair had more touches of silver than she remembered. And his eyes—

His eyes were the eyes of an old man.

"Billy?"

He reached out, his hand shaking. "Please, Evelyn. Olivia confided in you. You have to tell me. Can the dead really come back?"

Never had they discussed Olivia's magic or Evelyn's participation in it. They never really discussed Olivia's hope that her husband would return.

She dodged out of Billy's grasp. "Something happened. What?"

"Spence," he said.

"You saw Spence?" She could barely breathe. "But you said Addy was wrong, that it was some kind of hoax."

He shook his head.

She dragged him into the kitchen and turned on the light. The familiar room always comforted her. He glanced at the window, saw the ocean, and turned his back.

"How do you know?"

"I know," he said. "He knew things no one else knew. Only Spence."

She had to keep her hands busy. Lisa had done the spell for Zeke. That man had died, and Spence had returned. Spence, not Zeke. Spence, whom Olivia hadn't been able to revive. Maybe she had been right about motives.

Maybe she had been right.

Evelyn opened the refrigerator, pulled out a bag of ground coffee, and scooped out enough for them both. "Where did you see him?"

"At Ruthie's. I came straight here."

"So he's still there." Her heart had an odd lightness to it. Spence, after all these years. Spence.

"I don't know," Billy said. "He may be gone now. But I know how to find him."

She poured water into the lid of the coffeemaker, splashing it on her hands. Her hands had been one of her most beautiful features when she was a girl; smooth skin, long fingers, well-shaped nails. They had age spots now, and her knuckles were swollen with arthritis, the skin wrinkled and the color of parchment.

"Why did you come to me?" she asked.

"Because if you know how to bring a man back from the dead, you'll know if he's a real man or a ghost." Billy's voice still had that odd tremble to it. "You'll know if we can send him away."

"Away?" She flicked on the coffeemaker's switch but didn't turn around. She wasn't certain she wanted to hear Billy talk like this. "I hope you mean out of town."

"Just tell me, Evelyn. I saw Spence tonight. He looked twenty years old. He's been dead a lot longer than that. What is he?"

"I'd have to see him," she said. She wanted to see him.

"No." Billy said. "You tell me what he is."

197

She whirled. "You can't come into my house and order me around, Billy Malone."

He had one hand resting lightly on her kitchen chair. The ocean moved behind him, calmer after the storm. "You don't know, do you? You don't know what he is. Olivia never taught you anything."

"Olivia was a friend of mine," Evelyn snapped.

"She was a friend of mine too," Billy said, "but I didn't know a lot about her."

The coffeemaker groaned as the water heated. Then it hissed, and steaming coffee trickled into the pot. Evelyn could feel the heat against her back. She moved sideways so that she could watch the both pot and Billy.

She hated his allegations, but she wasn't sure how much she wanted to tell him. She had been keeping Olivia's secrets for a very long time. "Olivia believed people could come back from the dead," Evelyn said.

"I know that." Billy's tone had contempt laced throughout.

Evelyn decided to ignore it. "But that didn't mean she was right. Zeke never came back."

"Zeke didn't die here," Billy said.

"What?" She hadn't expected that. If that were true, then Zeke couldn't come back. Not with the spell. "Where ever did you get that idea?"

He shook his head. "It doesn't matter. Except that it's true. Al the time Olivia was waiting for him, Zeke was alive."

"Did Olivia know that?" Evelyn said. She couldn't reconcile the news with what she knew of Olivia.

He shrugged. "Does it matter?"

"It matters," Evelyn said. She turned around, took out two mugs, and poured coffee. Then she added cream for herself and sugar for Billy, just as she had done a hundred times before.

If Olivia knew her husband was alive, then she was playing a different game with her stares out to sea, a game Evelyn didn't understand.

Or maybe she did.

And that scared her more.

"Does it matter in relation to Spence?" Billy asked.

She brought the mugs to the table. "How do you know it's Spence, Billy? How do you know your mind isn't playing tricks on you?"

"Because when I came into Ruthie's, he was beating up a black kid who was as skinny as I had been at that age. And he thought that kid was me."

"Everyone knows that you and Spence didn't get along."

Billy shook his head. "There's more to it."

"But the town knows you were there when he died."

"Please, Evelyn," he said. "I can't say any more."

She pulled out a chair and waited for him to do the same. He picked his mug off the table but did not sit down. She wouldn't sit if he wasn't sitting. She picked up her mug as well.

"If you're so convinced that it's Spence," she said, "why do you need me to tell you that a man can be raised from the dead?"

"Because," Billy said, "I need some kind of logic here, Evelyn. I need some answers."

This time Evelyn did sit down. She didn't care if he stood or not. She was tired.

The day had been hard and he had awakened her from a deep sleep to ask questions about Olivia, to reveal secrets she was hoping she would never have to discuss.

But she had vowed to herself that she would move out of Olivia's sphere of influence, and one way to do that was to talk.

About everything.

"I saw the fight that day," she said. "I saw you try to save Spence."

"Oh, God." Billy slumped into the chair beside her. She grabbed his mug to keep it from falling.

"You think he's here for revenge?" she asked.

"I didn't push him in," Billy said.

"I never said you did. I saw it," Evelyn said. "He slipped."

"I shoved him," Billy said.

"The rocks were wet. He lost his footing. You were fighting."

"That's manslaughter, Evelyn."

"That's an accident, Billy. I'd testify to that." She set his mug down. "Is that what you're afraid of? That he'll try to get you arrested? He can't. No one will believe who he is except you and me and maybe Addy."

"And Charlie."

"Charlie?"

"He's with Charlie."

"Charlie Winter?"

Billy nodded.

"You tried to save Spence," Evelyn said. "I watched you."

"It doesn't matter," Billy said. "I failed."

"But he's here now."

"For what?" Billy asked. "That's what I need to know. For what?"

"Have you asked him?"

Billy shook his head. "I can't, Evelyn. To him I'm still the twenty-four-year-old nigger he was fighting with when he fell into the Churn."

She let out a long breath of air, then sipped her own coffee. She had put in too much milk. The coffee was cool.

"Evelyn, please," he said. "I know you can help me."

She pushed the mug away. "Olivia had powers, Billy. She had magic."

He frowned and leaned his chair back on two legs, as if distancing himself from the information.

"You listen," Evelyn said, "and you listen with an open mind, or I won't say any more."

"Magic, Evelyn?"

"Magic," she said. "You come here wanting to know if a man can be raised from the dead, and then deny the presence of magic?"

He set his chair down and sighed. "Good point."

"Olivia said she was born to the Churn, and that it was part of her. She would never say where she learned its magic, but there have always been stories about the danger in that section of coastline, and about the people who were able to harness that danger and turn it into power. I guess she learned from them."

Evelyn sipped more coffee, not because she wanted it but because she couldn't say everything at once, even though she intended to. She had to sort it out.

"I don't know the particulars of Olivia's history. I know that she and Zeke built the house to enhance her powers." And to lure the gods inside. Olivia had told her this long after Addy left, long after Zeke disappeared.

"Zeke knew of this?"

"He had to," Evelyn said. "Olivia never did anything to hide it. You could have seen it if you were looking, Billy."

He didn't meet her gaze, apparently not willing to accept the rebuke.

"The fights started over Addy. I walked in on one. Zeke was yelling that he didn't want to live with two witches. Olivia said that he would have to. It was just after that that he disappeared."

"And Olivia thought he died?"

Evelyn shrugged. "She seemed to. I remember her waiting for him. She let me think she was trying to bring him back. But she didn't. She did try to bring Spence back, and failed. She said she didn't have a pure heart. To be pure, she would have had to want to bring the dead back. She just wanted to use him to keep Addy in the Cove."

Billy scratched his head, obviously confused. "So when she looked at the ocean, was she looking for Zeke or for Spence?"

"She kept looking for something, but I don't know what it was," Evelyn said. "I think she might have been afraid she called up the wrong thing, and was worried that it would come to get her. It never did, but I think it worried her all the same."

"If that's true," Billy said, "why didn't she just leave?"

"And bring it inland? To Addy? No matter what Addy says, Olivia loved her. I think it wasn't until Olivia realized she was safe that she went to visit Addy."

"Monsters, magic, resurrected men," Billy said. "You believe all of this, Evelyn."

She nodded. "I've done some of it. Olivia taught me. But when I realized what it would take from me, I left. And then Olivia put her Book away."

"Her book?"

"She had notes, some really ancient, on all types of spells. She let me see them, and Addy. And Lisa."

"What are you saying?" Billy asked.

"I'm saying that if you believe you've seen Spence, someone had to cast for him. Someone had to use that old Book."

"You think Addy did it?" His voice was strangled, as if he couldn't get the words out.

"Or Lisa," Evelyn was shaking. This was the closest she had come to betraying a confidence. "Lisa was here. Addy didn't come until after Olivia died."

"But Addy saw Spence the day of the memorial."

"And it scared her."

"Because she cast the spell?"

Evelyn shook her head. "If she had cast the spell, she would have been expecting something. Lisa brought Spence back."

"Why?"

"Because she was trying to raise Zeke. For Olivia. She got Spence instead."

Billy pushed away from the table. He clasped his hands behind his back and paced. "You say that Lisa has the capability to raise the dead?"

"I don't know exactly. Olivia never trained me in this. I'm only telling you what I understand."

"But if Spence was at the bottom of that Churn for fifty years, he would be nothing but bones. That can't be him."

"The water's cold," Evelyn said.

Billy shook his head. "I saw him, Evelyn. His face was sliced open, his bones broken before he drowned. He looked just fine when I saw him tonight."

She bent over her mug so that he wouldn't see her face. "You're saying he's not human?"

"I guess." Billy had stopped in front of the window. She could see his face outlined against the dark night sky.

"Why does it matter whether he's human or not?" Evelyn asked. Her hands were cold, her palms damp. She resisted the urge to wipe them on her robe.

"Because he doesn't belong here," Billy said. "We have to send him back."

22

THE BOOK sat on the car seat between them like an accusation. Addy refused to look at it or at Lisa. Her daughter huddled in the passenger seat, her coat wrapped around her, her head turned away. She kept her distance from the Book as well, as if its presence burned her.

The Book wasn't really a book. It was a folder packed with loose papers, some bound by ribbon. The papers were written in different hands, and some of the paper was so old that it crumbled to the touch. The folder, once black, had water marks. The ribbon was a faded red. Most of the good papers were creased around the edges.

Addy drove as fast as she dared through the rain-slicked streets. Lisa had taken the call and then had gone into the basement. When she came up with the Book, she had tried to hide it. Addy knew. She insisted on going along.

It felt like years since she had been to Evelyn's, even though it had just been that morning. Billy was up there. Billy and Evelyn. They had called Lisa for the Book, and Lisa wouldn't say why.

Addy pulled into Evelyn's driveway, got out, and didn't wait for her daughter.

Addy was halfway up the walk before she even heard Lisa's door open. She didn't wait or knock. When she reached Evelyn's door, she opened it and walked in.

The house smelled of coffee. Billy and Evelyn were in the kitchen, Billy standing by the window, Evelyn sitting at the table. Evelyn was in her robe. Addy took a step backward, then decided that what had happened between them was none of her business.

"What do you want the Book for?" she asked.

They both turned. They hadn't heard her come in.

"I called Lisa," Evelyn said.

"I'm here." Lisa was standing behind Addy, cradling the Book against her chest.

"With the Book," Addy said. "As you requested. Now you get to tell me what you're going to do with it."

"The Book is none of your business," Evelyn said.

"The estate isn't settled yet. I'm in charge of the property until it's disbursed. Right, Billy?"

He was staring at her like a drowning man. His mouth was half open, his skin ashen. "Addy," he said, and the way he said it sounded like a cry for help.

She didn't move. "The Book isn't something for last-minute solutions or games. It has powers that shouldn't be used casually."

Evelyn stood. Her robe flowed around her, making her look taller. "Don't lecture me about the Book, Addy. I know more about it than you ever will."

"That's what frightens me," Addy said. "What are you going to do now? Try to raise my mother from the dead?"

"No." Billy still had that odd look. "No." He moved closer to the window. "We're going to try to send Spence back."

The name took all the energy from her. She leaned against the counter. "Spence?"

I'm not dead, Addy.

Billy nodded. "I saw him tonight. He tried to beat me up."

She closed her eyes. The line was unbroken. Things that were interrupted fifty years ago had started again. She tried to make light of it. "A boy slugging an old man."

"He hit a teenager. He thought the boy was me."

Addy opened her eyes. Lisa was beside her now, the Book too close. "Why would he attack you, Billy?"

"Billy was there the day he fell into the Churn," Evelyn said.

"He thinks you killed him?" Lisa asked.

"Does it matter?" Billy spoke softly, flatly. "He doesn't belong here."

"You're sure it's Spence?" Addy asked.

Billy nodded. "Positive."

"How did he get here?" Addy asked.

"We thought you could answer that," Evelyn said.

"Me?" Addy frowned. "I am a practicing Christian. I gave up my mother's ways the day my dad died." Things were moving too quickly for her. She grabbed a chair and sat, grateful for the support.

In the silence that followed she saw Evelyn glance at Billy. Billy didn't turn. He was staring through the window at the ocean, as if it provided answers. All of them were reflected in the glass. Billy, standing close, Evelyn to his side, Addy in the chair, and Lisa beside the counter, hugging the book.

"Resurrecting Spence seems like an odd choice, Lisa," Billy said. Again the calm voice. It was the voice he had used in the old days when someone picked on him for no reason. Addy had once called it his dangerous voice.

"I didn't resurrect Spence," she said.

"Then what were you doing?" Evelyn asked.

"Nothing," Lisa said. "I did nothing."

"Dark powers require a death," Addy said. She was numb inside. She felt like she had known this would happen and had done nothing to stop it.

"Why Spence?" Billy asked again.

"I didn't mean for it to happen!" Lisa's voice rose. "You have to believe me."

"Spence's return or Kowen's death?" Billy asked.

"Both."

Addy closed her eyes. *Mother, you corrupt everything you touch. Even my children. No one is safe from you. No one.*

"What were you trying to do?" Evelyn asked.

"Bring my grandfather back," Lisa said.

Addy frowned, opened her eyes, and blinked hard. Billy was watching her through her reflection in the glass.

"But you already knew your grandfather hadn't died here," Billy said.

"I hadn't read the report," Lisa said.

"Nice try," Billy said. "But you need to think faster than that to beat a lawyer. Even a lawyer like me."

"Billy," Addy said. "Let her be."

"Not yet, Addy." He turned. "Kowen told you that your grandfather died in Chicago, didn't he? Kowen showed you the pictures."

Addy whirled. Tears were running down Lisa's face. "Dad died in Chicago?" Addy asked.

"Two years ago," Billy said. "He was running from your mom."

"You have no proof of that!" Lisa said.

"It's obvious," Billy said. "He had a false name. He never came back to the coast. Forgive me for saying this so bluntly, Addy, but he knew where you were and never came forward."

"He could have been running from bad debt," Lisa said.

"He wouldn't have kept running for so long, and he would have made contact with Addy."

Addy couldn't wrap her mind around the news. She felt like she was still two steps behind the others. "He knew where I was?" she asked.

"He watched you in Chicago. The report even has a picture of the two of you in the same restaurant."

"And he didn't come forward?"

Billy shook his head. "I don't think he felt it was safe."

"But I wouldn't have told Mother. I wouldn't have."

"How would he have known that?"

"Besides," Evelyn said. "Olivia would have known."

Addy's mouth was dry. She licked her lips, but couldn't moisten them. "The blood tells," she whispered. Her mother had always said that. *The blood tells, Addy. I will always be able to find you and to know how you are. The blood tells.*

"What?" Billy asked.

"Olivia could track through flesh-and-blood links," Evelyn said.

"You make her sound all-powerful," Billy said.

Evelyn shook her head. "She was powerful only so long as she remained here. Her power was based in the Churn. She was afraid to leave to visit Addy. It wasn't until Lisa was born that Olivia felt safe traveling away from the Churn. She couldn't use her powers anywhere but here, but at least she knew they wouldn't leave her."

So much of what her mother did was making sense to her now, and she liked it even less than she thought she would. That fight, the morning her father had left. She could barely remember it. Pieces of it had haunted her dreams forever.

You can't sacrifice me. I won't let you. I'm not a pawn you can use. I'm Addy's father, he had shouted.

You've been a pawn from the beginning, Zeke. I can do anything I want with you, and I always will.

I won't stand for it any more, Olivia. I'm leaving. I'll take Addy.

No, Zeke. You can't take Addy. She's mine.

Addy had waited for him to come up the stairs to get her, but he never had.

Then she thought he would return and rescue her, but he hadn't done that either. He had been afraid of her mother, afraid that her lies were truth. It became easier to believe he had died because then he couldn't take her with him.

But he had abandoned her.

Left her.

With her mother.

"Addy?" Billy's voice was soft. "You all right?"

She stood and took a deep breath. If she had learned anything over the years, it was how to calm herself in a crisis. "Do you have more of that coffee, Evelyn?"

Evelyn nodded. She walked over to the coffeemaker and poured.

Addy had to get the focus off the past and onto the present. "So you knew, Lisa. What spell did you cast? What were you trying to do?"

Her daughter stared at her. They had always been different. Always. And so alike.

She had loved Lisa's determination. It had seemed so selfless, especially compared to Loni's selfishness and Marty's self-absorption. Maybe it had been selfless. Or maybe Olivia had had her hooks in Lisa from the beginning.

"I was trying to make him come back," Lisa said.

"Even though he didn't die here? The gods can't return what they didn't take," Addy said.

"You were trying to prove that Olivia was right, that Zeke did die here, weren't you?" Billy asked.

Lisa shook her head.

"Then what were you trying to do?" Addy asked.

Evelyn crossed her arms. "She was trying to prove to Olivia that she was powerful enough to raise the dead. It was an experiment, wasn't it, Lisa? Because if you could raise Zeke, wherever he was, you could raise Olivia, whether she died in the Churn or not."

The heat of the coffee had seeped into the mug's handle. Addy set it on the counter. Lisa's eyes teared. That had been it. That had been it all along. "What did your grandmother say when you told her what you had done?"

"I didn't tell her," Lisa said. "She would find out soon enough. She would have been happy, though. She would have seen him."

"That wouldn't have made her happy," Addy said.

"Yes, it would," Lisa said. "Gram said she didn't want to die with unfinished business. This thing with my grandfather was unfinished."

"You don't know that," Addy said. My mother kept secrets from everyone."

"Maybe," Billy said, "Olivia's unfinished business was with Addy's real father, not with Zeke."

Addy sighed. She hated that old story, and hadn't thought of it in years.

"Really, Billy. It's a lonely woman's fantasy, a myth from every culture that lives by the sea. Mother was delusional sometimes."

"Have you looked at your birth certificate?" Billy asked.

"Every time I need a new copy," Addy said.

"No," Billy said. "You have two certificates. The courthouse mails the second. Did you see it, Lisa?"

She shook her head. "I don't know what you're talking about, Billy."

"On the first birth certificate, Addy, the father's name is crossed out. It was in Kowen's report. I was meaning to check the original today to see if I could see what had been written there. Zeke's name is on the second."

Addy took a brownie off the stack Evelyn had on a plate in the middle of the counter. She ate it quickly, without thinking, needing, almost craving the chocolate, the way she sometimes craved cigarettes.

"What's the story, Mom?" Lisa's voice had a touch of panic.

Addy swallowed the brownie and wiped her hands on her slacks. "I'm surprised she never told you. Perhaps it wasn't a story she wanted her granddaughter to hear. Or maybe she was afraid you'd try it."

"She didn't want anyone related to you near the Churn," Evelyn said.

"Mother," Lisa said. "You're being mysterious."

Addy sighed. "My mother claimed to have been at the Devil's Churn at twilight. The sun cast a green glow across the waves and this perfect man walked toward her. They spent the night together, and as the sun came up, his legs grew into a tail and he dove into the Churn."

"A merman?" Lisa asked.

"My mother never saw him again. When she realized she was pregnant, she got my father to marry her. She once told me she was terrified in her ninth month that I would be born with gills and a tail." Addy shook her head. "I thought it a child's tale, something magical to make me feel special. Then, after my father left, I thought she told me to give me hope. I never thought it was true."

"She always did stare at sea for the green glow. She always said she was waiting for your father to return. She never said it was Zeke," Evelyn said.

"And she had to know that Zeke ran away from her," Billy said. "Although I can barely deal with the idea of witches. Mermen stretches things too far."

"There have been stories about sea men every since this coast was settled, and the local guides attribute that to people getting glimpses of sea lions, and not realizing what they've seen," Addy said.

"People always have a rationalization for magic," Evelyn said.

Addy sipped her coffee. They kept talking around the important things. She had to concentrate on what really mattered. Only she wasn't certain of that anymore.

Lisa was watching her, as if trying to see if Addy were any different. Addy nearly snapped, *I'm still your mother. I'm still human,* but thought better of it. If this night confirmed anything, it was that none of them were as they seemed.

Then the question came, the one that she needed to ask, the one that held the key.

"What spell did you use, Lisa?" she asked.

Lisa winced. Addy knew she had found the right thing to ask. Lisa was like Olivia; she didn't want to face anything until confronted. "A resurrection spell," Lisa said, "for a beloved."

"Yours?" Addy asked.

Lisa shook her head. "Family."

The conversation around them had stopped. Addy nodded. It made sense now.

Lisa had performed a resurrection spell, thinking it would work on Zeke, who had died in the prairies, trying to bring him back. But the spell was for a beloved, and Addy's mother had never loved Zeke. She had only used him to provide a name for her daughter in the days when such things were important.

"A beloved?" Billy asked. His voice had regained its flat tone. "And so your resurrection spell brought back Spence."

Lisa nodded.

Billy sighed. His whole body seemed to collapse in on itself. "I thought you said you didn't love him, Addy."

"I loved him," she said. "Just not the way he wanted me to."

Her words hung in the silence. Billy turned his back on her. Evelyn was watching them both. Lisa had that trapped look she had had earlier.

"So that brings us full circle," Billy said. "Spence doesn't belong here. How do we send him back?"

"He has to go back into the Churn," Lisa said.

Addy spilled coffee on her hand. The liquid burned. "Is that why you brought us up here? To find a way to kill Spence?'

"It's not like he's alive," Billy said. "He's already been dead fifty years."

"Then what tried to beat you up tonight, Billy? A ghost?"

"I don't know, Addy."

She set her coffee down and shook the drops off her hand. "Then just tell me one thing. Did you intend to kill him the first time, Billy?"

"God, Addy, you were there. You saw it."

"I saw what I thought was an accident. But it could have been murder. A little too much force on your part. Did you kill him?"

"Addy—"

"Did you?"

Billy sighed and leaned his head against the glass. "No," he said. "No. I never did."

"Then why are you trying to do so now?"

He brought his head up and turned, facing her not with the mask he had worn since she arrived but with all the yearning she remembered. "He doesn't belong here, Addy."

"You didn't either, once."

"You're defending a man who's already dead."

"No," she said. "I'm trying to prevent more tragedy." She walked over and took the Book from Lisa. "These powers in this Book are wrong. Spence died because of them the first time. Maybe this is his chance to get his life back. But you want to use this Book to take his life away again. I won't let you. I won't let any of you."

She whirled and ran from the room, clutching the Book. They were shouting behind her, Lisa, Evelyn, and Billy, Lisa saying Addy had no right to the Book, Evelyn entreating her to come back, and Billy calling her name.

She hurried out the door. The rain had started again, and the wind had come up, gale force, so strong it almost blew the Book from her hands. She got into the car, started it, and backed out of Evelyn's driveway.

The Book and its powers had led her daughter to resurrect a man who should have remained dead, to use another man's life force to do so. It had turned the most ethical man Addy knew into one who would contemplate murder. It had destroyed her mother.

Addy would do what she should have done decades ago, what her mother had tried to do and failed.

She would return the Book to its rightful owner.

Her father.

23

BILLY SLUMPED in the armchair beside the window. The women were still yelling after Addy.

"Let her go," he said.

They didn't hear him. They were arguing about who would drive after her.

"Let her go!"

The force of his words stopped them. Evelyn and Lisa turned to him, frowning.

"She's right," he said softly. "We're playing with things we don't understand. She's right."

"She took the Book, Billy," Lisa said. She made it sound like a crime.

"It's hers to take." He closed his eyes and leaned his head back. Addy had never been the moral center of his universe before. She was always the one he took care of, the one who had led him astray. She had caused the greatest heartache in his life.

"You said legally whatever was in the house was mine," Lisa said.

"Damn the law," he said quietly. "The law isn't always right."

"But it's what governs us."

He shook his head. The darkness behind his eyelids was safer than looking at the women in the room with the ocean visible through the window beside him. "The law doesn't govern us. Compassion guides us, or it should. The law is only there when compassion fails us."

"Compassion, Billy?" Evelyn sounded confused.

He opened his eyes. The women were still standing near the door. Lisa looked less like Addy, more like Evelyn. They both had an angularity, a sharpness to their features, a cruelty in their mouths that Addy lacked.

"Compassion, Evelyn," he said, allowing sarcasm into his voice for the first time that night. "You should recognize it. It's what's allowed me to listen to your problems night after night." He put his hands on the arm of the chair and pushed himself to his feet. "But then again, maybe you're not familiar with it. You wouldn't even open your goddamn door when I needed you tonight. I had to threaten to tear it down."

"You're in," Evelyn said.

"And you convinced me to call this miserable excuse for a human being to discuss how we can rid ourselves of another human being."

"We don't know if Spence is human," Evelyn said.

"We don't know he isn't."

Billy set his coffee mug on the counter, then walked around the women, heading for the hall.

"You were certainly frightened enough of him a little while ago," Evelyn said.

Billy nodded. "I am still frightened of him, Evelyn."

"You killed him, didn't you?" Lisa asked.

Billy turned, slowly, until he faced her. She was watching him, her dark eyes intent, as if his answer meant more than anything she had ever heard. "I didn't knock him over the head like you did Ian Kowen, but I was there when Spence died. I had as much a part of it as Addy did or Evelyn."

"I had nothing to do with it," Evelyn said.

"You watched, same as me. You could have stopped it before Spence fell."

"Men fighting—"

"Is an excuse," Billy said. Lisa was watching him, that intent look still in her eyes. "I notice that you haven't denied what I said."

"I wasn't anywhere near Ian Kowen when he died," Lisa said. She swallowed. "How can you defend me when you think I killed him?"

"I called a man from Portland who'll be here in the morning," Billy said. "I won't defend you, Lisa. I think there is no defense for taking a life."

"You don't know that I did."

Billy smiled. "I know that you did. Whether you were standing beside Kowen or whether you were at Mo's when he died, it doesn't matter to me. It takes a life to run the dark powers. You all said as much. A man died, and Spence returned. That's enough for me. Fortunately for you, that's not enough for the court."

"Billy!" Evelyn said as if he were a recalcitrant child.

He ignored her and her fake shock. He had been taking care of her too long.

He had been taking care of all of them too long.

"If the police summon you tomorrow, Lisa," Billy said, "you show up. Because if you don't, I'll hunt you down personally."

"That's supposed to scare me into appearing?" she asked.

"No," he said. "It's supposed to remind you that outside of your little magic world there is another, greater world."

"You think she'll get off?" Evelyn asked.

"Is that important?" Billy said. "She killed a man."

When they didn't answer him, he sighed. He had no idea if she'd go free, but if he told her she would, she would be more likely to stay in Dory Cove.

"If they have compelling physical evidence, she's in trouble," he said. "But if they only have her last meeting with Kowen, the report, and a body, then any attorney can get her free."

Even one who knew she had committed the crime. He turned and hurried down the hall before they could call after him. He already had one death on his hands.

He didn't need another. If only he hadn't represented her at the station, he would call the police right now and tell them to pick her up. But he couldn't. She was protected.

Although he could tell the police that Evelyn knew.

He might do that.

But he had something to settle with Spence first.

24

SPENCE HAD REFUSED to talk to Charlie since they had gotten home. The boy lay on the couch, eyes closed, arms resting on his stomach. His bruised knuckles looked raw and painful, and he had a scrape on his right cheek. The young black man he had beaten up had managed to get in a few licks himself.

Charlie sat at the kitchen table, his hands shaking. He had forgotten the unenlightened parts of his youth. Billy had become such a fixture in his life that it was hard to remember how out of place Billy had once been, how scary Billy had seemed then, with his thick, muscular arms, coal-black skin, and strange accent.

No one let him into the church, and only Charlie's father had been willing to help him when Billy arrived by giving him a room in the storage shed. For that, Charlie's father had received anonymous threats, and he had laughed them off.

People will always be that way about someone different, Charlie, his father had said. *The thing of it is that good people get beyond the differences. Good people don't judge a man at all. They simply accept him.*

Billy Malone, seventy-four-year-old lawyer, who raped Addy Hawthorne fifty years ago and pushed Spencer Chadwick into the Churn when Spence challenged him about it.

The idea made Charlie's skin crawl.

How could a man keep such a thing hidden so long?

Charlie remembered the uproar about Spence's death. If Evelyn and Addy hadn't told the police that they were there, that a huge wave had washed Spence out to sea, Billy would be in prison now.

But they had made that claim, and Billy had gone on to become accepted in Dory Cove, to get an education, and in the twilight of his life to become a professional of high standing.

He had never married, never had children, and never spoke of Addy or Spence.

Until today.

But Charlie had been there too. He had seen Spence stumble, seen Spence fall, and seen Billy try to rescue him at great risk to his own life. Maybe Billy had pushed too hard, but it had been an accident.

It had to have been.

A knock on the door made Charlie jump. He'd been expecting it. The knock sounded again. Spence sat up as if moving hurt him. Charlie got out of his chair. "Who is it?"

"It's Billy, Charlie."

"Go away."

"Please, open up."

Charlie glanced at Spence. The boy had gotten off the couch and was standing beside it, fists clenched.

"Don't touch him," Charlie said. "He's an old man."

"I have a right," Spence said.

Charlie shook his head. He hobbled to the door and pulled it open.

The wind had kicked up again, sending leaves and rain in a swirling dance around his door. Billy huddled as close to the door as he could get, his overcoat open, and his collar turned up. His hair shone in the porch light, and rain had beaded on his face.

"My grandson and I are about to go to bed," Charlie said, trying to keep the desperation from his voice.

"Grandson?" Billy raised his eyebrows. "You never married, Charlie."

"His grandmother was a girl I knew on Guam. He found me—"

"And you named him Spence? I think not." Billy pushed past Charlie and came into the kitchen. "Better close the door, Charlie, before the storm blows us all away."

"You weren't invited, nigger." Spence had come into the kitchen too. He stood, his legs apart and hands up as if preparing for an attack.

"That's always been my problem," Billy said. His voice had a calmness to it, a reasonableness that Charlie had never heard before. "But it seems to me that's your problem now."

"I don't have any problems," Spence said.

"Except that you lost fifty years of your life."

"I wouldn't have if it weren't for you."

Billy winced as if he had been struck. "True enough," he said. "But I think it's time we talk."

"You can't talk about killing a man. No one can be reasonable about that," Charlie said.

Both Spence and Billy looked at him in surprise. Spence had a slight frown on his face. "You think he tried to kill me, Charlie? You were there."

"You said he did," Charlie said. "Just a couple of hours ago. You called it attempted murder."

Spence put a hand over his face. "I was mad."

"Mad enough to accuse a man of murder?"

Spence shrugged, then looked at Billy. "I can't get you any other way."

"I doubt you can get me that way either," Billy said. "There's a slight matter of fifty years."

Charlie took a chair and slumped in it. This blood hatred made no sense, then. "But you want to kill him," he said to Spence.

"I want to beat the ever-living crap out of him," Spence said, "and make him stay in his place."

That last he directed at Billy. Billy had his hands in his overcoat pocket. He stood straight, his head unbowed. He still looked strong, but it was the strength of a man who had lived a full and rich life, not the physical strength of a boy.

"We fought that out once," Billy said.

"We didn't finish," Spence said.

Billy held up his hands in a surrender gesture. "We can fight now, if you want. You'll beat me. You have youth and strength and power. But I have understanding."

"I don't need anything from you, nigger."

"You need my apology," Billy said.

Charlie looked at Billy in wonder. In all the years they had known each other, Billy had never used that word. Once Billy had even said that apologies were the sign of a weak man.

"I think you owe the apology to Addy," Spence said.

Billy shook his head. "Addy and I made a sort of peace after you died. My business is with you."

"You're going to tell me she loved you," Spence said.

Charlie stiffened. How could he live so long in a town and not see anything?

"She told you, then," Billy said.

"She screamed it at me on the Churn, remember?"

Charlie remembered. He remembered Addy screaming something at Spence, Spence wrenching free from Billy's grasp, tripping, and falling into the water.

And taking forever to die.

Billy pulled the overcoat tighter around his middle. Charlie could see the young Billy in that gesture, the man who had come to Dory Cove because he had nowhere else to go. "She was going to return your ring," he said softly.

"She did," Spence said. "Just before you two went to the Churn to make out."

The wind howled around the house, rattling windows and slamming branches against the wood. Charlie wanted to slide his chair back and leave the kitchen.

The men weren't going to come to blows. Spence didn't need his protection.

Charlie felt like he was spying all over again.

Amazing how much he had missed by arriving a few minutes after Spence that day at the Churn. Spence had come to find Addy and Billy. He had. They had been making out. Spence attacked, and by the time Charlie had arrived, the fight was underway.

"I loved her, Spence," Billy said. He kept his head bowed. Something in this interaction took away Billy's years. It was as if, confronted with his past, he became the person he once had been.

"You overreached yourself," Spence said.

"I know. I have had a long time to think about this." Billy shrugged as if ashamed. "I think part of it was that I could have something that the great Spencer Chadwick wanted. Me, a poor uneducated black boy. I could have Addy Hawthorne."

Spence's fists clenched and unclenched. The past was still alive for him. The things Billy was discussing dispassionately from fifty years before had the immediacy of yesterday for Spence. Perhaps Charlie did have a place here. He seemed to be the only one who remembered that detail, the only one who knew that even in the best of circumstances, tempers flared.

"You didn't marry her. Charlie says mixed marriages are common now." Spence spoke the words as if they disgusted him.

Billy glanced at Charlie as if he had forgotten he was there. "She left the day after you died."

"You could have gone with her."

Billy shook his head. "She didn't want me. I was her rebellion against her mother, against all that was expected of her. Nothing more."

"But she loved you." Spence's voice broke.

"I think she actually loved you, Spence, but I think that frightened her more than I did."

Spence frowned. Charlie held his breath. Billy had spoken with the soft tones of conviction. "How do you know that?" Charlie said, hoping that Billy did know, that it would break the tension.

"Because," Billy said, "the spell that brought Spence back only worked if someone in Olivia's family loved him. Olivia was dead. Addy's children didn't know him. That left Addy."

Spence sank into a chair as if his knees were going to give out. He ground the heel of his hand into his skull. "She chased me away," he said. "When she saw me, she chased me away."

"You'd been dead to her for fifty years," Billy said. "That's a long time, Spence."

Spence laughed. There was no humor in the sound. "Believe me," he said. "I know." He slapped his hands on the table, then looked at Charlie, eyes bright with unshed tears. "I'd like to find her, Charlie, to talk to her."

Charlie nodded. "Get cleaned up," he said. "Then we'll go to Olivia's."

Spence pushed away from the table and ran to the bathroom. Billy watched him go.

"He's still a boy," Billy said.

"Yes," Charlie said.

"Younger than I remember," Billy said. "More hot-tempered."

"It mattered then," Charlie said.

Billy smiled. He took his hands out of his overcoat. They were shaking. "It matters now."

"Do you know why are you sending Spence to her?" Charlie asked.

The windows rattled again. The wind was even stronger than it had been a moment before.

"Because he haunts her just like he haunted me."

The pipes squealed as water ran in the bathroom. Outside, rain drummed against the roof. Charlie looked at Billy, really looked at him for the first time.

Charlie's counselor had once said that each man had a time that defined him.

A moment, a day, a year. That year for Charlie had been 1944. He still tried to shake it off, but when he thought of himself, he was a twenty-two-year-old kid tripping on a land mine, forever vulnerable, forever frightened.

Billy, for all his awards, education, and accomplishments, was still a young black man in a world where he was seen as less than human. Worthy of being an object of a woman's rebellion, but not worthy of her love.

"Maybe you should talk to her," Charlie said.

"Maybe," Billy said. He stood, pulling his coat tight. He hunched his shoulders, in a manner Charlie hadn't ever seen Billy do before, as if he suddenly felt the weight of all his years. As he opened the door, the wind snatched it away and slammed it against the side of the building.

"I think the Storm's finally here," Billy said and stepped into it.

25

THE WIND came up after Billy left. Evelyn stood beside the counter in her kitchen and listened to the gale whip around her home. Sea squalls were forming funnels of water above the ocean, like toy tops scattered across the surface.

"We need to get the Book," Lisa said.

Evelyn nodded. Compassion. Billy had accused her of lacking compassion. She had compassion. She had nursed her husband. She had lost a child. She had spent every Saturday at the Senior Center and every Sunday visiting shut-ins. She had more compassion than Billy ever did.

But she hadn't opened the door to him. She had never really thought of him as a man who needed anything.

He had needed her advice tonight.

And she had sent him to Lisa.

Lisa who, like Olivia, took what she needed and didn't care about the consequences. Olivia had taken Evelyn's whole life and had given her nothing in return.

Nothing except belief in a religion based on lies, and a fear that accompanied each waking moment.

The Storm was here.

And Lisa wanted to get the Book.

"Where do you think she took it?" Evelyn asked.

Lisa shook her head. "Knowing Mother, she would take it home. She's the executor. She knows the Book belongs to me."

Evelyn nodded, although she didn't agree. Addy had the strength of her own convictions, rather like Billy. They both seemed to have a gut sense about the difference between right and wrong.

Compassion. Did Addy have compassion? It seemed that way. She had tried to talk them out of sending Spence back. But she lacked compassion too. She had allowed Olivia to die alone.

Or had she?

Olivia had always made it clear that she felt betrayed by Addy, and that she loved Lisa. Lisa was at her side when she died. Lisa, the child of her heart.

Who had killed as easily as Olivia had.

"The Storm's coming up," Evelyn said. "If she's going to the house, we'll be able to get her when the Storm dies."

"The Book should be in the hands of someone who understands it during the Storm," Lisa said.

Evelyn's throat went dry. The Storm was here. The herbs in the Churn had done nothing. Nothing except perhaps delay it a day.

It would all happen again.

Only this time, Lisa would make things worse, not Olivia.

"You're right," Evelyn said. "Let me change, and I'll drive you there."

Lisa nodded. She walked to the window and stared out. The ocean was frothy and high, the water spouts blending the line between sea and horizon. The sky looked lighter. Evelyn didn't glance at the clock, even though she knew it had to be close to dawn.

She made herself walk to her bedroom. She turned on the clock radio, switching until she found a weather report, and she played that loud. Then she locked her bedroom door and, with shaking hands, punched the speed dial for the police station.

When Lois Gunther, the night dispatcher answered, Evelyn told her to get Jonah and to hurry. She carried the receiver as close to her closet as she could get it, and she barely managed to reach the slacks and blouse she had worn earlier in the day. As she waited, she slipped into the clothing.

The radio announcer mentioned a freak storm cited off the central coast. "It seems to be heading toward the stretch of shore between Florence and Yachats. The National Weather Service has closed Highway 101 in that area due to gale-force winds..."

"Jonah Huffman."

Evelyn let out a sigh of relief. "Jonah, I only have a moment. This is Evelyn. I have Lisa here. She confessed to me. Now she wants me to take her home. I think she's crazy. I think she'll go after Addy."

"She's at your house?"

"Yes, but she wants to leave."

"Keep her there," Jonah said. "We'll be right over." Then he hung up.

Evelyn replaced the receiver on its cradle and put her face in her hands.

Compassion? Turning a woman in, allowing her to go to prison, was that the kind of compassion Billy had been talking about?

"...suggesting that local residents shore up windows, go into basements, use storm cellars. If those aren't available, find a small area within the house, closets, tiny bathrooms..."

Evelyn's heart was pounding. She remembered the last time such a Storm hit the coast. Houses all along the ocean were destroyed.

"...water inches deep on the roads. Rain is coming down in torrents. But it's the winds..."

She left the radio on and let herself out of the bedroom, still buttoning her blouse. Lisa was standing in the hallway, waiting.

"Did you hear the news?" Evelyn said. "They're warning people to stay in."

"Things could get a lot worse if Mom misuses that Book," Lisa said.

Evelyn knew that too. But she couldn't trust Lisa with it either.

"I know," Evelyn said. "I've been through one of these before. But I think you'd better call your sister and have them leave the house."

"Why? I don't think Mother's a danger to them."

"She's not," Evelyn said. "The Storm is. The last time we had one of these, half the seafront houses disappeared."

"The house survived that Storm."

"The house had more yard then."

Lisa's eyes grew wide. "If I get there—"

"The roads have water inches deep. You may not be in time. Save them, Lisa."

Lisa shot her an exasperated glance, then picked up the phone. She dialed quickly and leaned against the counter while she waited.

Evelyn picked up her purse and dug for her keys as she would do if she were actually taking Lisa to the house. Her stomach was queasy with fear. If Jonah didn't arrive in time, then she would have to take Lisa out into the Storm. Evelyn wasn't a good enough driver to fight the winds and the rain. She lacked the strength. Besides, she didn't drive much at night anymore. Her night vision had always been poor.

Lisa had turned her back and was talking softly. Occasionally she would gesture with her right hand. Finally she snapped loud enough for Evelyn to hear, "Then use my credit card number. Hang on, I'll get it for you."

She set the receiver aside and grabbed her own purse.

"They don't want to go," she said to Evelyn.

"It's best if they do."

"They want to know why I'm not joining them."

"Have them get you a room. It'll save questions."

Lisa nodded. She went back to the phone and read the card into it. Then she hung up.

"Let's go," she said.

Now the moment had come. Evelyn would have to think of a way to stall her outside the house. She should have realized that she might have to do this before.

She put on her raincoat, handed one to Lisa, and they walked to the front door. She pulled the door open to find Jonah standing there, fist raised to knock.

Fitz was beside him. Two squad cars were parked in her driveway, but the police officers in the other car remained inside.

When Jonah saw Lisa, he pulled out his badge.

"Lisa Rustin?" he said as if he didn't know her. "You're under arrest."

She whirled at Evelyn. "You called them."

The wind swirled around them like an intrusive child. It grabbed at Evelyn's hair, pulled at her coat, and got inside her clothes. She shivered.

"You shouldn't have called them!" Lisa said.

"Miss Rustin," Jonah said. "You'll need to come with me."

"Mother's got the Book! You don't know what she'll do."

"Miss Rustin—"

"I trust Addy," Evelyn said, and was surprised to discover it was true. "She'll do the best thing."

"Miss Rustin, I need to read you your rights." Jonah had taken her arm. The rain was coming down in sheets, almost as if they were standing beneath a waterfall. The downpour had turned Evelyn's yard into a river.

"I can't go with you," Lisa said. "My mother's in trouble."

"Is that true, Evelyn?" Jonah asked.

Evelyn shook her head. She didn't know if Lisa was telling the truth or not.

Jonah took Lisa firmly and forced her to the squad car. She kept yelling as she went, but the wind snatched her words away. As she slid inside the car, the wind died down.

"Evelyn," she screamed, "you're damning us all!"

Then Jonah slammed the door, waved, and crawled inside. Fitz was still standing beside Evelyn in the rain. "We'll need a statement from you," he said. "I can do it now, or you can come with me."

She shook her head. "I still have some warm coffee inside. I'd rather be home during the Storm."

Fitz grinned. "Can't say as I blame you."

She held the door open for him. He went in. The first squad car backed out of her driveway, followed by Jonah's car. Lisa had her face against the glass.

If Evelyn had done that to Olivia, how different their lives would have been.

Olivia had confessed to killing the hobo, but Evelyn had ignored it, just as she had been prepared to ignore Lisa.

Lisa. Her arrest would crush Addy.

Evelyn shivered and walked back inside her warm house. Maybe she hadn't called the police in order to be compassionate. Maybe she was making one last dig at Adelaide.

Or maybe, at the age of sixty-nine, Evelyn was finally taking steps toward being her own woman.

She closed the door, and prayed that turning in Lisa had been the correct choice. For everyone.

26

B Y THE TIME ADDY turned her car into the Churn's parking lot, the water on the road was nearly a foot deep. She had boots in the backseat, and she slipped them on, as much for traction as for protection. She probably wouldn't come away from this trip alive. She didn't care, as long as the Book was gone and her family was safe.

Lisa had killed that man to bring her grandfather back.

Lisa. She had been such a wonderful child, full of sunshine and life. And then her father died, and Addy left the house every day. One day she noticed that Lisa no longer smiled much, and both Loni and Marty were complaining about how difficult the youngest had become.

Except when Olivia was around.

Addy had been right in the first place to leave her mother. But her new religion had commanded her to honor her parents, so she flew her mother to the Midwest as soon as she could afford it. She had brought Olivia into their lives.

The man she thought was her father, Zeke Hawthorne, had run away from Olivia, had abandoned Addy to her mother's powers.

Just as Addy had abandoned Lisa.

But it would end here. Tiffany would get a chance at a normal life. With the Book gone, the dark powers would disappear too. And Olivia's legacy would end.

The wind was so strong, it buffeted the car. The wind wailed around her, its sound a counterpoint to the thudding booms of the Churn. The rain cascaded in sheets, making the darkness under the trees into an uneven black gloom.

Addy reached into the glove compartment and took out the flashlight she had stashed there for emergencies. She flicked it on, its beam a small halo of light.

Then she picked up the Book.

It was warmer and heavier than she expected. She almost dropped it. But she had a mission. Something she should have done five decades before instead of running away. She should have destroyed the Book.

If she had done that, none of this would have happened.

She had to lean her entire weight onto the car door to force it open in the wind. The gale was strong enough to allow her to lean on it. Her heart was pounding hard, but she could only feel it. The Storm raged around her, magnifying the thunder of the Churn, the downbeat of the rain echoing in the darkness.

Her father had given her mother the Book. Her mother had told her after Zeke left, gloating, saying she had asked for power from the Churn and had received it.

Addy's father had given her mother the Book, the power she wanted, in exchange for a sacrifice.

That sacrifice must have been Zeke, who ran away. And then her mother had tried to groom Evelyn. When Spence died, she had tried to make Addy satisfied with that. And Addy had abandoned her mother then. Apparently her mother reconsidered and tried to raise Spence.

And failed.

Ahead of her, in her small beam of light, Addy could see only rain and water.

She would die here, but the Book would die with her.

The air was frigid. The wind cut through her clothes. She clutched the book close, its warmth like a live thing against her chest. She walked by long forgotten landmarks—the old oak, its roots exposed and still treacherous; the sloping path; the guardrail. When she reached it, she saw waves slamming into the Churn, large walls of water.

When she was a child, she could touch the water and calm it. Her mother used to marvel at that. Addy thought nothing of it then.

She understood whom she got that power from now.

She stared at the Churn. She would be able to walk down the path, but the stairs would lead her to the water's edge. The lava rock where she and Billy once sat trading secrets was now under the sea.

That made her trip a little easier. She carefully made her way down the path. The water ran in rivulets ahead of her; only her boots kept her steady. Twice she thought of chucking the Book over the side, but she was afraid she'd miss. If it landed on the ground, some kid might pick it up and the whole cycle would start again.

She had to finish this.

The wind blew her hair over her face. She was drenched, but the Book remained curiously dry. Once she slipped and caught the railing for support. She stood, her heart pounding, while she tried to regain her composure. Even if she fell, she would throw the Book away. She had to.

Around the corner the bench looked uninviting, wet and waterlogged. The waves slammed into the Churn so hard, the entire cliff face shook. The ocean frothed around her, its water wild and uncontrolled. Now she was walking into the wind and it took all of her strength to keep moving forward.

The rain tasted of salt.

Waves washed onto the stairs, and water ran down them, like a tiny waterfall.

She would drown, just like Spence did, and with the Book gone, no one could revive her.

No one would.

She had lived a long and full life, but in doing so had not made herself central to anyone. She would die, and people would mourn, and then they would go on with their lives as if she had never been.

That isolation was her legacy from Olivia. A legacy she had chosen to continue.

She reached the top of the stairs.

Below her the water churned. Waves as high as walls rolled in and slammed against the cliff face. The stairs were almost completely under water. She couldn't see the center of the Churn. She could only guess.

She tucked the flashlight into the waistband of her pants. The loss of its light seemed to make the sea's roar even louder. She was breathing hard, the air in her mouth cold and salty. With both hands she gripped the Book and waited for the wind to die down.

When the gusts eased, it was as if the world had taken a breath. She tossed the Book toward the center of the Churn with all her strength, stepping forward and nearly tumbling down the steps. Her feet shot out from underneath her. She landed on her back on the path, and as she slid, grabbed at the railing. Her hands slipped on the slick wood, but she finally managed to get a purchase.

She scrambled to a sitting position, bracing her body against the handrail, and scanned the water's surface, looking for the Book.

It was gone.

It had disappeared as if it had never been.

But the water in the Churn was completely still, and the wind was gone. It took her a moment to realize that the rain had stopped too.

She grabbed for her light. It had slid into her pants leg, but hadn't fallen out.

She pulled it free and flicked it on, grateful for the thin beam.

The water was a summer green and as flat as a stagnant pool. Rainwater still ran down the stairs, but didn't make a wave as it fell into the sea.

As she watched, a hand broke the surface.

It was holding the Book.

She nearly dropped the flashlight.

Her breath was coming in short gasps. She was too terrified to scream. She tightened her grip on the railing. Running would damn her. She would slide down the slick walkway right into that unnaturally calm water.

A head broke the surface, then a body—a male body, perfectly formed, and sitting on lava rock, his legs curled to the side like a tail. He was naked. His muscles rock hard and perfect, his shoulders wide and his face—

His face was hers with a masculine cast.

"You dropped this," he said. His voice burbled from him.

"I'm returning it," she said, amazed she could speak at all.

"You're not the one I gave it to," he said.

"She's dead."

He tilted his head. "Without fulfilling her promise?"

Suddenly the water around him rose in a funnel. A mini tornado in the center of the Churn. Droplets whipped off it, hit Addy in the face. His anger was visible in the wind, the storms.

She backed away.

"You!" he said, and the funnel stopped circling. It sank back into the calm sea.

Addy jutted her chin, held her ground, even though she was cold and frightened.

"You have the look of me in the face."

Addy shook her head. She wanted no part of this man, this thing that had seduced her mother, had stolen her mother's heart, and then her humanity, one day at a time. "I gave you your Book. That's all you need."

"You got the Book from her," he said. "You're hers. And mine."

She was shivering. The draw she always felt to the ocean, the pull that she hated and loathed and could barely resist, was stronger here.

"She promised you to me."

"No," Addy said.

"But she did. In exchange for the Book. She would make you. For me." He held out his hand and smiled. As he did so, the water became a deep blue. He stood.

He had the perfection of Michelangelo's David, the narrow lips, the long legs, and the allure of every man she had ever loved. "Come daughter. You're welcome in the deep."

She shook her head. "I'm not your daughter."

His laugh boomed like waves against the rocks. "You have my look. A man cannot deny what he sees. You are mine. She made you for me." Then he frowned. The water turned dark, and waves broke it surface. "And you're old. Very old. You have spent too much time with her people. She betrayed me."

Addy gripped a sharp stone. It offered little protection. Just as her mother had. Her mother hadn't betrayed him. Her mother had brought Addy to the Churn as a child and waited for him to appear. "No," Addy said. "She tried to give me to you. You never came."

His smile was pure triumph. "Then you are mine."

"No," Addy said. "I am my own person. I have nothing to do with you."

"You will," he said, reaching for her again. "We have need of you below. Your humanity can bring my people children. Come, daughter. I will make you young again."

She wrapped her arms tightly around the handrail. "No," she said.

"The men below are more beautiful than any on earth."

"No," Addy said.

"A woman needs children," he said.

"I have children," she said.

He froze. "Human children?"

She wasn't sure if she had jeopardized them or not. She couldn't tell. "Three human children. Beautiful human children. And they're mine. Not yours."

He brought his hand in, then sank back onto his lava rock. "She should have told you, daughter. Human children tie you to the earth."

"Good," Addy said.

"But I can still make you young. I can send you below, to see my world, be with my people. You cannot be of us, but you can visit us."

Addy loosened her grip on the railing. She could go into the ocean and return.

The best of both worlds. She stood.

"And you will remember," he said. "Unlike the human visitors, you will remember."

Human visitors. Spence. The chill that had been in her body moved to her heart. She grabbed the railing again. "How long do you keep your visitors?"

"Until someone wants them back." He leaned on his lava rock, the king on his throne. "Will someone want you, daughter?"

No. No one would want her. And if someone did, no one would be able to get her. Her father now had the Book.

"I'm staying here," Addy said.

"Daughter." His voice had softened. "Your mother always wanted to join me. Would you pass an opportunity that I can only give once?"

"My mother is dead," Addy said, "and I am not her. You and your *gifts* have caused more destruction in my life than anything else has. I don't believe going with you is an opportunity. I am human. I chose to remain so."

He stared at her for a moment, as if he could not understand her. Then he shrugged. "As you wish. But I am keeping the Book."

"I don't want it," she said.

He set the Book on the rocks beside him. "If you do not want power, what do you want?"

Such a simple question and such a complicated answer. She wanted love in all its forms: from parents who cared for her to children who believed in her. But she couldn't explain that to him. He had seduced her mother and abandoned her with a Book on power, thinking that was enough, leaving her mother dazed with longing for the rest of her life. Such longing that she was willing to sacrifice everyone to get him to return.

How ironic. All she had to do was toss the power away.

"I want you to leave my family alone," Addy said.

"Your family means little to me, daughter. I will give you a wish that is much grander than that, as a token of affection lost between us."

Addy shook her head. "My family means everything to me. Leave them alone. That's all I want from you. Leave them be."

"As you wish, daughter," he said. "But I shall not make this offer again."

He waved a hand over the lava rock and as she watched, his legs became a tail.

The rock sank back into the ocean. As the Churn swallowed him, he nodded to her.

She nodded back.

The rain was falling again, tiny misty drops that felt like a caress. The waves returned to the Churn, but the wind had died down.

The Storm had passed.

The magic was gone.

She had survived.

She got up slowly, using the railing to pull herself back to the top of the cliff.

It wasn't over yet. She still had Lisa to deal with, and Spence, and Billy's fall from grace. But in their way, these were human problems.

Things she could handle.

A future she could face.

27

WHEN BILLY FOUND HER, she was standing on the driveway that used to lead to her mother's house. The morning sun made the world look bright and new. The grass was bright green. The dampness from the night's storm made the trees, the leaves, the grass sparkle. Even the ocean twinkled in the sunlight.

The house was gone. It had tumbled down the hill in the strength of the Storm.

A neighbor he had spoken to just after dawn had said that the last big gust of wind took the house and crumpled it as if it were being crushed in a giant fist. The huge waves had stolen the walls.

All that remained was Olivia's new kitchen, lying in one solid piece on the ocean side of the hill.

Addy stood, her hands clasped behind her back, her clothes drying to her body, her curls plastered against her forehead, and stared at the ocean.

Billy came up behind her. "You always said it would go."

She turned. Her eyes were as bright as the ocean, and just as blue.

"I'm glad it did," she said. "It was an evil place."

He put a hand on her shoulder and she leaned into him. Her warmth surprised him. She had looked cold standing in the wind.

"We were looking for you."

"We?" she asked.

"Me and Charlie and Spence."

"Such an odd grouping."

He smiled. It was, he supposed, although by the time they called him, it seemed natural enough. "Spence was coming to talk with you. You weren't here. The house was dark."

"Loni took the kids to a hotel around midnight."

"Good thing," Billy said.

"It was Lisa's idea."

He recognized the sadness in her voice. "You know, then."

"Oh, yes." She sighed. "The neighbors told me, and the police. Evelyn turned her in."

He wouldn't have thought it the night before. Evelyn was making some changes herself. "Olivia taught Lisa well."

Addy shook her head and pulled away from him. He shivered at the loss of her warmth. "The mistake was mine, Billy. I wasn't there for her. She turned to my mother because she didn't have me."

He shoved his hands in his pockets. He wanted to touch her. Seventy-four years old, and around her he felt like a kid. "Lisa is almost forty. After a while a child becomes responsible for her own actions. You grew up with Olivia. You never followed her."

"No," Addy said. She continued staring at the sea. "I rebelled against her. That's a daughter's way. A granddaughter follows her grandmother. I should have known that."

"Would that we were always all wise," he said.

Addy laughed. The sound was not bitter, nor was it happy. It was an acknowledgment of the truth in his words. "Having you around keeps me humble," she said, and ran her hand along his arm.

He glanced at her in surprise. He kept his own hands in his coat pockets, away from her. He had been so worried when he couldn't find her, when the storm raged. And then when he had seen the house, he had thought she'd died.

His whole world would have ended then. Such a strange thing for a man to say about a woman whom he hadn't seen in fifty years. But it was true. He had become all he was in order to impress her. Now that she was here, he wanted at least to have that chance.

"The lawyer I hired out of Portland is the best in the state," he said and winced at the formality in his tone.

"Good," Addy said, letting her hand drop. "She'll need the best."

"What are you going to do?" he asked.

"Stay." She responded as if there were no other choice. "I can't leave her now."

Behind them a car pulled up, its engine rattling. Billy turned. Charlie's Olds blocked Billy's in the drive. Charlie shut off the car and opened the door.

"You found her."

"Safe and sound," Billy said.

"Good."

The other car door opened. Spence got out, his lanky body unfolding like a live action figure's. He was a handsome boy, even with the scrape on his cheek. The naked yearning on his face made Billy's heart ache.

"I think Spence wants to talk with you alone."

Addy nodded. She wasn't looking at Spence. She hadn't taken her gaze from the ocean. "My daughter's miracle."

Billy started to walk away, but Addy grabbed his arm. "Wait for me, Billy. I want to go to the police station, but I don't want to go alone."

He almost told her she was asking too much. He didn't want to see the reunion between her and Spence. It brought back too much, all the things about himself he had tried to change, to hide, to conquer. But he had learned last night that killing the past was the coward's way out. He had to face it and accept the consequences as they came.

* * *

CHARLIE WINTER watched Billy nod as he slipped out of Addy's grasp. The hillside looked odd without Olivia's house. Odd, but natural, as if the house had never really belonged.

"I don't know what to say to her," Spence whispered across the car.

Charlie leaned on the car door. This time he had no real advice. "It'll come to you," he said.

Spence straightened his shoulders and waited until Billy reached the car. Then he walked up the driveway to Addy. Charlie turned away. This was a private moment, one he didn't need to witness. If it went wrong, he'd know about it soon enough.

Billy came up beside him and leaned on the car, apparently not wanting to watch either. "Have you thought about what's going to happen to him?" During the night's search they had somehow become friends. Not close friends. Never close friends. But at least Billy and Spence had stopped hating each other. At least Charlie knew that they both had an ally.

"He's staying with me," Charlie said, "until he gets to know most of what he missed. I figure he doesn't need the history. Most kids his age don't have it. But he needs to know things like math and computers and video games. And movies."

"A few job skills would be nice," Billy said.

"He needs ID for that."

Billy frowned. "His grandmother lived on Guam, you say? How about his mother?"

Charlie shrugged, his heart rising. Billy would help, just as he had hoped. "From what I can tell, she skipped out when she remarried."

"Taking all papers."

"All the records."

"Of course, Spence wasn't born on Guam."

"No," Charlie said. "He was midwifed. As far as I can tell, the birth was never officially registered."

"Hmm," Billy said. "Could be a problem."

"Can a lawyer help with that?"

"If you know for certain he's your grandson."

"No doubt about it," Charlie said. "None at all."

"Then I'm sure we can figure something out."

They still hadn't looked at each other. Nor had either of them glanced behind them. Spence and Addy might make the entire conversation moot.

The sun was bright. It had climbed over the Coastal Range and was sending white light into the town. The morning had a freshness to it, as if the world were new again.

Charlie's leg was growing tired. He wished Spence would hurry. If the boy was going to leave with Addy, Charlie wanted to know soon. His heart had been open for three days. If he had to close it, he wanted to do it now, before it sustained more damage.

"Things are never quiet when Addy's around," Billy said.

Charlie nodded. "She's kinda like the ocean. Beautiful, but unpredictable as hell."

* * *

EVELYN WAS ALREADY at the police station. She had brought the remains of her baking from two days before; the brownies and the cinnamon rolls sat on the table beside the ancient coffeemaker.

The police wouldn't let her see Lisa. Evelyn figured that was probably good. She suspected she had brought food as an apology, and her heart told her that she didn't need to apologize. It was the old Evelyn who used food to communicate, the old Evelyn who was too frightened to speak for herself.

The new Evelyn was waiting for Billy. She wanted to tell him that compassion was overrated. And she wanted to thank him for giving her the strength to break free from Olivia once and for all.

The Portland lawyer had arrived. He was three-piece-suit slick, all business, and had dismissed Evelyn with a glance. He was with Lisa now, and Evelyn remembered what Billy had said about the magic explanations not holding up in court.

Part of her hoped he was wrong.

Evelyn would pay for following Olivia. Not the same way that Lisa would, but in a way that was just as painful. No one in Dory Cove would ever look at her the same again. No one would ever take her seriously. They would have names for her.

She would deserve some of them.

But she could live with that now. That's what Billy had given her. He had given her the ability to believe in herself.

* * *

IT WAS AN ODD REVERSAL. A few days ago it had been Spence standing in the yard wearing clothes soiled by the sea. Now it was Addy. She held out her hand, wondering how she had ever doubted him.

He looked so right.

He looked so young.

"It's me, Addy," he said.

"I know that now." She swallowed. Her heart was pounding. She was heavier than she had been, and her skin was wrinkled. Her hair was gray. "I'm sorry about the other day."

"It's okay. I—" his voice broke "—I was rude."

"You were scared."

He nodded. She wondered how she had ever thought that Marty looked like him, or Marty's father Drew. They never had that clear-eyed look, the air of confidence that Spence gave off even when he was frightened.

And he was frightened now. She wouldn't have been able to see it when she was younger, but she recognized the signs.

"I'm not what you expected, am I?" Addy asked. "I'm different."

He swallowed. "Fifty years is a long time."

"And I'm an old lady."

He shook his head too quickly. "You're still Addy."

She took his hand. It was smooth. No wrinkles, no age spots, no calluses. "Not the Addy you remember," she said.

He started to deny it, but she put a finger to his lips.

"I like what you remember," Addy said. "The girl you once said was too pretty to kiss. The way you held me the first time we danced. Keep that girl for me, Spence."

He kissed her finger, then moved it. "You're not going to give me a chance, Addy?"

She shook her head. "I screwed us up once, Spence."

"But that doesn't mean we can't fix it."

He was so sincere. His earnestness almost convinced her. Until she remembered:

At nineteen she thought she knew all she could about life. But she was just beginning. Spence's death had taught her about pain. Drew had taught her about choices. And her children had taught her about love.

"I've had fifty years," she said, "that I wouldn't trade for anything. Not even for the memory of my youth, Spence."

His cheeks were red, his eyes too bright. "But I love you, Addy."

"And I love you, Spence." She leaned over and kissed his cheek. A grandmotherly kiss. "Let's keep it that way."

She knew he didn't understand. She could see it in his face. But maybe, fifty years in the future, when he was nearly seventy, and she was long dead, he would look back on this moment and have the aha of clarity that she sometimes got.

The moment when an event that had seemed cloudy became clear. The moments when she finally understood the trial or the joy that life had presented her.

"You're staying with Charlie?" she asked.

He nodded.

"I'm staying in Dory Cove too." She had to now, for Lisa. "Maybe we can talk?"

"I'd like that," he said.

She smiled. "I would too."

He grabbed her arm and pulled her close, an embrace she had forgotten. He smelled of sandalwood and sea salt, just like he always had. For a moment she was nineteen again, and frightened, in love with Spence but attracted to Billy, and unable to reconcile all those whirling emotions.

She could reconcile them now. She eased out of the embrace. Billy was waiting for her by the car. Billy, who had lived a full fifty years too. Billy, who had taken her shouted advice on a heated afternoon to heart:

I can't spend my life with a man like you, a man with no education, no skills, and no hope. You're just a big handsome buck, Billy Malone, and that's all. And that's all you'll ever be.

Nineteen years old and wrong. Spence was the handsome buck now. Billy had skills, an education, and only a few years left.

And a wisdom she cherished. He was as willing to face his past as she was.

"Does this mean we're going to be friends, Addy?" Spence asked.

She put her arm around him and gently, slowly, walked him to the car. "Yes," she said, knowing he meant the casual friends a teenager had and she meant deep, lifelong companionship. "We'll always be friends, Spence."

Behind them the ocean sighed against the beach. She was no longer afraid of the coast, the Pacific, or the Churn.

She had finally made her peace.

About the Author

USA Today bestselling author Kristine Kathryn Rusch writes in almost every genre. Generally, she uses her real name (Rusch) for most of her writing. Under that name, she publishes bestselling science fiction and fantasy, award-winning mysteries, acclaimed mainstream fiction, controversial nonfiction, and the occasional romance. Her novels have made bestseller lists around the world and her short fiction has appeared in eighteen best of the year collections. She has won more than twenty-five awards for her fiction, including the Hugo, *Le Prix Imaginales*, the *Asimov's* Readers Choice award, and the *Ellery Queen Mystery Magazine* Readers Choice Award.

To keep up with everything she does, go to kriswrites.com. To track her many pen names and series, see their individual websites (kris nelscott.com, kristinegrayson.com, krisdelake.com, retrievalartist.com, divingintothewreck.com, fictionriver.com). She lives and occasionally sleeps in Oregon.

Also by
Kristine Kathryn Rusch

Sins of the Blood

Façade

Snipers

Spree

Alien Influences

www.ingramcontent.com/pod-product-compliance
Lightning Source LLC
Chambersburg PA
CBHW030402020726
47493CB00003B/917